BRONWYN SCOTT

The Bluestocking's Whirlwind Liaison

HARLEQUIN®
HISTORICAL™

ISBN-13: 978-1-335-72330-7

The Bluestocking's Whirlwind Liaison

Harlequin Enterprises ULC
22 Adelaide St. West, 41st Floor
Toronto, Ontario M5H 4E3, Canada
www.Harlequin.com

Printed in U.S.A.

Recycling programs
for this product may
not exist in your area.

Bronwyn Scott is a communications instructor at Pierce College and the proud mother of three wonderful children—one boy and two girls. When she's not teaching or writing, she enjoys playing the piano, traveling—especially to Florence, Italy—and studying history and foreign languages. Readers can stay in touch via Facebook at Facebook.com/bronwynwrites, or on her blog, bronwynswriting.blogspot.com. She loves to hear from readers.

Books by Bronwyn Scott

Harlequin Historical

The Peveretts of Haberstock Hall

Lord Tresham's Tempting Rival
Saving Her Mysterious Soldier
Miss Peverett's Secret Scandal
The Bluestocking's Whirlwind Liaison

The Rebellious Sisterhood

Portrait of a Forbidden Love
Revealing the True Miss Stansfield
A Wager to Tempt the Runaway

The Cornish Dukes

The Secrets of Lord Lynford
The Passions of Lord Trevethow
The Temptations of Lord Tintagel
The Confessions of the Duke of Newlyn

Visit the Author Profile page
at Harlequin.com for more titles.

For Apollo, most beloved of dogs.
July 4, 2011–December 18, 2021.
This was your last book and you sat with
me the whole time as I wrote.
I will miss you forever.

Chapter One

Haberstock Hall, Hertfordshire—Autumn 1856

Whir, click-click, whir, whish... Whir, click-click, whir, whish... These were the sounds of comfort, of order and predictability.

The little ballerina on her pedestal stopped in mid-pirouette. Rebecca leaned forward to wind her up again and sat back, watching the little figure bow and dance, raising her arms over her head as she turned. There was nothing as satisfying as a well-oiled machine whirring flawlessly through its routine: reliable, predictable. Safe. All the things the world was not. Except for here, in her cottage workshop. Here, there was order and calmness. This little space, with her worktable and tools, a fire in the hearth and a kettle on the hob, this was her retreat, where she could invent to her heart's delight all sorts of things that would help others live better lives and keep their own chaos, their own helplessness at bay.

The little ballerina finished her dance and Rebecca

pushed aside the temptation to wind it up again. She eyed the row of unpainted toy soldiers lining the shelf and pushed aside that temptation, too—the temptation to paint them instead of doing real work. She ought to be working on the pieces and parts of her latest project— a fused bifocal lens—which lay spread out on the table. A wind-up ballerina and toy soldiers were just that— toys—but a sturdy, reliable bifocal lens would enhance vision for people who felt they had to give up reading or close work as they aged because they had no choice. People like her. Rebecca took off her own glasses and set them aside.

She rubbed at the bridge of her nose out of habit more than an attempt to relieve discomfort. The little nose pieces she'd attached to the frame seemed to be working to reduce the friction against her skin. That was something, but it wouldn't match in scope what she could achieve for herself and others if she could fuse the lenses. So far, she'd not been successful in working out how to do it.

She closed her eyes, letting her mind walk back through her past efforts on the lenses. What had she overlooked? The currently used bifocal lens was notoriously breakable, something she'd proven time and again. Perhaps fusion would work? Maybe there was a better way to conjoin the two lenses? Perhaps if she…

A knock on the cottage door intruded on her thoughts. Drat! She grimaced at the untimely interruption. She'd almost been on to something. She looked up as her mother entered, shaking rain droplets from the hood of her cloak. A visit from her mother wasn't unwelcome, just unexpected. 'What a surprise this is.' Rebecca smiled. As interruptions went, this was of the more pleasant variety. Her mother usually gave her second-youngest daughter privacy, stopping by only on her way home from rounds in the village. But today was not a visiting day.

Rebecca's smile faded, fearing the worst. 'Oh, no, you've not come with bad news, have you? The girls are well? The babies are fine?' The past two years had seen a flurry of weddings and births in the Peverett household. Her three sisters, two older, one younger, had all married, two had children now and one more niece or nephew was on the way—Thomasia's second child was expected at Christmas. A more worrying thought came to her. 'It's not William, is it?' Her brother was a doctor with the British Army in the Crimea and while the war was over, William was still there, insisting on tending those who weren't well enough to travel yet.

Her mother set aside her cloak with a shake of her head and a laugh. 'Everyone is fine. Did it occur to you that I might bring *good* news?' She took a seat at the worktable. 'It's so cosy down here, I can see why you like it.'

The tension between Rebecca's shoulders blades eased knowing her siblings were well, only to be replaced with a faint twinge of resentment. Good news meant one of those siblings had done something extraordinary. Again. They were all paragons of social work while she had nothing to show for her efforts. It was poorly done of her. Rebecca shoved it away and jumped up, determined to be more generous of thought.

'I have tea. If it's good news, perhaps we should cele-brate.' She busied herself setting out two chipped mugs she'd purloined from the Hall years ago when she'd first set up shop out here, seeking sanctuary from the busyness that marked the lives of her family. 'I have a tin of biscuits, too.' If she could just find them. She rooted around in a cupboard, moving vials and tins of other less edible items. Ah, there they were.

She set the tea things and biscuits down and poured the hot water. 'So, tell me, who are we celebrating today? Let me guess. Anne is expecting? Or maybe William is coming home?' Or maybe one of them was taking on Parliament again, healing the unhealable or any number of the amazing things Peveretts were raised to do. All except her, who preferred her quiet workshop.

Her mother calmly took a mug, her smile contain-ing a hint of teasing smugness as she kept her secret a moment longer. 'No on both accounts, dear one. Why must the news be about someone else?' Because it al-ways was. Her brother and sisters lived boisterous lives, full of action and purpose. One of them was always advocating for a cause or facing down the dragons of social injustice. Her mother leaned forward. 'Why can't the news be for you?'

Uh-oh. 'That sounds ominous.' The tension be-tween her shoulders returned. She hoped 'good news' didn't mean her father had a friend coming to dinner who happened to be in possession of an unmarried son. She was the last of the Peverett girls to marry—assuming she ever did, which was an assumption she and her mother disagreed on. She'd given up on marriage. She was quiet, unlike Thea. She was plain, unlike Thomasia and Anne. She would not settle for the sort of man who wanted a quiet, plain wife just to say she was married.

Her mother pushed an envelope forward. 'This came for you. It looked important so I wanted to bring it right away. I think it's the people you've been waiting to hear from.'

Becca slit open the letter, noticing the heavy, business-like weight of the paper. Her hand trembled in excitement as she unfolded it, her eyes quickly scanning the contents. It was indeed from Howell Manufacturing. She'd contacted them last month about her latest invention, a handheld ophthalmoscope. She noted the signature at the bottom, Winthrop Howell, head of acquisitions and productions. Her eyes went back to the top of the page and she forced herself to read slowly, once, then twice to make sure she understood. She didn't want to get her hopes up. She'd applied for numerous patents before and been rejected each time until someone in the patent office had finally told her there was no chance of a patent being issued to a woman. She'd changed her tack after that, seeking to sell her device to a company and let them handle the patent. A man would get the patent, she was sure of it.

There was no mistake. She'd read it correctly. She looked up at her mother, incredulity in her voice. 'They want to discuss a contract for the ophthalmoscope. They want to come for a visit in two weeks.' Becca couldn't stop smiling. It was going to happen, *really* happen this time. Surely they wouldn't travel from

Manchester for something they weren't serious about. Her invention was going to be produced!

Her mother got up and hugged her. 'That is wonderful, you've worked hard for this. I'm so proud of you.' Her mother held her gaze and added seriously, 'But I am always proud of you. I think sometimes you don't understand that. Even if no one ever bought one of your inventions, you've still used them to make life for your neighbours better and that's what matters: doing the most good where and when you can do it. You don't have to be like Thea or Anne or Thomasia. You just have to be yourself.'

'I know, Mother.' Rebecca stepped back from the embrace, a little overwhelmed and a little embarrassed that her earlier thoughts might have been that transparent when it came to her siblings.

Her mother smiled and reached for her cloak. 'We'll celebrate tonight at dinner. I'll have Cook find something special for dessert.'

Becca sank into her chair after her mother departed, reading and rereading the letter, relief filling her. At last, perhaps this meant her life could truly begin, that she wasn't wasting her time in her cottage. She, too, could make contributions to the world. She admired and shared her siblings' values of social justice, but she wasn't like them. She wasn't loud, she didn't care to argue with others, which didn't mean she couldn't hold her own when she had to. She *could* argue if needed. Neither did it mean she didn't want to be part of the fight. She just wanted to do with her inventions what her brother and sisters did with their words.

Her inventions would speak for her, they would be her words, if only she could find someone to listen. Apparently, she had. Howell Manufacturing had lent their ear. This was her chance. The invention had spoken for her as she had hoped it would. The only obstacle standing in her way now was the visit and what they would find when they came. Or, more to the point, *who* they would find. After her experience with patents, she'd not dared to sign her full name. Howell Manufacturing was expecting to visit R. L. Peverett. She'd deliberately not alluded to her gender in the letter, but she was not so naive as to believe they hadn't assumed R. L. Peverett was male. She was also not so naive as to believe it wouldn't matter. The question was, how much?

How long before his brother would go spare? Jules Howell leaned back in his chair on the guest's side of the enormous, polished oak desk that signified the authority and power of the man who sat behind it, his none-too-clean boots propped on its pristine surface while he watched Winthrop's face turn red, explosion imminent.

'For heaven's sake, Jules, get your feet off my desk. This isn't one of those low-life taverns you frequent.' Ah, there it was. It hadn't even taken old Winnie a whole minute. His brother must be extra irritable today. Winthrop was only five years older than he was, but Win looked and acted at least a decade more.

'Father's desk.' Jules couldn't resist the correction, purposely making sure the heel of his boot bumped the white Carrera marble paperweight out of alignment with the inkstand as he swung his feet off the desk. *That* was for ordering him around. It was childish, he knew. But so was the way the family treated him. Was it any surprise he resented being summoned to the Howell Manufacturing offices when the family agreed he wasn't capable of doing anything more than tramping around Europe, wining and dining clients whose business was all but assured?

'*What* did you say?' Winthrop glared and Jules's short-lived satisfaction dissipated as Winthrop righted the paperweight.

Speaking of dissipated, Jules tipped his chair back on its hind legs and reached for the flask in his coat pocket. 'I said, it's *Father*'s desk.' That would needle Winthrop more than nudging his precious paperweight even if it was only technically true. Winthrop sat at the helm of Howell Manufacturing these days, with their father taking a more distant role, coming by only to check that the coffers were still spilling over with riches. Jules twisted the cap off his pewter flask and took a long swig, grinning at the look of horror he'd managed to conjure on Winthrop's face.

'Lucifer's balls, Jules, it's not even noon.' There, that was more like it. Lucifer's balls was a real man's expletive. He must really be getting to Win if his brother had forsaken his fussy 'heaven's sake'. There'd been a time when Winthrop hadn't been so proper.

Jules winked and offered his brother the flask. 'Want some?' He laughed when Win shook his head. 'Suit yourself, you're the one that called an early meeting.'

Winthrop cleared his throat. 'Yes, about that, we

have business to discuss. We're sending you to Hertfordshire to meet with an R. L. Peverett on the issue of acquiring production rights to a medical device he's invented.'

'Hertfordshire?' Might as well as send him to the moon. It was just as desolate, just as wild. What the hell was an inventor doing living in Hertfordshire? The area wasn't exactly known for its big cities. He took another long draught and swore. 'Dammit, should have brought a bigger flask.' He shook it in dismay. Four, maybe five swallows left. He'd need more than that to stomach this latest assignment. At least when they sent him to the Continent he knew all the good brothels.

Disgust crossed Winthrop's face. 'Watch your language, this is a place of business and you are the owner's son. Try to act like it.'

Jules set his chair down with a thump and swept the office with an exaggerated glance. He leaned forward and said in a mock whisper, 'I think we're safe, there's no one here but us.' He waved his flask. 'You sound like him, you know. Just like Father. I expected better from you, Winnie. You used to be a lot of fun.'

'Don't call me that. At least one of us has to be a credit to Father.'

That was it—the heart of every argument they'd had for the last five years. 'Father needs you *now*? You're still delusional, I see. Father doesn't need anyone. We used to agree on that.' They used to agree on a lot of things back in their twenties right up until Winthrop decided to be respectable, to grow up. Jules couldn't quite forgive him for that. Winthrop had given him up in order to chase Father's elusive favour.

Winthrop speared him with a hard look, unwilling to be shamed into backing down. Win was tough like that. 'It's different now, Jules. If you were sober long enough, you might have noticed that.'

If *he* could get Winthrop mad enough, Hertford-shire might fall by the wayside, he might even be able to walk out in a fit of pique, the trip forgotten entirely. 'Different?' Jules scoffed, taking another drink from his flask. Three swallows to go, he'd better make them count. 'You've got it bad.' Father had never noticed them and Jules had really tried, going as far as to be sent down from Harrow and then a series of England's finest public schools, each one slightly less prestigious than the last, all to no avail.

'Yes, it *is* different,' Winthrop argued. 'Father's sixty-five. He relies on me, on my ideas, to guide the business into this new age. Who had the idea to buy alpaca wool from that Viscount in Somerset? Whose idea was it to snap up those munitions contracts for the army at the first sign of trouble in the Crimea? We were in position while our competitors were still scrambling for crumbs from the military's table.' It was Winthrop, of course. He had all the best ideas. The implication was clear. Winthrop was the golden boy while Jules, who had all the same advantages of being born to the richest man in the north of England, had done nothing in the thirty years he'd been on the planet. That was worth another drink.

'He's just using you,' Jules said, wanting to be mean.

'Put that flask down. You've had enough. If it's too early in the day to drink, it's certainly too early to be drunk.' Winthrop reached across the desk to grab the flask, but Jules was too fast for him. He tucked it away inside his coat.

'I prefer "pleasantly pickled", and you're wrong. It's never too early for either.' Pleasant pickling was in fact a necessity these days. It took the edge off reality, the edge off looking in the mirror every morning and wondering when his life would begin. Or the greater fear that it *had* begun. Somehow it had started without him and this was it: doing his brother's bidding, entertaining clients because he couldn't mess that up too badly—usually—that one time in Amsterdam notwithstanding. Unlike his brother, serving the great machine of Howell Manufacturing interested him not one iota. The problem was, he didn't know *what* interested him and, as the years passed, he was starting to despair of ever finding it.

Winthrop tapped the file on the desk. 'Hertfordshire, Jules. Everything you need for the trip is in there including your train ticket. You leave in two weeks, plenty of time to read the papers regarding the invention and the contracts on what we're willing to offer.'

Jules scanned the file and winced. 'An ophthalmoscope? Lucifer's balls, Win, I can barely say the word.' He had no idea what one even was, but it sounded *boring*. 'Are you sure you can't send someone else? Maybe that new clerk, Daniel. He seems hungry and eager. Let him prove himself in Hertfordshire.' There, that seemed like a perfectly reasonable solution. Jules rose and made to leave, conveniently forgetting the file.

'Take the folder, Jules,' Winthrop called him back. 'I don't want Daniel to prove himself in Hertfordshire, I want you to. This is a big chance for you. It's not just wining and dining after the deed is done, it's making the deal.' What Winthrop meant was that it was his big chance to fail. Winthrop didn't have to say it out loud in order for Jules to hear that message. 'I mean it, Jules. This is it. Don't come home empty-handed. The company can't keep supporting you without getting something in return.' There'd be no arguing with Winthrop when he used that tone, and Jules did not miss the veiled ultimatum.

Win rose and thrust the folder at him. 'Dammit, Jules. Why can't you do your part like the rest of us? What do you do all day anyway?' It was a not-so-subtle reminder that the company paid for his town house, his carriage, his horses, his club memberships both here and in London, his tailor, his staff, his liquor, his gambling, his entertainments. He'd stop there. That last category encompassed quite a bit.

'You want me to go and earn my keep, is that it?' Jules felt resentment rise. 'I'm supposed to come running when I'm summoned and live at the disposal of the company.' Like Winthrop had. Winthrop had sold his soul to the company, all in the hopes of garnering their father's favour. Jules had chosen a different method of claiming their father's attention. It had not been successful.

'That would be a start. What I really want is for you

to *want* to go, to want to have some purpose, some direction, Jules.' Winthrop's expression softened and Jules felt the pressure of his brother's hand on his arm. 'You are thirty years old. It's time to stop thinking about what you will be when you grow up and *be* that person. None of us is getting any younger.'

What if I don't know who that person is? Jules nearly spoke the words out loud in earnest.

'Mary and I worry about you, Jules.' That was absolutely the worst, knowing that Winthrop had discussed him with his wife. He'd be fending off invitations for months to dinners where Mary just happened to fill out the table with unmarried daughters of Manchester's finest. It certainly made Hertfordshire look a bit better.

'I'm fine.' Jules danced away from his brother, brandishing the folder and summoning some sarcasm to part on. 'After all, I get to go to Hertfordshire. What could be finer than that?' Maybe when he was done in Hertfordshire, he'd go to Italy and paint, pretend he was an artist for a while. Italy always soothed him. Winthrop didn't know what he was talking about. *He* was living his best life, Jules told himself, while Win was the one trapped behind a desk. But despite the reminder to self, a tiny part of him wondered if just drifting through life had begun to lose a bit of its appeal.

Chapter Two

Jules was starting to worry about this latest errand Winthrop had sent him on. The further the solid, black travelling coach that had awaited him at Broxbourne station jolted into the countryside, the more his anxieties rose. He lifted the curtain and peered outside once more, hoping that somehow a town of some substance would appear. But it didn't work that way. The English countryside was populated with small, rural villages made up of churches, inns and a few shops.

The view outside the coach window only served to affirm that. Thus the source of his worry. Such surroundings seemed unlikely to produce an inventor of any merit. In his experience, inventors clung to cities where supplies were at hand and inevitable eccentricities were more readily tolerated, where there were universities and communities of similarly minded scholars: Amsterdam, Brussels, Paris, Lyon, Vienna, Florence, Milan, Rome. The English countryside was notably *not* on the list. What did his brother think he'd find in furthest Hertfordshire?

Jules yawned and stretched his legs across the coach interior. It was only afternoon and already it had been a long day capped off by an hour-long coach ride to Haberstock from the station. He'd spent the train ride pondering the situation his brother had dropped in his lap and he didn't like it. His brother had been adamant that he take this opportunity to prove himself. Jules understood what that was: an ultimatum. He was *not* to come home empty-handed or there would be consequences, at last, after years of living luxuriously on the company's pay in exchange for haphazard work.

On the surface, there seemed to be no risk of failing. He might not give two figs of interest in the company or the work his brother asked him to do, but he was good at wining and dining. He did have a knack for understanding people, for making them feel good about themselves. He knew how to woo, if his brother sought to put those charms to use for the company on occasion, Jules was paid handsomely for it. With that in mind, he ought to be successful in Haberstock. A country bumpkin would be easily flattered by the attentions of a representative from Howell Manufacturing.

The country bumpkin piece niggled at him. Places like Haberstock did not breed inventors, they bred farmers. Would he be disappointed in what he found in Haberstock? Would the invention be unreliable? His mind had reeled continually with what ifs. What if he *couldn't* close the deal? What if the deal wasn't worth closing and he returned home empty-handed against his brother's admonitions to do otherwise? Among those thoughts rose a darker one—what if his brother already knew it was a fool's errand? What if Win had made the ultimatum knowing full well the futility of finding anything worthwhile in a place like Haberstock? Was he being set up? Had Win decided to wash his hands of him, after all?

He might not need to come home from Italy in that case. He might not be *able* to, which prompted the question—what happened if Win finally despaired of him? What would he do if he finally got the independence he thought he'd craved for years? If his years of rebellion finally paid off and he could go his own way? Is that what he really wanted? Certainly, he hoped to be his own man when the time came—*when* he knew what it was he wanted out of life. It had to be on his terms, not Win's. He didn't want it because he'd been cast out or because he'd sold out like Win. Jules shoved the thoughts away. They were complicated and confusing and he hadn't the time for them at the moment. The white steeple of a church came into view, signalling their approach to Haberstock Village. Time to focus on the deal at hand.

His approach would depend on what sort of man R. L. Peverett would be. He closed his eyes, trying to imagine Peverett. What kind of man lived in the countryside, inventing things miles from a train station and even further from a major town? A slightly unkempt man, perhaps. Hair a little long, like his own. Greying. *Not* like his own. His appearance not quite polished because his inventions claimed his time and energies, not the mirror. Perhaps retiring in personality, rusty manners not often used. A man who lived in seclusion. No doubt R. L. Peverett was crusty and crotchety. Maybe that was what Win was hoping for. A man who lived in seclusion would be less likely to be aware of his own worth. He'd be a man who could be paid less for his invention.

Jules leaned forward and hazarded a glimpse at the village as the coach passed through. It was a neat village, with the church at one end, a large inn at the other, shops in between them lining the green sward in the centre that acted as the village common. He thought of the dwindling contents of his flask. At least the inn looked like a promising watering hole. 'Haberstock Hall in one mile,' the coachman called down to him as the village disappeared behind them. It was meant as a warning to give him time to make himself presentable. After the better part of a day spent on trains, Jules didn't think there was much he could do in that regard. He took out his flask and took a swig of fortification.

The coach made a turn around the driving circle in front of the hall's entrance and came to a halt. Jules drew a breath and stepped down on to the gravel drive, steeling himself for his first glimpse of the hall. It, at least, did not disappoint and in fact exceeded expectations. Haberstock Hall was impressive, a brick Elizabethan structure surrounded by manicured parklands and autumn-leafed oak trees whose height and girth spoke of having been planted centuries ago and come of age with the estate. At first glance, it did not *look* like the home of a hermit inventor.

A man stood at the top of the steps. He raised a

hand in greeting and made his way towards Jules, giving Jules a few precious seconds to establish his first impressions, all of which shattered the image he'd fixed in his mind. 'Hello, I'm Dr Peverett, you must be Mr Howell.' The man extended his hand, his grip firm. 'Welcome to my home. Won't you come in? You must have had a long journey today.' The man smiled, warmth and invitation in his eyes as they mounted the steps. Jules took in the man's clothing—well tailored if plain by city standards. He'd been right about the greying hair, but nothing else. This man bore none of the markings of the inventors Jules was used to meeting.

If Jules had to guess, this was a country gentleman. It was a guess borne out when he stepped inside the Hall. This was no ramshackle bachelor hermit abode. The oak banister gleamed with polish and a cut-glass vase of autumn florals adorned the hall console. Dr Peverett led him down a hallway, saying, 'My wife has arranged for refreshment in the music room. We are all looking forward to meeting you.' Some of Jules's anxiety eased. Dr Peverett seemed an intelligent, reasonable man, who lived in a prosperous home. Perhaps his worries had been for naught. Perhaps he might even enjoy his time in the country?

The music room was a well-appointed space done in blues and cream, with a polished Broadwood piano against one wall and long windows that overlooked gardens and let in plenty of natural light. But it was the cluster of furniture near the fireplace with its cosy heat that held Jules's attention. Two women sat on the sofa, one an auburn-haired woman possessed of a mature beauty and a younger woman whose features were saved from plainness by smooth dark hair and warm eyes the shade of rich cognac. They were both dressed as Dr Peverett was—neatly in well-tailored clothes that favoured plainness over embellishment.

The younger woman wore a merino wool gown of a deep maroon trimmed in white cotton lace at the wrists and neck. The maroon was a stunning colour on her, bringing out the walnut hue of her hair and the cream of her skin. She had a calm air to her, sitting quietly with her hands folded in her lap. Although, to his eye, she had the potential to be a beauty in town with a modiste to see to her and a few cosmetics applied to highlight that skin. But that was as far as he allowed his thoughts to wander. He didn't dally with the daughters of clients, although willing wives were, on occasion, a different story. For now, it was enough that their presence eased the last of his worries. He'd been making trouble where there was none.

Dr Peverett made the necessary introductions. 'Ladies, allow me to present Mr Howell. Mr Howell, my wife, Mrs Peverett, and my daughter, Miss Rebecca Peverett.' This last was said with immense pride and Jules made sure to respond accordingly.

'Charmed.' Jules bent over each of the ladies' hands and flattered the quiet wallflower and her mother shamelessly. 'Dr Peverett is a lucky man to be surrounded by such beauty every day. Please, call me Jules. Mr Howell is my father. I wouldn't know whom you were speaking to.' They laughed and everyone took their seats. A tea tray followed almost immediately and that, too, was gratifyingly delicious: lemon cakes, ham sandwiches and strong tea. This was looking better and better all the time.

The Peveretts were interested in Howell Manufacturing and Jules was happy to oblige with the usual things he told clients about the company—how his father had started out as an investment banker who'd quickly seen he could make more money by cutting out the middleman and acquiring products for himself; how his father was a self-made man. Inventors tended to like that aspect of the story. No one listening to the great story of the Howells would ever guess at the family strife behind it, at the price the family paid for one man's success, or of two little boys who grew up without a father's attention, each of them warped in their own way by the affection they sought and never received. 'But what of yourselves?' Jules was careful not to talk too long. He wanted to learn about the Peveretts and he'd long believed that listening to others was an underrated conversational quality. 'This is a lovely home.'

'It is—I think it's the reason my wife married me,' Dr Peverett joked and the warm look that passed between he and his wife suggested nothing could be further from the truth. There was genuine affection in this room, Jules noted. 'There's been a Peverett at Haberstock Hall since the sixteen-hundreds,' Dr Peverett said, offering him a brief history of the family.

'All of you have been doctors?' Jules enquired, sincerely interested.

'Yes, all of us. Not only has there been a Peverett

at Haberstock Hall, but there's also been a healer here for centuries as well. I feel especially blessed...' Dr Peverett shared with a nod to his wife '...that my wife is a gifted herbalist who has devoted her life to the health and welfare of our tenants and the villagers in addition to giving me five children. My son, William, will eventually be the next healer at Haberstock, but he is currently away serving as a doctor in the British military.' A smile tinged with pride and sorrow passed between the doctor and his wife. They missed their son. They worried over him. How wondrous to be missed, Jules thought. How wondrous also to be worried over for oneself, not just because of how it reflected on the family.

'I hope your son is home soon,' Jules offered, although he was curious why the son wasn't home already. The peace had been settled in March, several months ago. He sensed there was a story there, but he didn't dare pry. He didn't generally pay attention to world affairs unless it affected the supply of brandy across the Channel. He offered the family a broad grin, 'Perhaps he'll be home in time to celebrate the production of your ophthalmoscope. Howell Manufacturing has great plans for the invention. We think the portability of the device could make it a tool that every physician will begin to carry as matter of fact in their medical bags, not just here in England, but internationally as well.'

'Internationally? Truly?' It was the daughter, Rebecca, who spoke for the first time since being introduced. Her face shone with delight at the news. 'How incredible, how wonderful!'

'It is and I am here to make sure that all happens as smoothly as possible.' Jules smiled briefly in her direction and turned his assurances back towards Dr Peverett. 'I would love to see the device first-hand. I've seen the drawings and the prospectus that were sent, of course.' Not technically a lie—they were in the folder Win had given him and he had thumbed through it this morning on the train after he'd read the newspaper. But he was no expert on the device although ultimately that didn't matter. It only mattered if he got Dr Peverett's signature on the contract.

The daughter rose, still beaming, much to his surprise. 'I would be happy to take you down to the workshop.'

Jules stood, not wanting to be rude, but definitely perplexed. This seemed an odd development. 'Will you be accompanying us, Dr Peverett?' His gaze drifted between the doctor and his daughter. Something was afoot.

'I think Rebecca can handle it,' Dr Peverett said confidently. 'It's her invention, after all.'

'Hers?' Jules enquired politely, smiling through his shock, his mind reeling. He'd misjudged her. She was more than a wallflower. Quite a bit more, in fact, and that was alarming. His anxiety returned as he began to piece the revelation together. The daughter was the inventor?

'Yes.' The daughter's cognac eyes flashed in challenge. 'I am R. L. Peverett.'

'Well, this is indeed a surprise.' It was, perhaps, the

first complete truth he'd told since arriving. The inventor was a woman. What would Win say to that? This was the catch he'd been on alert for. Jules needed time to think, to gather his thoughts, to decide how to proceed.

'Perhaps I could have a moment?' It was not the most gracious exit. He excused himself and hurried through the hall back towards the entrance, out on to the wide front steps and stopped. He should probably keep going. Haberstock Village was only a mile down the road. He could get a room at the inn and catch the first train in the morning back to Manchester. And Win would be furious. Or right. He was indeed a failure just as the family had long decided. How could he leave empty-handed? But how could he bring a *woman's* invention back to the company? Either way he was doomed. Contracting with a woman would make him look like a fool, but coming back without the contract would prove he was just as useless as everyone thought.

The dark thought of earlier niggled again. Had Win known this would happen? Had he been set up to fail once and for all? He reached for his flask. Damn it all. It was empty at the worst possible time. He absolutely needed a drink. What was he going to do now?

He felt a quiet presence behind him. *Her.* Rebecca. The inventor. The girl whose face had lit up like a candle when he'd talked of international sales and worldwide success. But he'd been thinking the invention was Dr Peverett's then. He could not offer her the same things. He could offer *her* nothing. Anger rose up. 'You lied.'

'I did not. R. L. are my initials.' She was cool, unperturbed, not nearly as bothered as he was. 'Rebecca Louise. I have lied about nothing.' Her sangfroid was admirable.

'You know what I mean,' he ground out. She had played the company and he was taking it personally because it was his head on the block over this. How dare she do this to him? Not just the surprise that could ruin his task here, but how dare she take him unaware? He was usually a fairly accurate judge of people and he'd misread her entirely—she was not a wallflower when she was left on her own. All that quiet stillness of hers belied a rather fierce demeanour he'd not expected.

'I do know what you mean. You mean that it's my fault *you* drew erroneous assumptions about my gender. You mean that it's my fault that you don't think a woman's invention is good enough for your company when you know very well that your company liked the invention well enough before you knew my gender. Liked it well enough, in fact, to travel all the way to Haberstock. My gender does not change the competence of the invention nor should it change what you have come to offer.'

He'd been wrong in thinking she was a polite, reserved young lady. Her audacity knew no bounds. She might say things in quiet tones, but they were no less shocking for it. He did turn to look at her then, meeting her with the full force of his gaze. 'You have no idea of the position you've put me in.'

Chapter Three

'The position I've put *you* in?' Becca met his gaze with an incredulous stare, her hands going to her hips. 'What of the position you've put me in? Howell Manufacturing wrote to say they liked the invention and was sending a representative to discuss the acquisition. That is the most wonderful news an inventor can receive. It's a complete validation of their time and effort and now you are reneging on the company's word.' Did he have any idea of how that made her feel? After two weeks of anticipating his arrival, of anticipating his offer, to have the rug pulled out from under her feet, especially after all his talk about international sales.

He'd buoyed her up with his vision and with his presentation. She had to admit he'd been impressive and persuasive from the moment he'd walked into the music room, filling the quiet afternoon with his energy. He was well dressed in the way men from the city were, sporting a waistcoat in a coppery beige silk, patterned with dark green vines beneath his jacket and a complicated knot in his cravat, the folds decorated with an emerald stickpin. Men in the country didn't wear jewellery in the daytime and he was positively dripping in it: the gold ring on his little finger, the watch chain winking beneath his jacket and, of course, the cravat pin. Every inch of him male sartorial beauty personified.

His words were as polished as his clothes. When he'd bent over her hand and brought those mossy green eyes up to meet hers as he uttered that single word, *charmed*, she'd felt his touch, his voice, his gaze, all the way to her toes. His conversation had been polished, too, as he'd shared stories of the company and taken an interest in the house. She'd felt as if she could listen to him for hours and never grow bored. Perhaps it was because he knew not to dominate the discussion. He knew when to let others tell their stories. As a result, she felt connected to him, as if she'd known him far longer than the span of an afternoon tea.

But now here she was, staring into the loveliest green eyes she'd ever seen and arguing for an acceptance she'd already thought she'd achieved with him. 'I am counting on you, sir.' No matter how polished he was, he had to answer for this volte-face.

'That is your misfortune, Miss Peverett.' He gave her a curt nod, his expression grim. 'I regret any inconvenience I may have caused you.'

Inconvenience? Oh, this was far more than a mere inconvenience. This was the dashing of dreams. 'You truly do not understand, do you?' Of course not, he was a man. No one had likely ever told him he couldn't do something because of his gender.

'What I understand, Miss Peverett, is that I've been sent out to remotest Hertfordshire to acquire an invention, only to discover that the situation is not what we at Howell Manufacturing thought it was. I have been sent on a wild goose chase and now I am faced with the task of returning home empty-handed, with nothing but wasted time to show for my effort.'

That bothered him. She could see it in his eyes. Those green depths weren't merely grim, they were troubled, upset. There was a window of opportunity in that. This visit mattered to him. He didn't *want* to go home empty-handed. She could guess the reasons for it; perhaps his pride was at stake, maybe there was pressure being applied by the company. Perhaps something deeper, not that it mattered. Whatever the reason was, she could work with that.

He took a step backwards towards the stairs. 'Now, if you'll excuse me, I'll be on my way. I'll take a room at the inn and catch the first train to Manchester tomorrow.'

That was unacceptable. A certain level of panic gripped her, tempered only by her anger. If he left, her hopes went with him. 'You can't leave.' They were the knee-jerk reaction words of her logical mind asserting itself through the panic.

'I know you're disappointed, but there's nothing more to be done.' He gave her a look that bordered on pitying. That only fuelled her anger. She didn't want his pity. She wanted his contract.

Pride came to her rescue and Rebecca drew herself up. 'It's not that, Mr Howell. You really can't leave. To-

morrow is Sunday. There are no trains that come here.'
Unlike the city, where there were trains seven days
a week. The look on his face said he hadn't thought
of that. Resignation settled in his eyes as his mind
registered the idea of spending a day stranded in the
Haberstock Village inn. This man gave up too easily,
accepted fate too easily. She wouldn't have any of that,
either. Resignation was akin to complacency. She was
an inventor, a scientist—it was her job to solve problems others couldn't, to see solutions where others saw
obstacles and impossibilities. She'd just bought herself another day. Now she had to do something with it.
Becca racked her mind. What did she say to a stranger?
How did she appeal to a man she'd just met and barely
knew? The only thing she knew about him was that
he didn't want to go home empty-handed. Her mind
latched on to an idea. Perhaps it would be enough.

Her arm reached out reflexively, her hand gripping
his forearm with some force, enough to make him
glance down at her hand on his sleeve with concern.
'Don't go to the inn. Stay here instead. Have a good
supper, a good night's sleep and in the morning, we'll
go down to the workshop. Afterwards, I'll show you
around the Hall's land. Perhaps we could throw in a
picnic. You've come all this way; it would be a shame
not to show off the Hall in all its autumn glory.' She
was being bold now, painting in word pictures, but this
was her future on the line. She needed to fight for it.
No one else would, certainly not Mr Howell, who gave
up too soon. Perhaps he'd never had to fight for any-

thing he desperately wanted. Perhaps the world came easily to the handsome Mr Howell.

'Things will look better tomorrow.' At least, she hoped so. If he could see that she had other inventions, that she wasn't a woman who'd happened upon a singular idea, but a serious inventor, he might think differently about offering her the contract.

He shook his head. 'Why do you think anything will be different in the morning?'

Becca lifted her chin and met his green eyes squarely. 'Because, Mr Howell, you and I are not so vastly different in this moment. Right now, your problem is that you see us being on opposite sides. I want a contract that you don't want to give me. But I think you're looking at it all wrong. We aren't on opposite sides at all, we're on the *same* side.' She watched his brow furrow, his gaze sceptical of her logic.

'How do you reason that, Miss Peverett?'

'We want the same thing. You don't want to go home empty-handed and I don't want you to either. We are in this together and you give up too easily, Mr Howell.' She stuck out her hand. 'Do we have a deal? Stay the night, spend Sunday at the Hall and you can decide what you like on Monday.'

The grimness in his features faded and Becca would have given a small fortune to know what thoughts ran behind his eyes. 'Well, if there's a picnic involved, I can hardly say no.'

He should have said no. That one thought drummed through Jules's head as he was shown up the polished

oak banister to a chamber where his trunk had already
been unpacked and expertly put away, his cufflinks in
a trifle tray, his shirts neatly tucked into the drawers of
the Queen Anne highboy and his brush and razor laid
out beside the washstand. He should have got into the
coach, gone straight to the inn and nursed his disap-
pointments with a never-ending stream of ale until the
trains started running. What he *shouldn't* have done
was let himself get talked into the comfortable room
where he already felt at home amid the careful arrangement of his things, or the promise of a good meal, or
given into the challenge she'd thrown down with her
words, *you give up too easily, Mr Howell.*

But he'd done all those things instead of the one
thing he ought to have done, all because he liked to
be right. He would stay and prove to her that he did
not give up too easily and that, come morning, things
would not have changed. In another twenty-four hours,
Rebecca Peverett would still be female and he could absolutely not sign a contract with a woman. His brother
would see it as proof of his unsuitability for even the
simplest of company tasks.

The consequences of such unsuitability were com-
plex. On the one hand, he did not care. The family
business did not appeal to him. On the other, he supposed he didn't want to lose his access to the money.
He was a Howell, after all, and the prospect of *not*
having money was frightening to a Howell. But there
was also the prospect of letting his brother down, the
one person who had ever believed in him. At least at
one point in time Winthrop had. Perhaps, too, a part

of him didn't want to fail himself any more than he already had. Again, came the insidious little thought that drifting through life on the family's money was no longer his idea of success or that it never had been, he'd only convinced himself it was.

Jules tested the water in the ewer beside the wash-stand. It was pleasantly hot and he could already imagine how delicious the hot water would feel against his face, washing away the dirt of the day. He poured the water into the basin and stared at the face looking out at him from the mirror. What the hell was he going to do? He was thirty years old and he had no idea what to do about the ophthalmoscope he was supposed to contract and no idea about what to do with his life. He'd need an idea for the latter once Winthrop heard about this little debacle.

Jules washed his face and stripped out of his shirt to shave. There were a lot of things he should have said no to. Most of all he should have said no to *her*, but Rebecca Peverett had taken him unawares on the front steps with her arguments. Women seldom argued with him—there was usually no need. But she was something of a surprise, this polite quiet miss with the smooth walnut hair who wasn't really polite or quiet after all. Behind those steady cognac eyes was a quick mind and a sharp wit. She'd not been afraid to challenge him, to take aim at his pride and his assumptions. He'd not been prepared for either. The women he knew either wanted to bed him or marry him. The one group weren't interested in thinking and the other wanted to reform him. Rebecca Peverett wasn't interested in either option, which made her something else altogether. He didn't have a category for her.

He ran his razor down one side of his jaw and then the other, thinking about her words. *We are on the same side, Mr Howell.* It was ages since anyone had been on his side. Not even Winthrop was on his side these days. He missed that. Growing up, he and Winthrop were always on the same side, the two of them together vying for their father's attentions. In truth, the loss of Winthrop's support hurt the most.

He shook the soapy foam off his razor and dipped it into the hot water for another pass. Rebecca Peverett might have persuaded him to stay, but he was on to her. She meant to wine and dine him into compliance. That was the biggest reason he should not have stayed. By staying, he'd sent the message that perhaps he could be wooed, that he was willing to play their game, and that he had a price. Maybe he did. He was here, after all. He'd sold himself to Howell Manufacturing years ago in exchange for expensive clothes, a luxurious town house and pockets full of money. Perhaps that made him not so different from Winthrop, after all.

Jules wiped his face with a towel and strode to the wardrobe, carefully selecting a dark jacket and trousers and a waistcoat of watered green. Well, he knew better now. Forewarned was forearmed. He'd be ready for Miss Peverett's next volley.

Except that he wasn't. He'd been braced for a showy supper full of courses served on china plates and wine flights poured into crystal and the Peveretts dressed to impress. Nothing could be further from the reality that met him in the Haberstock Hall dining room. The four of them sat at one end of the table, platters and bowls set down the middle between them amid the heavy silver candlesticks and crystal goblets so that they could serve themselves at will on china plates, an interesting contrast between the formal and the informal. Like himself, Miss Peverett had changed for supper, but he felt positively gaudy next to her plain forest-green gown—not of silk, he noticed—but of a soft wool. Her hair was pinned up to reveal the long slim column of her neck and frame the curve of her jaw. Hers was a quiet, understated beauty that would be overlooked in places like London and Manchester.

'The china service is beautiful,' he complimented Catherine Peverett as they began to fill their plates.

'It's my great-grandmother's. It was part of my trousseau when I married.' Catherine smiled, glancing at her husband warmly. Jules did the multiplication. A dish set that was nearly a hundred years old. How many meals it must have seen! Unlike his mother's china, which was rotated out every few years to keep up with fashion. Just another sign of how deep the roots ran at Haberstock Hall.

Dr Peverett poured him a glass of red wine. 'My son-in-law's family sends this to me. Tell me what you think of it.'

Jules tasted the wine, surprised by its quality. 'It's excellent. Definitely French, I'd say.'

'Have you spent much time in France, Mr Howell?' Miss Peverett enquired, her cognac eyes resting on him, assessing him. 'I hear French women have more liberties than English women.'

He had the distinct impression he was being set up. 'I could not say, Miss Peverett,' he said, dodging the question diplomatically. The women he associated with in Paris were certainly free with their liberties, but that wasn't what Miss Peverett was asking about.

'I look forward to the day when women can attend Oxford,' Miss Peverett continued, her gaze steady on him as she pursued her argument. 'My sister, Thea, is studying medicine in Germany. She's a countess and it's still not enough to get her into a medical college here,' she announced, suggesting that England lagged behind the Continent in terms of women's education. 'It's ridiculous she has to go so far away simply because she's female.' Just as it was ridiculous that her contract was pending because she was a woman. Jules did not overlook the subtle message intended for him.

He also did not overlook another, perhaps unintended message: she missed her sister. She didn't like her sister being so far away. His family preferred him far away. He doubted he was ever missed. He could hardly imagine Winthrop pining for him over dinner. Then again, he could hardly imagine his family sitting down to a supper where everyone served themselves and spoke openly about women studying at a university alongside men.

Catherine Peverett offered him a benevolent smile. 'Have we shocked you with our manners or perhaps the lack of them? No doubt you are used to more formal affairs. If it's any consolation, this is rather tame.

You should see it when they're all home, spouses and grandchildren included.' Her smile widened, suggesting that she looked forward to that time. Jules chuckled, picturing the long table filled with the five Peverett siblings, their spouses *and* young children. What a raucous meal that would be. His father would absolutely hate it. Perhaps that was why he suddenly yearned to see that spectacle. He'd made it a practice to like the things his father despised.

Careful, Old Boy, the warning whispered in his head. *You're here for business. You're not here to like them.* Even he knew sentimental attachment was not the best grounds on which to do business.

Catherine Peverett rose. 'We'll leave you gentlemen to your brandies.' Jules felt a strange sense of deflation filter through him at the thought of the meal coming to an end. Usually, he looked forward to brandies, the best part of the meal, really. But not tonight. He was relieved when Dr Peverett set aside his napkin.

'No need for that, my dear. We've been at the table longer than usual. Why don't we all adjourn to the music room? Rebecca and I have been working on a duet.'

An evening of music. How very country. How very *different* than the high stakes, high-priced evenings he was used to in Manchester, whiling away the nights at expensive gaming hells with expensive women sitting on his lap while he poured expensive champagne down their throats. By rights, the thought of a musical evening should have sent him running, but Jules found he couldn't muster the usual distaste for a home-grown night in. Perhaps it was the novel idea of watching a father and daughter sit down at the piano, participating in a pastime together, that had his curiosity piqued. How interesting, foreign even, to watch parents and children, even grown children, doing something together and enjoying it.

'Do you play an instrument, Mr Howell?' Rebecca asked as he fell in step beside her.

'No, I'm afraid not,' he confessed, feeling as if he'd somehow disappointed her or that he'd come up lacking. Again. He ought to be used to it. He'd been lacking for years in his father's eyes. But something unexplainable didn't want to disappoint this woman he had just met.

'We all play. My father believes music has healing properties. Thea and William both play the cello. My father, Thomasia and I play the piano and Anne sings. Thea's husband plays the piano as well. He could tour Europe if he wanted. He's that good.' Of course he was. Of course, Thea, the countess who was studying medicine in Germany, had a married a man—an earl, no less—who was perfection itself, Jules thought uncharitably. He'd never even met the couple and he was jealous of them. 'You admire your sister.' As she did not admire him; yet another reason to be jealous of them. Rebecca Peverett would not do business with a man she didn't respect.

Miss Peverett flashed him a brief smile. 'I admire all of my siblings, sir.' Yet another difference between them. He'd once admired Winthrop, looked up to him. But then, Winthrop had sided with the enemy.

'I sing a little,' he offered without meaning to. Whatever had prompted him to say that? He hadn't sung in ages, not since his father had determined singing was for sissies when he was twelve, back when he still cared what his father thought, back when he *wanted* to please his father instead of irritating him. They entered the music room and Miss Peverett gave him a polite nod that said she doubted his claim. 'What is it, Miss Peverett—don't you believe me?'

She cocked her head to one side and studied him. 'No, it's not that, Mr Howell. I'm just trying to figure you out. It's what inventors do.'

Chapter Four

She could *not* figure him out. Rebecca peered over the sheet music as she sat at the piano beside her father. What a puzzle Jules Howell was. He was nothing like she'd anticipated. When she'd imagined someone coming from Howell Manufacturing, she'd not thought of them sending one of the owner's sons. Instead, she'd pictured a smallish man of middle years who wore wire-rimmed glasses and a tweedy suit, not this man who matched her father in height, with broad shoulders that filled out his city-tailored jackets, hair long enough to border on unfashionable and green eyes a girl could get lost in. Plenty of girls probably had. He was roguishly handsome and from the way he turned on his smile he knew the power of his charms.

But what to do with him? He wasn't the usual company representative and that had her searching her mind for a way to convince him to take the invention.

Was he even a man of science and invention? Did he understand how machines worked? She'd been relying on her workshop and other inventions to intrigue him, but she'd been expecting a man of science who would naturally be interested in such things. He looked as if he was more interested in card games and…well, more rakish pursuits. She would leave it at that.

She watched surreptitiously as he took a seat by the fire and flashed her mother another of his charming smiles. What did those smiles hide? Was he bored already? Was he wilting inside at the thought of a simple evening of music at a country house? Or was she thinking too much? Was there anything at all behind those smiles? In London, a charming man was quite often only charming with no bottom beneath him. A very disappointing sort of man.

Her father nudged her leg. 'Are you ready?' She gave a nod and they launched into a lively version of '*Eine Kleine Nachtmusik*' arranged for four hands. The piece was quickly paced through its opening, although she had the easier part, leaving the more intricate runs to her father, but the energy of the piece was irresistible and she found herself smiling and laughing with her father as they played. They were breathless with laughter as they finished to the applause of their small audience.

'That was spectacular, well done,' Jules Howell enthused, coming to his feet and bestowing a wide smile on her that she felt to her toes along with a look she couldn't quite decipher—part-admiration, part-incredulity perhaps? It was the last she couldn't quite name. Amazement? But at what? Certainly not her. She'd never been the type to amaze a man, certainly not such a handsome one—that was Thomasia's talent. Men usually looked right through her as if she weren't even there.

Rebecca rose and made a laughing curtsy, the thrum of energy still humming through her veins, making her bold. 'It's your turn now, Mr Howell. Come and sing for us.' A glance of challenge passed between them as they smiled at one another. Would he demur? Find some excuse? She more than half expected him to. She rather thought he'd been bluffing in the hallway earlier. But he surprised her yet again, coming to stand beside the piano and riffling through the music.

'I am familiar with this one.' He set the music on the rack and gave her a private smile that set his eyes to twinkling. Now it was he who was calling her bluff. 'You'll accompany?'

She sat back down at the piano bench with a nod and played a few introductory measures. He'd selected a ballad called 'The Irish Soldier' that had become popular during the war in the Crimea. It was not a complicated song, making up for its simplicity with the poignancy of its lyrics as it told the story of an Irish soldier who fell in love on the eve of leaving for battle against the Russians.

It was a sad song of young lovers parted, awaiting an uncertain future, and Howell did not disappoint. He had a pleasant tenor that brought the story to life and drew all eyes to him. It was a good thing her hands knew their way around a keyboard because she couldn't take her eyes from him as he sang. He'd not lied. He could indeed sing. More than that, she noticed, he *enjoyed* singing, it was there in his face, his smile, his gaze. Watching him, listening to him, was mesmerising. She managed to coax two more songs from him before she had to give him and the magic he wove up to the tea cart.

He lowered the lid on the piano as she put away the music. 'Did I pass muster, Miss Peverett?' he asked quietly.

Rebecca blushed, feeling foolish for her earlier doubt. 'You know you did. You sing splendidly.' She wasn't so petty that she couldn't admit when she was wrong.

He rewarded her with a smile. 'Thank you for your modest validation.'

If only that validation went both ways, Rebecca thought as they sipped tea and wound down the evening. She'd need his validation tomorrow. In the morning, she needed him to get past his bias regarding her gender and appreciate her as an inventor.

Rebecca's nerves were entirely on edge by the time they tramped down to her cottage workshop the next day. She'd spent the morning trying to convince herself this was a Sunday morning like any other. There'd been the large Sunday breakfast to get through followed by the short journey to the village for church. She'd spent the service seated beside Mr Howell, who smelled of freshly shaved male, all juniper and sandalwood with perhaps a hint of vanilla beneath it to keep the scent from being too sharp. He'd dressed in the suit he'd worn upon arrival yesterday and had garnered plenty of appreciative looks from the female members of the congregation, all of which he answered with one of his broad smiles.

Sharing her prayer book and listening to his beautiful tenor sing familiar hymns had done nothing to settle her jangled nerves. She was far too cognizant of him, sitting so close to her that their hands, arms, even legs, were bound to brush against one another during the course of the service, each touch sending a warm jolt of renewed awareness through her. How was she to focus on church or her inventions when his very presence seemed to steal all of her attention?

Finally, it was time to go to the workshop, Mr Howell offering to carry the picnic hamper as they made the journey to the cottage, tramping over leaf-strewn paths beneath a lowering pewter-coloured sky that boded ill for the picnic she had planned. She would worry about that later. Right now, she had to impress him with what lay beyond the cottage door.

'Here we are, my workshop.' She couldn't keep the pride out of her voice as she pulled out her key and unlocked the door. She stepped inside, Mr Howell following, suddenly seeing her prized space through his eyes. Doubt speared her. How would a man from a big city, with an enormous factory at his disposal, see her cottage? Would he laugh? Would it be too informal for him? Would he see nothing more than a cottage with a worktable and second-hand furniture instead of a place where dreams came alive?

She busied herself stirring up the fire. Keeping her hands active helped settle her nerves at last, but not her doubts. She was tempted to offer excuses: *I know it's not much, it's the best that's available.* But those wouldn't only be excuses, they'd be lies. This was her place and she was proud of it and the work that happened here. She would not demean it with apologies. Becca hung the kettle over the fire out of habit and brushed her hands against her skirt. When she turned to face him, she was determined. She would show Mr Howell just how proud she was of this place and of herself.

'This is where the magic happens.' Becca strode to the worktable where the bifocal lenses were laid out in pieces. 'Along with the ophthalmoscope, I am working on developing a more durable bifocal lens.' She explained the fusion process she was contemplating and moved on to the rubber and metal parts that made up her latest foray into stethoscopes. 'I've been thinking about the possibility of expanding the purpose of the stethoscope by creating a two-sided chest piece that can listen to both the lungs and the heart. When my brother-in-law returned from the Crimea, he suffered respiratory problems. It would have been helpful to be able to listen to his lungs as well as his heart.'

'What's this?' Howell picked up a glass cylinder.

'The beginnings of a more refined hypodermic needle.' Rebecca nodded at the items in his hand. 'I think glass might serve better than the current reliance on a metal tube.'

'A syringe, you mean?' Howell held the cylinder up, studying it.

'They're different, Mr Howell. A syringe extracts, but a needle injects. There's a doctor in Dublin who came up with the current design about ten years ago, but I think we can do better. As an instrument of study, we've been trying to refine the needle for centuries, millennia even.' She reached for the parts, roughly assembling her prototype. 'All needles operate with the same three parts: a plunger, a barrel and a piston. The Egyptians knew this and yet, here we are, not much further advanced except in the materials we have to work with.'

'To what purpose, though?' Howell furrowed his brow. 'What do we need to inject people for?'

'To better administer pain medication, for a start.' She put the needle down and went to her bookcase, rummaging for an article. 'Here it is.' She handed him the paper. 'Dr Rynd in Ireland was able to directly inject a woman with pain-relieving medication and within minutes her pain was gone. That's far faster than we can deliver medication and make it interact with the symptom orally—by mouth,' she clarified. 'I think about the future of immunology, too.' Again, his handsome brow furrowed and she backtracked. She was forever assuming everyone was as invested in the medical field as she was. It was an easy assumption to make when one's whole family were healers. 'Do you know Edward Jenner? The man with the smallpox vaccine?' She was relieved when he nodded. 'I think that's just the beginning. There are likely other illnesses that can be prevented by vaccination and a hypodermic needle could be the way those vaccines are delivered.' He was looking at her oddly and she feared she'd said too much. Would he think she was a crazy woman inventing crazy contraptions in a cottage, not even a real inventor's laboratory?

He delivered his verdict with considering, solemn green eyes. 'You are singularly the most interesting woman I've ever met, Miss Peverett. You play the piano, you read medical journals and you envision a future few haven't dared dream of.'

Rebecca flushed. 'Thank you, Mr Howell, I will take that as a compliment.'

She was far too trusting, sharing too much in her enthusiasm or perhaps in her efforts to build her credibility with him, and he was taking unfair advantage of her. Jules wanted to stop her, to tell her to keep her amazing ideas and her incredible world to herself, that she was tempting him beyond measure. If his brother knew what he'd stumbled on to here in the unlikely wilds of Hertfordshire, Winthrop would want it all, every last invention she had on the table and whatever else was in this rustic cottage in order to impress their father, and once his father got hold of them… Well, that was a recipe for disaster.

His father would not pay her for them—even if he did offer her some compensation, it would not be what they were all worth. He would use her gender as a reason to pay her less, or worse, his father would take the ideas and put the company men on them and she would get no acknowledgment. Jules had seen it happen before with a Frenchman who had a high-powered portable telescope. His father had politely turned the gentleman down and then put his own designers on the product and come up with his own. It would be too easy to do the same to Miss Peverett. Easier, in fact, because she was a woman and had no legal status to begin with.

Jules supposed he didn't have to tell Win about the things he'd seen here, but that didn't help his own cause. Other inventions aside, it also still didn't address the immediate situation with the ophthalmoscope. He'd still be going home empty-handed instead of going home with a treasure chest that would make Howell Manufacturing a fortune for generations to come.

'It is a compliment, Miss Peverett, but you should be careful who you tell such things to. These are innovative ideas and you should make sure they remain your ideas.' He would at least try to warn her. He'd never asked her to trust him and he'd never offered that trust. Business was business and he had his own head to watch out for. It was already on his brother's chopping block.

Jules walked away from the table, making a circuit of the cottage. A woman's workshop was quite different from a man's. This place was cosy, warm, homely, orderly. He wished some of that orderliness would translate to his thoughts. He tried to sort through the riot in his head. What to do about the inventions? What to do about her—this intelligent, open, honest, young woman who, for all her intelligence, had put her trust in him, the very last person who deserved it.

'Out with it, Mr Howell,' Rebecca demanded from the table, her hands on hips. 'You seem lost in thought. What is troubling you?'

He decided to meet her directness with directness of his own. He stood with his backside to the fire, letting its warmth ease him. 'If you were a man, Miss Peverett, I'd be offering you a contract for your ophthalmoscope and more. Your inventions and ideas are impressive. But you're not a man and I haven't any notion how to go on in a way that will get you what you deserve.'

'Does anyone *have* to know? At least not right away? Not until the deal is done and the invention has proven itself?' She offered him a half-smile. 'You're not the only one who's been thinking about our dilemma.'

The idea surprised him. She'd been so adamant about a woman being a man's equal yesterday, he'd not thought she'd settle for anything but outright recognition, that she'd want the fame. 'I'll have recognition, only delayed,' Rebecca explained. 'Sometimes we have to use the doors we're given, even if they're back doors. You can go home with a contract, which is what both of us want.'

His mind began to work. It could be done, although it came with a large sacrifice on her part. It did make him wonder why she was so willing to defer her acknowledgment. What was he missing? Did the family need money? Money was the only motive he could think of. In his world it was the great motivator for everything—it was what drove his father, drove his brother, it was what he feared losing if he failed on this mission. Money was the water of life for the Howells. Without money, they crumbled. It seemed that Rebecca Peverett was made out of sterner stuff. What was *her* water of life? What was the one thing that sustained her? He found he wanted to know.

Overhead, the weather announced itself, rain drumming loud and insistent on the cottage roof, the grey clouds finally giving up their bounty. Rebecca glanced up at the ceiling with a grimace. 'I was afraid of that. Our picnic will have to be postponed. I had wanted to show you the waterfall. It's quite a sight to see in autumn with the scarlet maples in flaming colour.'

'I would have liked to have seen it,' Jules said, realising he meant it. He wasn't ready to go back to the house yet. He was still sorting through his thoughts and her rather surprising idea. Of course, she wouldn't be the only one making a sacrifice. His own level of risk would not be insignificant. Could he fool Win with their temporary charade? What would happen when Win found out? He needed time to think. He didn't want to return to the house and play the good guest just yet. 'We can at least salvage our picnic. We'll do it here, indoors before the fire.' He went to retrieve the hamper from where he'd left it by the door, one thought continuing to haunt him in regard to her proposal. 'Why are you willing to defer your acknowledgment, Miss Peverett?'

'It's simple, Mr Howell. I'm not doing it for fame. I'm doing it because it's my purpose. It's how I can contribute to the world, how I can make lives better. It's what I was born to do.' He'd never been more jealous of anyone than he was of Rebecca Peverett in that moment. She worked in anonymity in a stone cottage in the middle of nowhere and she had everything he'd ever wanted.

Chapter Five

She had what she wanted—the contract—and she'd got it mostly on her terms. The bubble of elation that fizzed through her as they laid the picnic blanket before the fire was tempered only by the small compromise of having to hide the totality of her identity for a short while. But surely that price was worth it. This was the first step towards living her dream, towards offering her innovations to the world beyond the village. The greater good was worth the temporary sacrifice.

Now, she was faced with another dilemma—since their business was resolved what was she to talk about with Mr Howell? There was still the whole picnic to get through and she had no idea how to make small talk. Asking a question here and there at dinner was one thing, as was making an argument in the heat of the moment, but making deliberate small talk for an extended period of time was another beast altogether and one she'd not mastered during her brief Season in London a couple of years ago. There wasn't much need for such a skill when one spent one's days working alone. But she was in desperate need of it now.

She had planned on the walk to the waterfall to supply its own conversation. They could have talked about the trees, commented on the autumn foliage. She could have told stories about the Hall. They might have spied a deer or two. But what was there to speak of but themselves? *He* might be an interesting subject, but she definitely was not.

Becca opened the hamper and laid out the food: ham, fresh bread, a half-wheel of cheese, a carefully wrapped portion of chocolate cake left over from dessert two nights ago and a jug of cider. They'd need mugs for that. Becca rose to retrieve them from her cupboard, wishing her sister, Thomasia, was here. Thomasia always knew what to say. She came back to the blanket, holding the mugs aloft. 'I think we've got it all now.'

He smiled up at her from his seat on the blanket, looking entirely at ease. She envied him that ease. She'd noticed it last night at dinner, too, how easily he conversed with her parents and again today at church, greeting all the villagers. He had already made himself busy, slicing bread and carving ham. He passed her a plate. 'I took the liberty of giving you a little of everything. It looks delicious. After breakfast I didn't think I could eat another bite all day, but the sight of this food makes my stomach rumble.'

Becca sat, tucking her skirts about her as she took the plate. 'Thank you. The bread is fresh from this morning.' What a foolish thing to say. 'The cheese is from our own dairy as well. My mother has a special way of curing it.' Another foolish statement. What was it Thomasia always said about the key to conversation? Ask a man about himself and he'll talk for hours. She groped for a topic that might inspire conversation. 'What do you enjoy most about the manufacturing business, Mr Howell?'

'Jules, please. I do believe I've insisted on it before.' He smiled, perhaps thinking to put her at ease, although that smile did just the opposite. She felt those smiles to her toes and they set butterflies flitting in her stomach, but they weren't so distracting that she didn't notice he hadn't answered the question.

'Jules, then.' It felt daring to use the man's first name. 'Do you invent as well?'

'No.' He seemed inordinately busy building a sandwich for himself. 'I travel for the company. I am seldom at home.'

'Do you enjoy that? I suppose it must be interesting seeing different places.'

'It keeps me out of trouble, usually.' There was something about the way he said it that made her cock her head in contemplation. He wasn't entirely joking.

'Those are hardly the words of a man who likes his work,' Becca ventured. 'If you don't enjoy it, why do you do it?'

'Howell Manufacturing is a family business,' he explained. 'In order to *be* a family business, the family must participate. Perhaps not unlike the healers of Haberstock Hall? All of you are in the family business of providing health care.'

Becca laughed. 'The healers of Haberstock Hall. I like that. Of course, we all chose that path. We are drawn to our work and that makes all the difference. Does the family expect you to take over the company?'

He chuckled. 'Heavens, no. That's my brother Winthrop's job. He sits at the helm now that my father has stepped back. No, the family has no such expectations of me.'

She couldn't tell if that saddened or gladdened him. One moment he seemed resentful of the family business and the next he resented the idea of being put outside it. And yet, yesterday on the porch, he'd been quite determined to not go home empty-handed. A man who truly didn't care wouldn't be desperate for a deal. There were turbulent depths behind those laughing green eyes. 'What would you do if your time was your own?' She was genuinely curious now and the questions were coming fast.

'That is the burning question, isn't it?' he said with all seriousness. 'I haven't allowed myself to ponder it in years.' He smiled, but she was ready for it. He would not disarm her so easily this time. She felt a competition brewing between them. How long could he dodge, how far would she press?

'There must be something, Jules?' Becca persisted.

'*Must* there be?' He laughed, still trying to disarm her.

'Yes. Everyone has a passion.'

Sombre green eyes held hers. 'Not everyone is like you. You are lucky to have found yours while you're young.' He leaned towards the cloth-covered dessert.

'But if you insist I have a passion, in this moment it is chocolate cake. May I cut you a slice?'

She retreated, letting him think he'd won the round. She took a few bites of chocolate cake before launching her ambush. 'But when you *did* ponder it, what did you imagine doing?'

He stopped in mid-bite of his cake, his expression a mix of startled resignation. 'You do not play fair, Rebecca.'

Neither did he. The sound of her name on his lips, spoken before a cosy fire while rain pelted the windows, brought a different sort of heat, a heat that made her feel reckless and heady. 'Call me Becca. Everyone does.'

'Is that what we are? Friends?' His voice was soft and dangerous. 'After only a day? Do you know me so well, then?'

Becca felt her temper spark. 'I'd like to, although you make it rather difficult with your refusal to answer any of my questions.'

'Not everyone is worthy of your friendship, Becca. You should be more careful who you offer it to. Besides, hasn't anyone ever told you not to mix business with pleasure?' He was being cruel now, treating her as if she was a naive dupe with childlike notions of the world, or at least he was trying to.

She couldn't fully believe it. It seemed out of character for the man who'd joined in the music last night. He was defending himself the way a cornered animal protected itself, by striking out with ferocity. 'For the record, I don't think you're mean. I think you're unhappy.' Perhaps his unhappiness was the cause of those turbulent depths she'd glimpsed for only a moment.

He gave a sharp laugh. 'Why ever would you think that?'

'Because I once found a dog out wandering in the woods, lost and hurt. He was limping, thin, half starved. His ear was torn. He'd been in a fight with something. He was in no condition to hunt for himself. He needed help or he wasn't going to make it. He'd just lay down and starve to death. Surely he knew that. Dogs are smart. And yet, when I approached, offering help and comfort, an answer for all that ailed him, his hackles went up and he snarled. He backed up against a tree and prepared to resist with all he had left.'

'Perhaps he resisted giving up his freedom. What you offered didn't come without price,' Jules argued and her heart melted just a bit. He could not see, perhaps, how much alike he and that dog were. 'Well? Are you going to tell me the rest of the story?' he prompted when she fell silent. 'Did he run off and die of his stubbornness?'

'No, he lives in our stable, proudly patrolling our stalls since he's retired from running to the hunt,' Becca announced with a surge of pride. 'I named him Thomas, for Doubting Thomas in the Bible.' She began to gather up the picnic things, but Jules's hand gently closed about her wrist.

'You don't get away so easily. Sit down and tell me the story. How did you do it? How do we go from snarling with his back to a tree to being a beloved, ageing hunting hound?'

Becca put the plates down and resumed her seat. 'I waited him out. I sat down with a piece of meat in my hand and waited. And, yes, it took most of the day. I tossed him a bite first and then other bites, each bite landing closer to me than the last until, finally, I stretched out on my belly, my hand extended with a morsel and he took it from me. Then another and another from my hand until he let me put a rope about him and lead him home. Patience and tenacity are the two best tools anyone can have.' They sat in thoughtful silence for a while. Had she gone too far? Even if her assumptions were correct, he might not care to have her bruiting them about out loud. Perhaps she should have taken more care until her name was actually on the contract.

Rebecca Peverett had proved her boldness once again. In doing so, she'd managed to strip him bare and not in the usual way he was stripped bare at picnics either. He ought to say something glib and witty that would cut her story down to size, but Jules found he only wanted to sit there before the fire, thinking over what she'd said, every word of it. Especially that story about the dog. He'd thought the questions about his interests were bad enough, probing into the empty depths of his soul. Didn't she see, he was protecting her with his reticence? When a gentleman didn't tell a lady something it was because he didn't want her to be disappointed or shocked. He'd tried to warn her away from the abyss of him. But then she'd ambushed him.

I don't think you're cruel, I think you're hurting. 'You think I'm like that dog?' he said at last.

'I think you share some similarities,' she answered calmly.

'I don't think men are like dogs,'

'Well, you might be surprised.' She smiled softly at him and they both laughed. Out of habit, his gaze dropped to her mouth. This would be the perfect moment to steal a kiss, to take advantage of the quiet intimacy that had sprung up between them and see where it led, because that was how he knew to respond to such a moment.

But Becca Peverett wasn't that sort of girl. She was a good girl and he knew where things led with good girls—right down the aisle to the altar, the last place on earth he should end up with a girl like her, who would expect romance and responsibility from the man she married. He could manage romance, but not love, and the two were definitely *not* the same thing. He had nothing to offer such a girl, only heartache and disappointment when they realised he couldn't change, that perhaps there was nothing in him *to* change.

The Howells knew nothing of love, only money. Quite the opposite of the Peveretts. Rebecca had been raised surrounded by love. He'd only been here a day and already he knew that much. Love, care and concern oozed from every pore of Haberstock Hall. Just the simple way Catherine Peverett had spoken of her family around the dinner table had signified as much. His own mother wouldn't be caught dead professing such an unguarded depth of feeling for her family. No, he could offer a girl like Becca nothing she deserved. He ought to stay away, ought to resist the temptation.

Curiosity whispered none the less. What would she do if he leaned across the blanket and stole a sweet kiss from those soft lips? Would she slap him? Or would she open to him, let him taste her goodness for a moment? That moment would ruin everything. Would she feel she *had* to kiss him, that it somehow would affect their deal? Would she feel if she refused him that he might refuse her the contract? He never wanted to kiss a woman who felt she had to *endure* his attentions. Jules rose from the blanket, tamping down on his temptation.

'Let me help you clean up,' he offered in gruff tones. Reluctant as he was to leave the workshop, he needed some space and perhaps some fresh air to clear his head from this business discussion that had become quite personal.

'Shall we sign the contract tonight?' Becca asked as she put the mugs back on the shelf. Apparently, she was also looking to restore some balance to the afternoon.

'Of course,' he replied briskly to indicate that he, too, was back to business. It had been easy to set that aside, to forget, amid the lovely ambience of the fireside picnic. 'Best to get it done since I'm leaving in the morning.' The last was meant more as reminder to himself. His work here was complete. He had what he needed, what Winthrop required of him, and what Becca wanted.

On all accounts, he ought to be pleased to return to Manchester, a signed contract in hand. And he was.

It was the speed of that return that had him less excited about it.

It was only ever supposed to be an overnight trip, he reminded himself. *You didn't even want to come. You were still resenting the venture right up until you got out of the carriage.*

When had that changed? When had he started to *want* to be here? He supposed the answer didn't matter. He was leaving tomorrow, regardless. He would return to Manchester, deliver the contact and seriously contemplate decamping for Italy before winter set in.

He offered to carry the now-empty basket, but she waved him off, insisting she could manage. 'In that case, this is where I leave you. I think I'll take a walk.' He wanted time to clear his head, to separate his business from the pleasure of the afternoon.

'Do you want me to come with you?' she offered quickly.

'No, I've taken enough of your time.' He didn't miss the flicker of disappointment in her eyes, as if she suspected he was making an excuse to be apart from her. Nothing could be further from the truth. He liked her company, perhaps a bit too much for a business arrangement, and he was of a mind to find the stables and track down a certain dog. 'Thank you for this afternoon, Becca.' For an afternoon that had been illuminating, that had made him think for the first time in a long time about his own passions, the things that once upon a time made him come alive.

'All right, if you're sure?' she asked once more before setting out.

He watched her go and when she'd gone a certain distance, he called out to her, 'Becca!' She turned and he raised his voice to be heard. 'Painting. If I could do anything, I would paint.'

'Not sing?' she called back.

He cupped his hands about his mouth and shouted, 'Maybe I'd do both!' Why not? Just the thought of it made him laugh, a little bubble of joy welling up inside him. What a life that would be. A life lived just for him.

His inner voice mocked him. *Isn't that what you have now? Are you not living your best life? You told Winthrop you were.*

But drifting through life hadn't ever been for himself, had it? It had been to gain his father's attention and when that had failed it had been to spite him. But it had not been for himself, not like singing or painting had. These were deep contemplations, all brought on by a single question from Becca Peverett. *What do you want?* He wasn't quite sure he knew any more.

Chapter Six

'Are you sure this what you want?' her mother asked as they adjourned to the music room after supper table, leaving the two men to their port and brandy. Supper had been a festive affair and there'd been champagne aperitifs beforehand to celebrate the successful conclusion of Jules's business. She'd fully disclosed the parameters of the arrangement with her parents. She would not lie to them about the nature of the agreement and there was no reason to. They'd taught her to think for herself, to be herself, but they'd also taught her that there would be a price for that. The world did not necessarily value the same things the Peveretts valued, to the world's detriment.

'Are you disappointed in me?' Becca took a seat on the sofa and smoothed her skirts. She'd opted to wear her rose silk tonight for the occasion. To celebrate, nothing more. She'd not worn her best dress for any other reason, certainly not to impress Jules Howell. She'd been firm with herself on that point. After all, the impressing was already done. The quality of her work had spoken for itself just as she'd hoped it would. The contract was signed. Business was done. She could influence it no further. Besides, it was superficial to seek a man's validation based on one's appearances. A woman was more than a doll, an ornament.

'Are you disappointed in yourself?' her mother countered. 'It does not matter what I think. I'm not the one making the compromise.'

'Sometimes a compromise is the only way to move forward.' She had given it much thought before she'd proposed the idea to Jules. 'I think if I had not put the idea out there the contract would not be signed. I don't think a stalemate would have worked in my favour. It's only temporary, so it's not entirely a compromise, merely a delay in revealing the person behind the initials.'

'You're not being pressured or *persuaded* in anyway?' Her mother looked worried and Becca suddenly wished she hadn't worn the rose silk. She didn't like the way her mother said 'persuaded'. Did her mother think she'd worn the gown for reasons other than celebration?

'I can't imagine what you mean by that.' Becca gave a laugh that sounded a bit too forced to her ears. But she knew very well what was behind her mother's suggestion. She did feel a connection with Jules. It was easy to talk with him, to argue with him, easy to crave more of the casual touches he tossed out as he escorted her to dinner or out to the workshop. Such touches came naturally to him and he used them abundantly.

'This is a mutual agreement. He doesn't want to

go back empty-handed and I need this. This opens up a whole new opportunity for me.' The chance to help people beyond her village and eventually the opportunity to be taken seriously as inventor. Perhaps she might even travel with some authority to places like France and Switzerland and see their great mechanics now that she had something to offer in return.

'Mr Howell is a charmer and it's no secret why the company sends him out to secure business. I can't imagine a dinner table that wouldn't benefit from his company. All I'm saying is that you wouldn't be the first female to have her head turned by such a man, nor the first to be taken advantage of. I would not want to see that happen.'

Rebecca bristled at the notion. 'I am a smart woman, Mother. You needn't worry that I would be taken unawares. Keeping the initials was *my* suggestion. He was going to leave and forget it all. If anyone is taking advantage, it is me.' Her mother smiled, but Rebecca didn't think she was convinced.

'It's only that you're young and you haven't much experience.' Her mother sighed. 'I worry for you. You spend so much time alone when you should be out socialising and meeting young people your own age.' They'd had this discussion before.

'Being alone doesn't mean I'm naive. Don't worry, Mother. You've raised me better than that. Everything will be fine.'

The gentlemen entered, finished with their port. 'Cards tonight?' her father offered. 'Howell here claims he's a fair hand at whist and I'm of a mind to call his bluff.' Her father chuckled, clapping Jules on the shoulder. 'Catherine, shall you and I show these young folk how it's done?'

It was the work of minutes to set up a card table and fetch a deck of cards. Rebecca took her seat across from Jules as her father shuffled the deck and dealt. Jules gave her a wink and she smiled, some of the magic of the afternoon returning, but that magic was tinged with doubts.

She tried to focus on the cards as a means of pushing those doubts away. To some extent she was successful. Cards with the Peveretts was an all-consuming activity, demanding a player's attention, and Becca hated to lose even to her parents, especially at whist. It was the one thing she did better than her siblings and Jules was a strong player. They took the first set, but her parents took the second, forcing a rubber match. But there were moments when she'd look across the table at Jules and the doubts would come roaring back.

She *wanted* to believe her brave words to her mother that everything would be fine, that she knew what she was doing. More than that, she wanted to dismiss her mother's concerns that Jules had manufactured a connection, perhaps even *feigned* a connection in order to secure the contract. That couldn't possibly be the case when the idea had been hers all along. Yet, the idea nibbled away at her throughout the evening, fed by her own self-doubts.

She was the plain, quiet Peverett. Why would a man like Jules Howell look twice at her when he could 'look twice' at any woman he wanted and they would look back? Watching him was like watching the very antithesis of herself. He was comfortable among strangers, easy in a crowd, whereas she only came alive in private. She was not a public person.

Jules threw down the jack of hearts with good-natured resignation as the clock on the mantel struck eleven. 'By Jove, sir, you've finessed the last card you need from me.' He gave a shrug. 'I'm sorry, my dear, there's nothing we can do to stop them now. The last two tricks are theirs.' The endearment warmed her although she knew it meant nothing. He threw out endearments like he threw out his charm; indiscriminately and without a care for the wild hope it might sow. Another, less astute female would take those words to heart, Rebecca thought.

Her father laid down his hand with a satisfied grin. 'It's a smart man who knows when he's beat. Well played, though. We haven't had such good competition for a long time.'

Jules rose and stretched. 'I enjoyed that very much.' He made a small bow in her direction. 'You are an excellent partner, Miss Peverett.' He shared his smile around with the group. 'I have enjoyed my time here beyond measure. I will regret leaving in the morning.'

'You are welcome any time.' Her father made the necessary gestures. 'I'll have the coach ready for you at seven. That will put you into Broxbourne at eight o'clock and there will be plenty of time to get your ticket and see to your trunk. I do apologise, I won't be on hand to see you off. I have rounds to make and I will have an early start myself.'

'Thank you, sir.' Jules shook her father's hand. 'Ladies, if you will excuse me? I'd like to go up and make sure all is in order for tomorrow.'

Was that it, then? Rebecca watched him exit the room, feeling deflated as if he'd already left. But what had she expected? That he would have a special goodbye for her? What would that goodbye be? Certainly not a teary goodbye, or one that ended with an embrace or stolen kiss. Just thinking of such a farewell was ridiculous in the extreme. They were operating on an acquaintance of barely two days. They were business partners, nothing more. Weren't such feelings, such expectations exactly what her mother had been warning against?

Still, she couldn't let him go without a final word. She was waiting for him at the breakfast table the next morning. It was too early for her stomach to be interested in eating, but she nursed a cup of hot coffee.

'Becca, what a surprise.' He entered the dining room with a smile that widened at the sight of her. It made getting up early worth every inconvenience. He looked wide awake, too, more awake than she felt. He was dressed for the city in a brown suit of fine wool, a coffee-coloured waistcoat and a silk cravat to match. The faint, pleasing scent of his sandalwood and spice toilette mixed with the scents of breakfast. She would look pale and sleepy and drab beside him. Perhaps she shouldn't have come down. Perhaps it would have been better to have his last memory of her be from last night in her rose silk.

'I wanted to be sure you had everything you needed, to be sure there were no last-minute papers,' she improvised a plausible reason for rising early. In reality, she wasn't ready to let him go. The last two days had been exciting not only because of the contract, but because of *him*. It made her realise how long it had been since she'd had company, or even a close friend, someone to be with, to talk to. She had her family, of course, but now they were married with families of their own or were off to war or living in London. Their absence emphasised more poignantly the lack of her own personal social circle.

He piled a plate with eggs and sausage and took a seat near her. 'I have everything I need. But I appreciate the company. It's no fun to eat alone. Shall I go over again what will happen when I get back to Manchester?'

Becca listened, just to hear him talk. She'd memorised the process the first time he'd told her. There would be meetings to analyse the scope's construction, parts to be made, machines to be calibrated for assembly, and then, finally, production would begin. 'Any questions?' he asked when he'd finished. Only the one question she couldn't ask: *Will I see you again?* But she could not ask that without ruining everything. Only a silly, swoony girl would ask such a thing. It would suggest that she saw their time together as something more than business and it would prove why women didn't do business—they couldn't remain objective, they'd read more into an interaction than was actually there. In truth, what had he done to make it seem otherwise?

'No, no questions. You've explained everything very well.' The clock in the hall chimed the half-hour and Becca set aside her coffee cup. This was it, then. Time for him to leave. 'The coach will be out front.'

She walked beside him to the front steps where the travelling coach was indeed waiting, the horses' breath steaming in the late-autumn air. She stuck out her hand to shake. 'Thank you for this opportunity.' It seemed a very business-like thing to say—a very *objective* thing to say—but he took her hand and bent over it with a smile, pressing a kiss to her knuckles as if they were at a grand ball, the gesture sending a warm jolt of awareness through her.

He let his gaze linger on hers, warm and green like summer moss. 'I think this is the beginning of a wonderful partnership. I will be in contact when there's news. It shouldn't be too long.' Then he was gone, folding his long form into the coach and shutting the door behind him. But he'd given her something to hold on to: he would be in contact. There would be a letter. She would hear from him. He wasn't gone from her entirely.

She waved once as the coach pulled out of the drive circle and then felt foolish for having done so. The gesture was nearly as foolish as her thoughts. If she was so desperate for company she should pay a visit across the village to Rosegate where her sister, Thomasia, lived. Perhaps an afternoon with her sister and her little niece was exactly what she needed to put Jules's visit into perspective. She was lonely, that was all, and it had her acting out of character.

* * *

He ought to be excited about returning to Manchester. Dreading going back to the city was entirely out of character for him. He *thrived* on city life, on the dining, the parties, the shops, the gambling hells, the opera and the theatre. Jules settled into his first-class seat by the window and tried to find some enthusiasm. By tonight, he could be in the family box at the Theatre Royale, watching whatever production was in town at the moment. Afterwards he could go to the Manchester Union Club on Moslel Street and shoot billiards with friends, perhaps pay a visit to Clementine's on Peter Street where the girls were always happy to see him. But the thought of Clementine's or the Union Club failed to stir a single iota of interest in him.

His mind seemed determined to stay fixed not on one of Clementine's exotic girls, but on an alabaster face with soft eyes that shone like candlelight on cognac. What would she spend the day doing? Would she be in her workshop by now, working on her stethoscope creation? Or would she go out to the stables and take a bone to that hound of hers? He leaned back in his seat and closed his eyes, letting his mind imagine her going through her day and when it was done with that, he pictured her as she'd been last night in the rose silk, sitting across the card table from him. They hadn't played for stakes, but the game had been one of the most enjoyable he'd played. She'd been an astute partner and they'd paired well together against her parents. She'd been a fierce competitor, too.

At first glance, one did not expect fierceness from

Rebecca Peverett, but it was there. He'd seen it displayed on the front porch the first night, proof that one only judged that particular book by its cover at one's own risk. She intrigued him. It had been a while since anything had held his interest. That explained his nascent obsession. She was a novel discovery. He opened his eyes and laughed at himself. He definitely needed to seriously consider Italy if a plain girl was his new definition of intriguing. He could still leave for Italy before winter set in.

She's not plain, came the whisper in his mind. *She's smart, she invented a portable ophthalmoscope—what have you invented besides trouble?*

That was just it. Rebecca Peverett was far too good for him: too smart, too trusting, too decent. For those reasons, he needed to keep his intrigue in Rebecca Peverett and Haberstock Hall to himself and eventually the spell both had woven about him this weekend would pass. His interests always did. Since he'd given up his singing and his painting, he had no direction, no staying power with anything. His passions altered with the wind. The only thing that had been constant about him in years was his inconsistency. For the first time in two days, he reached for his flask, realising with some surprise that he hadn't missed it until now.

Chapter Seven

'Father, what a surprise. I did not expect to see you today.' Or any day. Jules had not expected his sire to attend the meeting between him and Winthrop. He was on full alert as Stefan Howell settled in a chair set before the wide desk he used to occupy daily, a tall, lean man of sixty plus years with a full, sleek, leonine head of white hair and sharp green eyes. Jules had often thought looking at his father was like looking at himself in the mirror. His paternity was etched in every line of his face, something which had once pleased him until he realised his father took no pride in that shared likeness.

'I am eager to see what Hertfordshire has coughed up.' His father didn't bother to rise and shake his hand, but remained seated, crossing one leg over a knee and folding his hands across the flat of his stomach expectantly. It seemed if he had not exactly been missed, his return had at least been anticipated. And along with that return, had they been anticipating his success or his failure?

Jules took his customary seat in the guest's chair, feeling very much the prodigal. He was glad now, in a petty sort of way, that he'd made them wait for his report instead of rushing over the moment he'd disembarked from the train. He'd pointedly ignored the dinner invitation that arrived an hour after his return to Manchester yesterday, opting instead for privacy in order to savour his trip to Hertfordshire a little while longer.

'Did you get the contract?' his father asked. There was no preamble, no general enquiry, 'how was the trip?' or 'how are you?', just straight to business.

'Yes, I got the contract.' Jules began to divest himself of the materials he'd brought, keeping his nerves in check. This would be the moment of truth. Had Winthrop and his father set him up? Had this trip been concocted between them to ensure his failure? That made more sense. He couldn't quite believe it of Winthrop acting alone. He could believe it of his father, though. His father had always been one to test them, to push them, to play them off one another, offering a prize only one of them could win. Was this another of those cruel games? Jules supposed he would know soon enough.

Jules pushed the folder forward on the polished surface of the desk, deliberately making a show of bypassing his father in preference for Winthrop. His father's cold gaze rested on him, letting him know he'd not missed the subtle reminder as to who was in charge now. Jules waited, half expecting Winthrop to burst out with, 'Ha! *You* signed a woman! How could you think of such a thing? This proves how incompetent you truly are. Couldn't you stand your ground and say no?' But there were no recriminations, no revealing of a secret agenda. Winthrop merely shut the folder and nodded. Only then did he pass the folder to their father.

'Very good. I assume you brought the prototype with you?' Winthrop nodded towards the pouch at Jules's feet and Jules breathed a little easier. The first hurdle was passed for him and for Becca. Being set up for failure didn't serve either of them.

Jules took the ophthalmoscope from the pouch and unwrapped it, carefully laying it on the desk. Winthrop picked it up, holding it aloft to study it from all angles. 'This is excellent work, not too many little pieces. It should be easy to replicate. I'll have the men get right on it, figuring out the cost of manufacturing and crafting pieces for assembly.' Winthrop set the scope down on the desk and fixed Jules with an approving stare that immediately had Jules feeling guilty for thinking the worst of his brother. Winthrop hadn't been out to get him. 'I was worried when you didn't come to dinner last night that you'd not got the contract.'

'I wanted some time to myself,' Jules offered obliquely with a shrug to say his decline of the invitation was of no import. He hadn't wanted to be among the others of his usual set: Winthrop and Mary, his friends at the clubs. He'd stayed in for the first time in months, shocking his cook and housekeeper. He'd spent the evening sitting before his fire, his mind miles away in Hertfordshire, wondering if Becca was doing the same. Was she working late in the cottage or sitting in the music room with her parents?

'Well? Is that all you have to say?' Stefan interrupted. 'How was our new client? Is he an agreeable man?'

Agreeable was not a word he'd use to describe Rebecca Peverett. Creative. Driven. Tenacious. Those suited her much better. 'Our client is pleased to do business with us.' He could say that much without lying.

'Is there any potential for future business?' his father asked. This was the moment Jules both hoped for and dreaded. The hope was for Becca. She would be thrilled if Howell Manufacturing was interested in more of her work. He could imagine her face lighting up at the news. He would be thrilled, too. It would mean more visits to Haberstock Hall, a thought that he would not have enjoyed entertaining a week ago. It would mean no Italy this winter.

The dread came from knowing that the little deception he and Becca had wrought would continue, it would start to take on a life of its own if he said yes. But what else could he say? If he said no, he'd be letting Becca and her dreams down and that sat inexplicably poorly with him. She was counting on him, which in itself was a novel idea. No one had ever really counted on him. There was dread in that, too. Dread that she would not be treated fairly by his family and he would not be enough to prevent it. 'Yes, I do believe there is. There are other items we might be interested in.'

'Any of them patented?' Stefan's gaze was hawkishly alert and Jules knew what his father was thinking.

'No.' His father would be glad of that. The company could acquire the patent and then own the item for themselves. There'd be less haggling over rights and profits, the sale more straightforward. Becca had known that and she would be counting on him to protect her interests because she couldn't negotiate on her behalf without giving herself away. That made Jules nervous. His father had behaved unscrupulously in the past when it came to patents and permissions. The situation with the Frenchman rose in his mind.

Winthrop's gaze split between him and their father, sensing tension, but perhaps not guessing the reason for it. 'You'll need to go back, then, and stay for a while, long enough to look over each item and bring back drawings so we can determine which or if any of the products would be right for us. Give me two weeks with the ophthalmoscope and then you can take the prototype back.

'I can deliver payment in person, too.' Payment had not been discussed yet and Jules did not want it 'slipping' anyone's mind. Payment would delight Becca. Jules did not want to see that delayed. He could already imagine her face lighting up when he presented her with it, not because she valued money, but she valued what payment for this would stand for.

Winthrop gave him a queer look and he quickly schooled his expression. 'I'll have a cheque written immediately.'

A cheque would not do. Jules thought quickly.

'Make it cash instead. There's no bank nearby. Cashing the cheque would require a trip to London.' Something Becca Peverett was not likely to do. He wouldn't have her sitting there with a cheque that was all but useless to her. He rose, eager to end the meeting, eager to get away from the piercing stare of his father. 'Well, I think that covers everything. I have things to take care of.' Fortunately, no one asked him what those things were.

'Come to dinner, Mary has finished the new re-model of the dining room and drawing room. She's dying to show it off. Please do try to admire it. It cost a fortune.' Winthrop chuckled, playing the indulgent husband.

'Stop by to see your mother. She'll want to know you're home and take time to comment on the new chandelier. It's Baccarat and no duke in London will have as fine a one this year,' his father said, preening a bit. Not because she'd worried over him while he was gone, but because she was probably lining up a social commitment or three that involved him. Jules sighed.

'I'll stop by this afternoon.' Best to get it out of the way and try to waylay any plans before they could run away with him.

Jules's mind was racing with lists and plans as he took the stairs and exited on to the street, his body and mind infused with the hum of purpose for the first time in…well, in a long while. He needed to send a letter to Haberstock. The thought of that letter brought a smile to his face as he tossed a coin to a street sweeper. He could imagine Becca reading it, her face glowing with joy over the news—about the inventions, of course.

Whether she was overjoyed about his return was immaterial, he told himself, just as his own warm pleasure at the idea of seeing her again was immaterial. This was business.

His inner voice nudged him. *Admit it, old chap, you're thrilled to be going back, you're wondering what startling questions she'll ask you, what challenges she'll throw down? Beware your expectations. A second visit can't possibly be as good as the first. The bubble will be off Dr Peverett's exquisite wine. A few weeks in Haberstock will remind you why you hate the country so much. You'll be champing at the bit to get back to town, back to your entertainments.*

Well, maybe he would be. Maybe the novelty he associated with Haberstock simply came from the need for a break from the usual routine of his life and had nothing to do with the quiet magic he'd felt at Haberstock, the inner stirrings it had provoked within him. Certainly, the excitement of going back had nothing to do with who was waiting for him on the other end. Rebecca Peverett was an outspoken bluestocking, hardly an endearing quality for the long run, and yet he couldn't get the image of her out of his mind.

Adelaide Pembridge was nothing like Rebecca Peverett, other than their surnames both started with P. Jules was rather regretting visiting his mother so promptly upon his return. He'd quite forgotten his mother's 'at homes' were on Mondays and now he was paying the price. He'd arrived at the very end, just in time to encounter Miss Pembridge and her mother finishing their tea.

'Your father said you'd come by.' His mother came forward to greet him, accepting his polite kiss in the air somewhere near her cheek. He'd learned early as a young boy with sticky hands that his mother didn't like kisses marring her coiffure or her cosmetics. She smelled of the rose petals that made up her various facial creams and money. 'I've been wanting to introduce you to my dear friend and her daughter for ages.'

'Charmed,' Jules said perfunctorily, bending over Miss Pembridge's hand and taking a seat at the tea tray. Most men *would* be charmed by Miss Pembridge in her fine ensemble cut in the highest of fashion and the newest of styles, her blonde ringlets done up superbly beneath a fetching little hat, her blue eyes as sparkling as her laugh—a tool she employed quite often, Jules noticed, along with a little toss of her head that made her pearl earrings bounce. In fact, he might even have been charmed by her for a short while last week. But today, she seemed long on affectation and short on sincerity. Once a man got past that laugh and the expensive couture, what would be left of her? He feared very little. Unlike the plainly dressed Rebecca with those eyes that didn't hesitate to strip him bare and a mind that sought to understand him.

Jules sipped at his tea and helped himself to a seed cake, answering questions about his recent trip, aware that Miss Pembridge was giving a strong imitation of being impressed. 'You're a man of business then,' Mrs Pembridge said approvingly, her gaze wandering the

Howell drawing room, no doubt calculating the worth of the brand-new curtains, the Turkish rugs and the silk-upholstered furniture with nary a stain or snag on them. Her own husband, Jules knew, had made a respectable fortune in textiles. The man who married Miss Pembridge would have access to a healthy dowry. And not much else.

The clock struck the quarter-past mark and the Pembridges rose to take their leave. Miss Pembridge's gaze lingered on him as they made their farewells, silently imploring him to make an appointment to call. He knew that look and he would not cater to it. He was not interested in what Miss Pembridge had to offer.

'Adelaide is very pretty,' his mother said after the Pembridges had left. 'You should have offered to escort her to the Damson fête. The two of you would make a striking couple.'

'I'm not interested in matchmaking, Mother. You can save your efforts,' Jules said succinctly. It was best to be direct with his mother and not leave her any room to manoeuvre or she would. She would have been a formidable general.

His mother sat on the pearl silk sofa and fixed him with a hard stare. 'You should be, Jules. You're thirty. It's time to settle down, take a wife, a woman who will look good on your arm, run your house for you, have your children, and be a credit to you the way Mary is to Winthrop. That was an *excellent* match.' Such an excellent match they'd been married five years and no children in sight. Perhaps his mother had overlooked that detail and what it might signify: two people leading two separate lives.

'And love, Mother? Should I not marry a woman who loves me and whom I love in return?' He'd said it more to be peevish, but it did resonate with him. There'd been love at Haberstock Hall between Catherine and Alfred Peverett and that love had been transmuted to their daughter.

'Love?' She laughed coldly, dismissing the idea. 'What does love have to do with marriage, Jules? What a silly notion you have. Marriage is about money, about alliances. Can you imagine what it would mean to have the Howells and Pembridges joined together? Manchester's two greatest manufacturing families?' She waved a hand to indicate the opulent drawing room with its elegant curtains and pearl silk furniture, the new Baccarat chandelier and the tabletops covered in expensive collections his mother had curated for effect. 'This kind of living takes money, pots of it, Jules.'

'What kind of living is that, Mother?' The question sprang from his lips without thought.

'Wealthy living, Jules. Leading the society of Manchester, having the best of everything, the latest fashions, the finest cook, superior entertainments,' she explained in a scolding tone. 'Money drives the world, not love. Love does not serve a woman. What woman ever benefitted from love? Not Cleopatra, not Heloise, not Ines de Castro, not Anne Boleyn.'

'I don't think Anne Boleyn loved the king,' Jules said and his mother shot him a sharp look that said she didn't appreciate his wit. He rose, suddenly eager to be away. Wealthy living was not gracious living, however. Once, he might not have distinguished between the two. But he'd seen the difference. Haberstock Hall was gracious hospitality defined. The Howell town house was a cold show piece. No expensive collection of figurines could change that.

There's been Peveretts at Haberstock Hall for centuries.

There'd been Howells in Manchester for twenty-five years. His father had bought this town house ten years ago when this neighbourhood had become more elite. 'Thank you for the tea, Mother. I must be off.'

It felt better to be outside, his feet finding their own way home. If he couldn't be at Haberstock Hall with its history and its warm oak staircase, its comfortable music room and Catherine Peverett's inherited dishes that had served generations of Peveretts and their guests, he could at least write to it. He would stay in again tonight, give his cook a shock and write his letters.

Chapter Eight

The letter came during afternoon tea with Thomasia and little Effie-Claire. 'There's a letter for you, Miss Becca.' Mrs Newsome, the housekeeper, bustled in, all excitement, waving the envelope in one hand. 'Do you think it is from the invention people, miss? I know you've been combing the post. I wanted to bring it straight away.'

Becca took the letter, flustered. 'Thank you, Mrs Newsome.' She *had* been combing the post. It was over a week since Jules Howell had left. Surely, it wasn't too soon to expect a note, an update on the project, nothing more. She studied the handwriting on the envelope, thinking it would provide her some clue, but that was fanciful. She had never seen Jules's handwriting; she wouldn't recognise it. At any rate, even if the note was from him, it would be a business missive, nothing more. She'd reminded herself of that each day the post had disappointed her. What was she hoping the post would bring?

Becca opened the letter, noting the Howell Manufacturing letterhead at the top, her eyes dropping to the bottom of the note, her pulse making a little irrational hop at the scrawl there. Jules Howell. It wasn't just the company that had written. He had written. On business letterhead to be sure, a good reminder that although she was having difficulty not conflating business and pleasure, he was not. She schooled her features and forced herself to read carefully.

'Well, is it good news?' Thomasia pressed. She reached down to give her daughter a biscuit to gnaw on.

'Yes, very good news.' Becca regrouped and refocused. 'The company would like to pursue some of my other inventions. Mr Howell is coming back to look at them.'

Effie-Claire began to cry. Thomasia scooped her up and made room for the little one on her slowly disappearing lap. 'I won't be able to do this much longer.' Her sister laughed and patted her round, seven-month-pregnant belly. Effie-Claire settled, Thomasia turned her attentions back to the conversation. 'Is Mr Howell the same representative who was here the last time?'

'Yes.' Becca folded up the letter and put it back in the envelope.

'Well? When's he coming?' Thomasia bounced Effie-Claire on her knee. 'You're being awfully close-mouthed about this.'

Becca unfolded the letter and looked at the date it was written, just two days after he'd got back to Manchester. Then it had taken five days for the letter to reach her here. 'At the end of the week.' She glanced up at Thomasia. 'That's so soon.' Especially since this was to be a much longer stay. 'He says he'll be staying for a few weeks.' Through the end of the month and into the early part of the next. He would see Haberstock Hall in all its autumn glory. There would be time for that walk to the waterfall and he'd be here for the cider pressing. Oh, but that was not what she should be thinking about. This wasn't a holiday, this was business.

'You must have Shaw and I to dinner while he's here. I absolutely must meet this man who can fluster my imperturbable sister.' Thomasia laughed.

'I'm not flustered,' Rebecca protested. 'There's just so much to do. There are copies of sketches to draw up and prototypes to finalise. I must be sure of my dimensions and the materials that are best suited to these designs.' But Thomasia tossed her a smile that said she didn't fully believe it.

Thomasia rose with Effie at her hip. 'We'll leave you to your plans, then, and look forward to a dinner invitation. Mother mentioned Mr Howell was charming and I admit to being intrigued at the idea of an acquisitions agent having any charm at all instead of being a dried-up stick.'

When Thomasia had gone, Becca took out the letter once more, letting her gaze fix this time on the postscript.

I'll be on the three-fifteen train on the nineteenth. You should come to the station with the coach.

She should not read anything into the invitation. It would be a chance for them to discuss business privately. And yet, there would be several chances to do just that down in the workshop over the course of his stay. It was difficult not to read it as a personal invitation to greet him, difficult not to read into it that perhaps he was looking forward to coming back as much as she was looking forward to having him here.

But to what end, you silly goose? she chided herself, folding the letter into the envelope once more. Did she really think such a handsome man, such a charming man, would be interested in her beyond business? She invented things. She spent her days with predictable machines while he spent his days meeting with clients, travelling, negotiating deals. Her life was quiet and his, well, his wasn't. She would bore him given enough time, while he would turn her dizzy with his charm and energy. Opposites might attract, but they didn't stick. It was simple science. That was fine. She wasn't looking to marry, wasn't looking to give up the freedom of her workshop in order to run a man's home.

Your sisters have all married and they've given up nothing.

The old arguments didn't carry the strength they used to. Her sisters had indeed proven her worries over marriage to be unfounded. The right man wouldn't make the woman he loved sacrifice her interests for him. The right man would share her with her passions.

It was just that Becca had given up meeting the right man. He hadn't been in London and he certainly wasn't in Hertfordshire. She'd lived her entire life here and hadn't encountered him. Nor would she. Hertfordshire was just twenty miles from London, but it was so entirely rural it might as well be a hundred. Liberated men who saw women as equals didn't come to the country and she had no desire to live in London surrounded by busyness, noise and stench and men who were more interested in fashion and entertainment than the health of their neighbours. It was better this way. She had her nieces and nephews to dote on, the collection of them growing every year, and her workshop. Falling in love would complicate things, perhaps even steal her creative energies away, like Samson's strength.

She would be happy enough knowing that she pursued her own passions. One couldn't truly miss what one had never had. But some days, when she watched Thomasia with Effie-Claire, or caught one of her brothers-in-law watching one of her sisters and their eyes would meet across a crowded room, she wondered what she was missing. What had she given up? What would it feel like to be the centre of someone's attention so that they simply *knew* when you were in the room? So that their gaze could find you wherever you were? So that you were their magnetic north? So that you were never lost but always found? What a feeling that must be. She could only speculate. Perhaps it was like the feeling of watching cogs and wheels turn in unison on a machine, working together to create a smooth, fluid action.

The reaction that welled up in her when she contemplated Jules's arrival was neither smooth nor fluid.

It was a jumble of energy and excitement that eclipsed the rational reminder that he was coming for the inventions, not for her. That would assume far too much. But it didn't stop her from being at the Broxbourne station, waiting in the rain, at quarter past three five days later.

Would she be there? Jules searched the platform at Broxbourne the moment it came into view, looking for her, even though the rain spattering the train window suggested that if she had come, she'd be waiting inside the dry interior of the coach. Propriety suggested it, too. A gently bred young lady would not be standing out in the open alone at a train station. But perhaps she had not come alone? Perhaps her mother or father had come with her for that very reason? That would deflate a bit of the surprise he had for her. Still, he hoped it would only be her at the station. She was of an age where, especially in the country where rules might be a bit more relaxed, she might go somewhere alone with the coachman to vouch for her safety. Jules dared to hope that would be the case.

The train rolled to a stop and he disembarked, turning the collar of his coat up against the insistent rain and scanned the platform for her: tall, dark-haired, straight-backed, that proud jut to her jaw. There she was! A swift stab of excitement speared him. She *had* come. She stood apart at the end of the platform, dressed in a long forest-green wool coat, a little hat to match perched atop her head more for decoration than protection, beneath an umbrella. 'Miss Peverett, you are a sight for sore eyes!' He strode towards her, drinking her in, watching her gaze light up at the sight of him.

'Mr Howell, welcome back.' She gave him a warm smile and stuck out her hand to shake. He shook it, but did not release it. Instead, he tucked it through his arm, all the better to navigate the mud and puddles between the platform and the Peverett coach. He hailed a porter and gave directions for his trunks.

'Shall we dare the mud?' He grinned at her and they began picking their way across the slog of the station yard while she attempted, mostly unsuccessfully, to hold the umbrella over them both. 'I'm surprised you were on the platform.' He held open the coach door for her as she closed the umbrella and shook off the droplets. 'You could have stayed in the coach and been dry.' He followed her in and shut the door behind them.

She laughed. 'I'll tell you a secret. I *did* stay in the coach right up until the train arrived.'

'That explains why I didn't see you at first.' He let his gaze hold hers a moment longer than necessary. 'I was looking, you know.' Despite the rain and the mud, it felt good to be back already. It was a ridiculous notion given he'd only spent two days here prior. Overhead, rain drummed on the roof of the coach and he imagined Haberstock Hall full of inviting warmth, hot fires in the grates and warm cider in mugs or perhaps a mulled version of Dr Peverett's very good red. 'How have you been, Becca? Tell me everything that's happened since I left. Have you invented a hundred new things?' He stretched his legs and they made small talk as his trunks were strapped to the coach.

'I'm glad you came, Becca,' he said as the coach lumbered on to the road, beginning the hour-long drive back to Haberstock. 'I've brought you something that I wanted to give you in private and I wanted to give it to you right away.' He watched her cognac eyes light up with delight as he'd hoped they would. He'd imagined giving this to her here in the coach, just the two of them. 'Close your eyes and hold out your hands.' He withdrew a thick envelope from the inside pocket of his coat and placed it in her palms. 'Now you may open them,' he instructed with a smile.

She looked down at the envelope and then back up at him. 'What's this?'

'Open it and see,' he urged.

She opened the envelope and her eyes went wide at the sight of the pounds inside. 'This is for me? All of it?' Her awe warmed him.

'It's the advance on the ophthalmoscope,' he explained. 'I wanted to bring it in cash, not a cheque. I thought it would be easier for you that way.' He'd wanted the money to be hers alone. He could not recall seeing a bank in Broxbourne and there certainly hadn't been one in Haberstock. Even if there had been a bank closer than London, women didn't have their own accounts. Her father would have deposited the cheque for her, but Jules had wanted this moment to be entirely hers, the payment and the sense of accomplishment that went with it, entirely hers. Cash was the only way to do that.

'Thank you.' Becca glanced up at him with glassy eyes. 'Do you have any idea what this means to me?'

'Some.' He gave a small smile. 'Freedom, perhaps.' And in ways he'd not contemplated before. He'd not realised until he'd thought about how to present the money to her—a cheque or an envelope—of how much he took his finances for granted. He had an account at a bank in Manchester where he drew on his funds at leisure. He had access to money whenever he desired it. Becca Peverett did not. Even if she earned her own money, she had no account for it. She was an unmarried woman living under her parents' roof. They would give her what she wanted, he had no doubt, but it was the point that she had to ask that had struck him. Asking was not freedom.

'What will you do with it?' he enquired, watching her tuck the envelope safely into her coat pocket.

Her eyes danced. 'For now, I will save it. I might take a trip to visit some inventors in France doing work on eyeglasses. It's interesting to me that so many inventors are concurrently working on similar projects without each of us knowing about the others. It seems to me that we would be more productive if we pooled our expertise instead of working in isolation.'

'Perhaps you should be the one to organise them,' Jules suggested. He could picture her arguing them into submission. Reclusive, eccentric inventors wouldn't know what had hit them. Hell, he wasn't even sure what had hit *him*. But here he was, back in Haberstock and feeling pleased about it.

She shook her head. 'I'm not the person for that job. I doubt they would listen to a woman.'

'Well, you are the person for the job at Howell Manufacturing. I am to bring back anything that might be of interest.' He smiled broadly at her. 'Does that please you? There will be more envelopes.'

Chapter Nine

More envelopes. More *Jules*. It was the latter that pleased her more. Becca wasn't sure which temptation was the greater. Perhaps it was the temptation that she didn't have to decide. She could have them both. He was as charming as she remembered and just as handsome with his lean, rakish grace shown to favorable effect in his town-tailored suits and silk waistcoats. And just as energetic. *Life* flowed from him effortlessly even in the confines of the coach—his laugh, his smile, the easy flattery that slipped from his lips.

It was all part of his charm, what made him so intoxicating. Only she was smart enough not to drink too much from the cup. She knew it was just his way. Lord have mercy on the woman who didn't understand that. But Becca had never overestimated her charms. She knew flattery from the truth. Still, it was a treat to bask in his presence, as long as one was careful not to get caught up in it and the drive to Haberstock sped by inside the coach even if the road was muddy and the rain unrelenting outside. 'I do hope it doesn't rain the entire time.' Jules grimaced as the rain came down more forcefully on the roof.

'It won't. The rain should pass in a day,' Becca offered confidently. 'Tomorrow we'll look at some things at the cottage and make a plan and then, the next day, we'll go out to the waterfall.'

Her confidence was rewarded with a strange look from Jules. 'How can you be so sure?'

'I've been doing some weather study. I'll show you that, too, tomorrow.' The coach pulled into the circular drive of Haberstock Hall and Becca felt a twinge of disappointment that the ride was over. She'd have to share him now. Oh! That reminded her. She touched his arm, stalling him as he began to open the door. 'Before you get out, I should warn you that we'll have company for supper. My sister, Thomasia, and her husband are coming.'

A glance passed between them and for a moment she imagined they were both thinking the same thing: *but tomorrow, we'll have the cottage to ourselves.*

Jules smiled as he opened the door. 'The more the merrier, I say. I will look forward to meeting other members of your family.'

He hopped down and reached a hand back for her. She took it, letting the familiar warmth of his touch suffuse her. There were only a few seconds of privacy left to them. Already, her mother and father had gathered at the top of the steps to welcome their guest. She wouldn't have him to herself until tomorrow. With her free hand she touched the pocket holding her envelope. 'Thank you again, Jules, for this most wondrous gift.'

He held her gaze and tucked her arm through his, his voice low for her alone as if he, too, wanted to make these last moments count. 'It was absolutely my pleasure.'

The evening passed pleasantly enough. Thomasia and Shaw were always good company and Jules had the knack of getting along with anyone. There was music afterwards with piano playing and much singing. Thomasia's husband had a good voice and Jules sang again. There were gifts, too, that Jules had brought for the family in token of Howell Manufacturing's appreciation of the Hall's hospitality: brandy for her father, a large box of confectioner's chocolates infused with fancy liquors for her mother which was shared around the group.

There was much laughter as they tasted the different flavours and exclaimed over them. The box came her way and Becca bit into a chocolate and a sweet flavour flooded her mouth. 'What is this one?' she asked, licking her lips where a drop lingered. 'It tastes like oranges.'

'Cointreau,' Jules supplied, laughing beside her. He reached a thumb up and brushed the corner of her mouth. The shock of his touch rippled through her and she drew back, confused.

'You had a drop right there.' He tapped the corner of his own mouth, his eyes soft on hers for a fraction of a moment before he drew in his pocket and extracted a handkerchief. 'Perhaps this would serve better.' He chuckled and reached for a chocolate of his own. 'Champagne in this one, I wager.' He bit into it. 'Yes, it is champagne. Try the rest of it.' He popped the remaining piece into her mouth before she could protest.

It tasted sharp and crisp on her tongue. A bubble of laughter welled up inside her as she finished the chocolate. She had not been this happy for a long time. Tonight, with Thomasia and Shaw here, and little Effie-Claire, it almost felt like old times when her family was all together, before William had gone to war, before Thea and Anne had gone to London, before Thomasia had suffered at the hands of a careless man. The world had pulled the Peveretts away from Haberstock Hall. Over the last three years, Becca had wondered if the family would ever be whole again, if all the fractures could be put back together. It felt entirely possible tonight, watching everyone laughing together, playing music together.

She caught Jules watching her as she watched everyone else. 'You're staring at me,' she murmured.

'You're happy.' He smiled. Around them, the family began to organise themselves to retire for the evening. Thomasia and Shaw were spending the night instead of driving home with a sleepy toddler. Becca took a lamp from her mother, and the family filed towards the stairs, she and Jules bringing up the rear.

'This is a good night. Thank you.' She looked away, not daring to meet his eyes for too long for fear of forgetting herself, for fear of forgetting that this was just another piece of his charm. It didn't mean anything.

The attention he showed her was no different than the attention he showed Shaw or Thomasia.

She'd watched him tonight. He'd fit into the fabric of the evening effortlessly, listening to Shaw talk about Parliament, asking questions, doting on Effie-Claire. 'People feel comfortable around you, Jules. I think that is your great gift.' He put people at ease, made them feel valued. He knew when to talk and when to listen, when to turn the attention from himself to others. There were a lot of men in London who needed to learn that skill.

He made her a little nod and took the lamp from her, adjusting the wick as they climbed the stairs. 'You are too kind, Becca. I enjoyed the evening very much and tomorrow will be even better.' They reached his room and there was a round of quiet goodnights as everyone sought their own chambers. 'Goodnight, Becca,' he said quietly with a look she felt to her toes as she made her way to her room.

She should tell him to stop doing that. He didn't *need* to flatter her. This was a business arrangement and she expected nothing more from him. Likewise, he should expect nothing more from her. It would not serve either of them if the lines between business and pleasure became blurred. One of them—her most likely—would end up hurt. That particular thought lingered as she made ready for bed. This was where she was smarter than other girls. How many other girls had been wooed by those green eyes and subtle touches? How many other girls had forgot themselves? Doing whatever it took to keep his attentions, not understanding those attentions weren't unique to them? But she knew better.

Becca slipped a nightgown over her head. Oh, she didn't think he was flirting with her deliberately for the express purpose of befuddling her. It came so naturally to him he probably didn't realise he did it at all. But he *did* do it and they both needed to be wary. They had too much at stake to wreck their business arrangement because she'd lost her head over a few smiles and touches.

And kindnesses. He's gone out of his way for you, bringing cash and not a cheque.

She slid beneath her covers and turned down the lamp. It was a little more difficult to discount his attentions when faced with that reminder. Bringing cash had been thoughtful in the extreme. And then there'd been the touch of his thumb at her lips tonight, the way his fingers had brushed her mouth when he'd fed her the champagne chocolate. All of those things were more than polite kindnesses he might dole out to anyone. She fluffed her pillow. Those were pleasant things to go to sleep on, nothing more. It had been a lovely evening. It would be back to business-as-usual tomorrow morning.

They spent the morning in the workshop, going through her designs that held the most promise and were closest to completion. That meant moving ahead on the hypodermic needle and the two-sided stethoscope but waiting on the bifocal lenses. She would dedicate her time during his visit to drawing up design plans and a prospectus for each of them, detailing their uses. Rebecca took out a notebook to draft out a time-line while he wandered the cottage, peering at shelves and nosing through cupboards. For such a small space, the cottage held all sorts of hidden treasures.

'What's this?' Jules spied a ballerina on a pedestal and gently cocked it sideways to look at the underside. The little engine beneath was elegantly simple.

Becca looked up from the worktable. 'It's just a toy.'

'And these?' Jules took down a set of soldier figu-rines five inches high and brightly painted. He brought them to the table and wound them up. 'They march!' he exclaimed, amazed at their movement. 'I would have loved these as a boy.' He took down another one and wound it up. 'This one raises his bayonet, how splen-did.' He set a drummer opposite the bayonet and wound them up, watching them walk towards each other. 'Did you make these?' A boy could delight himself all day long setting up armies that moved.

'Yes, I make them for the children at the Royal Mil-itary Asylum in Chelsea. Ferris and Anne do a lot of work there and I make them for children in the vil-lage at Christmas time. It's just a hobby, something I do for fun. My mother gives people herbs, I give chil-dren toys. I suppose it's my contribution to the gen-eral welfare.'

Jules picked up a soldier and studied it. 'How long does it take to make a soldier?'

'Not long, assuming I have all the parts. I start making toys in September and by December I have enough.'

She was generous with her time and her money,

Jules thought. Paints and metals and parts would cost. 'Show me the mechanism. What makes them move?' He was all curiosity now, his mind starting to race with ideas. What she needed months to do could be accomplished by machine much faster and on a much larger scale.

Becca left her notebook and went to a drawer. She pulled out pieces and spread them on the table. 'The mechanism is just old-fashioned automaton parts: a crank, ropes and pulleys.' She shrugged off the technology as if it were nothing. Jules disagreed, watching fascinated as she showed him an assembled rope and pulley skeleton. 'I just change what the pulleys do in order to get different movements. Some raise arms, others move legs, others thrust a bayonet forward,' she explained. 'Then, the metal pieces enclose the pulley system.' She demonstrated how to slide the parts around the ropes, enclosing the system. 'Then, I attach the crank right here, and paint them. My brother, William, would send back descriptions of the uniforms from the Crimea and I would do my best to duplicate the colours. The boys like that.' She wound up the newly assembled soldier and he walked across the tabletop to join the pile of his comrades. 'It's simple, really.'

'It's an amazing application,' Jules insisted, impressed. 'However do you come up with such ideas?'

Becca shrugged, uncomfortable with the praise. She was inordinately modest and humble about her talents, he was coming to realise. 'Well, this idea came from the Italians.' She went back to the drawer and took out a painted wooden doll with a hard wood body and thin, jointed arms and legs held together by strings that jerked when a cord running through the doll's body was pulled. 'I got to thinking—if this simple arrangement could move arms and legs, what could it do if it was refined? Then, I remembered my da Vinci.' She was in motion again, going to a bookshelf and taking down a battered tome. 'Da Vinci was a great inventor, not just an artist. He invented things that most people don't even know about.'

She set the book down on the table and stood beside him, flipping through worn pages. He could smell the clean, homey scent of cinnamon and vanilla soap on her skin, his eyes drawn to the long curve of her neck left exposed by her no-nonsense bun. That neck begged for a hand—*his* hand—to stroke it, for fingers to gently run its length and raise its little hairs in desire. 'Here it is, da Vinci's mechanical knight and his lion. Best of all, da Vinci left his instructions.' Not in an orderly fashion, Jules noted. One would have to have patience to sort through them in order to reconstruct them. Becca turned a page and pulled out a folded sheet of paper. 'From what I gleaned, there's a spring that controls the movements. It's a sound idea and I tried to replicate that for some of the soldiers with more complicated movements.'

Jules sat down hard on a stool, overwhelmed. *She* was overwhelming. The things she knew, how she thought, how she researched something as simple as how to construct a child's toy and then elevated it. He'd not learned half as much in all the schools he'd attended as she'd learned on her own. That wasn't to say Dr Peverett hadn't educated her. There was every sign she'd received an extensive traditional and classical education. But this love of learning came from within, it couldn't be taught or beaten into anyone. Otherwise, he'd be a genius. As it was, she put him to shame.

'When you go to France,' he said, thinking out loud, 'you should keep going. You should go to Italy and study with the toymakers in the north. And Switzerland,' he added. 'The last time I was there, I saw incredible music boxes.' Too expensive to make wholesale importation worthwhile, but she could learn how to make them, and Howell's could manufacture them. He rose and retrieved the ballerina. 'Could we make a music box small enough to fit beneath her pedestal? To give her music to dance to?'

'Probably—it would need to be a simple tune.' Becca's brow furrowed as she thought, but he could see the idea intrigued her. 'I don't have the parts, though. I'd need one of the new metal combs, and pins, and cylinders and gears. I can make them myself and there's a blacksmith who forges pieces for me on occasion, but it would be very time consuming. There are more parts to a music box than you might realise.'

'How do *you* know that?' he asked and was rewarded with a laugh.

'My uncle gave me a music box as a gift once. It was very beautiful and meant to be enjoyed, but I took it apart because I wanted to know how it worked. I had it spread out all over the dining room table. My mother was furious and she made me put it back together. It took me days to get it right. But when I did, she was very proud of me.'

Jules furrowed his brow, considering. 'Becca, these toys you make—have you ever thought of selling your design to somewhere like Howell's? We can mass produce these toys and sell them throughout England.' Maybe even throughout the Empire, but he didn't want to get ahead of himself. He envisioned a collectible set of soldiers where every middle-class boy would want to get the complete set and they'd be priced to where that was not an impossibility. There'd be dancing ballerinas with a music box beneath them for girls. 'Or what about a baby doll that could open its mouth and be fed from a spoon?' Dolls that resembled babies were still relatively new. This would be an innovative way to capitalise on the new doll trend.

'No, I've never thought of that.' She suddenly became brisk, gathering up the toys and putting them back on their shelf. 'The toys are just something I do for the local children. They're only toys, Jules. They don't improve the world, they don't help people walk, or live better lives.'

'Don't they?' Jules folded his arms. 'Giving a child happiness is no small thing, Becca.' But he knew better than to press his luck. Somehow, he'd hit upon a sore subject with her. He would bide his time. For now. He leaned back on the stool and glanced out the front window. 'You were right, it's stopped raining.' Maybe the best thing to do now was to leave the cottage behind for a while. He flashed her a winsome smile. 'You keep promising me that waterfall, but I'm starting to think it doesn't exist,' he teased.

'Let me get my satchel and we can go. I will prove to you it does exist,' Becca teased in return, climbing up a ladder to the loft above. He liked her being teasing and open. She was that way with him when they were alone, but she wasn't that way with her family.

He'd worked hard to draw her out last night. He'd had the distinct impression that she put herself in the role of spectator at family gatherings instead of active participant. Last night, she'd been quite willing to let the conversation flow around her, to let Thomasia dominate the discussion. It would be easy to do. Becca's younger sister was a vivacious beauty even at six months gone. One could not help but notice her, to be engaged by her.

It was not something Thomasia did on purpose, it was just who she was and yet Jules had felt surprisingly protective of Becca. He'd fought the urge to nudge her forward, to prompt her into more conversation, to make *her* the centre of attention. She needn't play second fiddle to anyone. But it wasn't his place to do that nudging or his decision to make.

Becca came back down, satchel in tow. It looked heavy and Jules offered to take it, but she refused, saying, 'I have surprises for you inside.'

'For me?' The idea that she'd planned a surprise for him was…sweet, warming. He couldn't recall the last time someone had planned a surprise with him in mind. When had anyone taken time to know him well enough to know what would please him?

'Yes, but don't go guessing. I won't tell you. You'll just have to find out,' she said firmly. 'Come on, let's go find that waterfall.' Jules held the door for her, thinking, for a chance to spend the day with her and whatever magic was in her satchel, he'd follow her anywhere.

Chapter Ten

He fell in behind her as they set out, happy to let her lead the way through the autumn trees. The path cut through a field and ran alongside a river. They passed a bench Becca referred to as Old Man Anderson's bench and continued, veering back into a forest of trees. 'It's beautiful out here.' He lifted his gaze to the crimson canopy overhead. The sky had cleared and the sun had come out in a bright blue autumn sky. The colours were striking and the air was crisp. 'The air in Manchester isn't as clean as this. One forgets what good air is like.'

He took a deep breath. One forgot how it felt to be out in nature when one spent all of one's time in gaming clubs and buildings. He certainly had and it was something of a surprise to realise he liked it—the nature, that was. He was *enjoying* tramping through a forest.

Was it the nature he was enjoying or was it the company?

'We're nearly there,' Becca called over her shoulder, tossing him a smile. They entered a clearing and he could hear the rush of water as they approached. 'The falls will be running hard today after all the rain we've had.' Becca seemed pleased about that; her voice held an excited lilt. 'You'll get to see the falls at their best.'

Her excitement did not disappoint. The falls came into view in all their natural splendour, crashing over the rocks in full, pounding force and spilling into the pool at their feet. The spray caught him in the face and he laughed, taking a step back. 'They're magnificent!' And they were—the rushing water rimmed by old oaks, tall and sturdy, their crimson foliage filtering the bright sunlight as it danced off the water. Magical. That was the word for it. The colours were resplendent. The old itch came to him, to paint the colours, to capture on canvas the sights around him and perhaps, by doing so, also capture the noise so entirely different than the clamour of a city street.

'In the summer, we used to swim in the pool. The falls aren't so full in the summer, just a pleasant trickle. We'd stand beneath them with our mouths open and have a cool drink.' Rebecca had taken up residence on a flat rock a safe distance from the spray.

'Used to?' Jules strode over to join her, wiping his face with his sleeve. 'If I lived here, I'd still be swimming in the pool.' He could imagine nothing more delicious than one's own private pool to cool off in on a hot summer day. 'Why did you stop?'

'We didn't stop on purpose. We simply grew up, we got busy. They went away.' Her voice trailed off. She fell silent, but he could fill in the gaps. She was fond of her siblings. She would take their absence hard.

Jules sat down on the rock beside her. 'You miss them. But you have Thomasia close by.'

'I am lucky to have Thomasia close. She and I have always been together. She's only two years younger than I am. I don't remember a life without her in it. But it's different now. She has a husband, a home of her own, a child and another on the way. She has less and less time for me.' Becca shook her head. 'I think what I really miss is how things used to be. How we all did everything together.' She gave him a rueful smile. 'But now they've all gone ahead and I am still here.'

Jules nodded. He knew a little something about that. Winthrop had left him, too. Winthrop had chosen their father over their brotherhood. 'I've never known life without my brother either. Even though we're not close any more, we used to be.' The old Winthrop would have liked the waterfall pool.

'What happened?' Becca asked, her brow furrowing.

'He grew up, took an interest in the company. He had less time for me.' Jules shrugged. 'It was bound to happen.'

'But you miss him even though he's still technically "there". I feel that way with Thomasia especially. We spent a difficult year in York together not long ago. We were all each other had. At the time, it felt like we'd always be that close, but then we came home and everything changed. For the better, of course,' Becca was quick to add, and Jules smiled. How like her, not wanting to criticise anyone. She was kind that way, he was noticing. 'We're all happy that she married Shaw,' Becca said, but he heard the other feelings embedded beneath the words, the feelings of betrayal, of being left behind, of being traded in for someone else. Perhaps he heard them because he'd felt that way, too.

'The day Winthrop was named the head of the company, I felt an immense sense of loss, that an era had come to a close, that my childhood had come to an end. Things would never be the same again and they haven't been.' How odd to discover they had this thing in common beneath the surface of their differences. The rogue and the wallflower, two very different personalities, one larger than life and one quiet and hidden, but both hiding the same fear of being lost inside one's own family.

Wallflower? No, that was not Becca, not really, it was only what she let people see. He studied her profile as they sat in silence, watching the falls. Wallflowers were plain, bland girls. The girl who'd spoken of da Vinci's automaton in the workshop this morning was neither. She was alive and vibrant and interesting. And he wanted…her…this…with an intensity that usually eluded him.

She turned her head to look at him. Their gazes held and the last of what little reason he possessed was undone. He let his eyes skim the fullness of her mouth, let his mind wonder one last time about the taste of her. He leaned in, ready to claim that taste, to put the wondering to rest. He saw her breath catch, saw her mouth part in the slightest of invitations, as he captured her lips, heard the faintest of gasps escape her as he took, as he tasted, and then she was tasting, too, tentative sips of him at first, growing slowly bolder.

Ah, this was the nectar of the gods, so sweet, his hand was at the back of her neck, his body moving to deepen the kiss, but she gave another moan and drew back, her eyes full of emotion, of questioning, of shock over what they'd done even as that shock mingled with unmistakable longing. Whatever they had done, she had liked it.

Her cognac gaze lingered on his, her fingertips going to her lips. 'Why did you do that?'

'Because you're beautiful.' He cradled her cheek in the cup of his hand. She stared at him, then, in awed amazement as if he were a crazy man, or as if she'd been seen for the first time, and there was no sound for a long while except the roar of the falls. He would claim it as something of a coup to render Rebecca Peverett speechless.

'Did you call me beautiful?' She could barely speak, her voice a mere whisper against the rush of the falls. Had he even heard her? She didn't think she could summon the courage to ask a second time or the wherewithal. Her wits were scattered from that shattering kiss, it had caught her by surprise and not let go until she felt it to the tips of her toes and the reaches of her fingertips, until no part of her body was left unaffected by it, not least of which was her brain, the one part of her she prided herself on and even that seemed to have betrayed her, so thorough was that kiss. The echoes of his kiss thrummed through her, refusing to depart, leaving her thoughts disbanded and her nerves raw.

'I did.' His words were quiet, too, although for a dif-

ferent reason. He seemed perfectly in control of himself
and his feelings. Of course, he'd been kissed before.
Not so her. Twenty-four and never been kissed, not
even in the fun of a parlour game. Perhaps kisses became less sensational the more of them one had. Not
that she'd get to test that theory. To date, gentlemen had
not lined up to kiss her and the one who had kissed
her absolutely could not repeat that performance. Jules
needed to understand that.

Becca covered his hand with hers where it lay
against her cheek. She let herself savour the warmth
of his touch and the luxury of being able to do such a
thing in the quiet intimacy that connected them here
in the grove where the trees hid them from sight and
the falls hid them from sound. They were in their own
world, able to do or say anything, be anyone and there
was no one to see. But that world couldn't last. She
set his hand away from her skin. 'You must never say
that again. You must never *do* that again,' she gently
rebuked him and silently rebuked herself. She should
not have allowed it to happen, nor should she have let
it go that far. One kiss had become several kisses. All
because her curiosity had got the better of her.

He chuckled, his eyes merry. 'Do you have something against the truth?' He wasn't taking her seriously. Perhaps because he had not meant his words
seriously. This was a game to him. Of course it was.
Flirting. Kissing. Flattering. It all came so naturally to
him. He'd probably done no more than make the most
of the situation.

'The truth is, I'm no beauty. Thomasia and Anne are

beauties. Thea is striking. But I am neither beautiful nor memorable. I am plain. I know what I am and I'm honest about it. You needn't pretend otherwise.' She'd seen the gentlemen's eyes in London skim right past her and rivet on Thomasia night after night.

'There are many types of beauty.' Jules reached out a hand to tip her chin towards him, but she slid away and rose. She'd just got her wits back. She would not let them go so soon a second time. Her wits were all she had.

She raised her voice to be heard over the falls. 'Did you hear nothing I said? You cannot do *that* again.' No matter how much she wished him to.

His green eyes flared and he rose, following her in order to be heard. He was becoming irritated with her. '*That.* You mean our kiss. Can't you even say it? Now who has an aversion to the truth? You're acting as if it didn't happen.'

'It would be best if it hadn't.' She whirled on him, forcing him back a few steps. She needed her distance or she'd be in his arms again. 'The more we discuss it,' she said pointedly, 'the more real it becomes, the more credence it has. It doesn't matter if I'm beautiful or not, you cannot go about kissing your business partners. Weren't you the one who warned me about mixing business and pleasure?'

'Sometimes rules are made to be broken.' He gave her a lopsided smile that turned his handsome rogue's face boyish. 'Don't tell me you weren't curious about it, about what it would be like?'

His grin was infectious, and she could not stay

angry with him. She felt her face give way, breaking into a smile of its own. 'We have satisfied our curiosity and now we must be on our best behaviour for both our sakes. Friends don't hurt friends.' And more kisses *would* lead to hurt. *Her* hurt. He might be capable of light flirtations, but she wasn't.

She strode back to the rock and picked up the satchel, eager to put the kiss and the conversation behind them. 'Friends do, however, remember that other friends like to paint.' She dug into the satchel and brandished a fist full of brushes. 'I thought you might like to paint the waterfall while the light is good.' She produced brushes and paints and thick tablets of heavy paper. 'It's just watercolours, but it will do.' Apparently, it was her turn to stun him. If his kiss had left her speechless, her act had done the same for him. His eyes gleamed with a suspicious light, showing what his words could not, and his response touched her, just as it made her wonder why such a small act had such a significant impact on a man who had money aplenty, affluence aplenty, who wanted for nothing materially.

'You remembered,' he said at last, taking his seat on the rock beside her once more. He flipped open the tablet and gave her a smile. 'Thank you.' Then he began to paint.

She ought to have bent to her own painting, but Becca found her gaze drawn not to the magnificent falls but to the man beside her, a man cocksure and full of confidence, who teased and laughed easily, who had a way with people and yet that man had been humbled by a simple gesture. There was a certain humanity to him, a certain vulnerability that she'd glimpsed today.

'How's *your* painting coming?' He looked over at her and she clutched the tablet close for fear he'd see she'd not accomplished a thing. Too late. He'd guessed her secret. 'What have you been thinking about so intently that you've not put brush to paper at all the entire afternoon?' He set aside his brush and fixed her with a merry stare.

'You. You're quite good.' She nodded towards his painting. Better than good, actually.

He shrugged and shook his head. 'No, I'm not. I haven't painted in years, not seriously anyway. I think the last time I even held a paintbrush was in Italy three years ago.'

Becca frowned. 'Why not? If I was that good, I'd paint all the time.' Surely it wasn't for lack of supplies. Perhaps it was time. It was neither and his answer surprised her entirely.

Jules leaned back on his elbows, his gaze serious. 'My father doesn't approve. Painting is not a manly pursuit for a Howell. In other words, it does not generate money, not in the amounts that he deems suitable.' He gave a half-chuckle. 'I can see from the look on your face that you can't imagine such a thing. You have your parents' support in all that you do, the encouragement to follow your dreams, not theirs.'

True. It was hard to imagine. He'd mentioned before how driven his father was, how his father had been inspired to build Howell Manufacturing from the ground up. But never once had she thought about the cost of that. 'I'm sorry, it must have been a difficult way to grow up.' The Peveretts were all healers of sorts, but of their own accord. Thomasia, for instance, had no interest in actual medicine, but her interest in the politics of health care had always been encouraged. Not one of the five of them had been forced into a mould that didn't fit. But Jules had been. When people or things were forced into moulds, one of two things happened: the mould broke or the person did. Which had it been for Jules?

She studied him thoughtfully, thinking back to other conversations like the day she'd accused him of not enjoying his work. 'Why do you do it, then? Why do you work for them?' But she knew the answer even as he spoke.

'They're the only family I've got. Where would I go? Where would I belong if I wasn't with them?' There was a desperate little boy behind those words, a boy who wanted a father's acceptance so badly he'd given up his painting and…another memory stirred…perhaps his singing as well…in order to please an implacable parent. And in doing so, what else had he given up? Her parents had taught them when people gave up their passions, they gave up a piece of their souls.

'What about your mother?' He never mentioned her. 'What's she like?' Surely his mother had been a source of support.

'She's a perfect match for my father. He makes money and she spends it. He wants status and recognition and she hosts fabulous parties to ensure he has it.'

Becca felt her hope deflate at the response. 'I'm sorry, Jules,' she said softly, treading carefully around the pain that must be there so close to the surface. 'I'm sorry they don't appreciate you. I'm sorry you had to give up the things you loved.' The people he loved, too. Winthrop, his one ally. Her heart hurt at the depth of betrayal he must have felt, even as an adult, at losing his one ally, his one anchor in a family that valued ambition over people.

He chuckled. 'My family disappoints you, Becca. I hear it in your voice. They are simple to understand. Money is at the root of everything that drives them. Once you know that, you know all there is to know about the Howells of Manchester. They're not like Peveretts.'

'The question is, are you like them?' she asked. After all his sacrifices, did he feel part of his family or detached from it?

'I like money as much as the next person. But I haven't my father's obsession for making it.'

'Obsession? Not passion?' She was quick to note. There was a world of difference between the two. Obsession was about preoccupation to the exclusion of all else while passion was about a desire, an enthusiasm for something.

'Obsession, definitely.' Jules gave a hard laugh. 'My mother is obsessed with Manchester society and my father is obsessed with money. They're a good fit for each other.'

'I think they should appreciate you more.' She

leaned her head against his shoulder, unable to resist the physical closeness.

He laughed. 'Should they? And why is that? Perhaps they're right and I'm nothing more than a smile and a charming word.'

Part of him truly believed that, Becca realised, and she felt compelled to disabuse him of the idea. 'You have a good mind, very intelligent, very versatile. In the workshop today, you were excited about the toys. You have vision.' Although she sensed he was rather unaware of it. His family was, too.

He reached for his tablet and she thought for a moment he was uncomfortable with the compliment. 'Well, what do you think? Have I captured the waterfall?'

It was beautiful. He'd used blues and lavenders to capture the cold water in contrast to the warm blue sky above and the canopy of warm orange autumn leaves. 'You've an eye for colour,' Becca complimented. She nudged him with her elbow. 'You're a man of many talents, Jules Howell. You sing, you paint.' *You kiss like temptation itself.* Although she dared not say that out loud. 'I wonder what other talents you might be hiding?'

'I think if we put my talents with yours, we might add up to one da Vinci.' He chuckled. 'We could be our very own Renaissance ma—ah, I mean person.'

'You're learning.' Becca smiled up at him and they laughed together, her head resting easily on his shoulder. Shortly thereafter, his arm slipped about her and they sat that way for a long time, not speaking, just watching the water play in the autumn sun. It felt right to lean against him as they sat on the rock. It was a rare moment on a rare day full of rare colours and even rarer experiences. Too soon it would be winter. Too soon, Jules would be gone again. She wanted to enjoy both while they lasted.

The shadows of early evening had begun to fall, the bright afternoon light changing to more muted tones, the bright blue of the sky slowly darkening to indigo when they finally stirred. She lifted her head from the solid pillow of his shoulder. 'We need to get back before dark.' But her body was reluctant to act on those words.

Beside her, Jules made no move, his arm remaining about her. 'I don't want to leave here. Today has been extraordinary. I want more days like it.'

'We'll come back. We have plenty of time,' Becca promised. 'Next time we'll bring food.' They'd missed lunch *and* tea. She was starting to look forward to dinner with a rather strong sense of anticipation. Jules was probably ravenous. 'I didn't think we'd be gone quite so long.' But she was glad they had been. Even hungry, she was still reluctant to leave.

She took her time gathering up their paints and carefully stowing their now-dry watercolours in her satchel. She was different from how she'd been a handful of hours ago. She didn't want to step out of the grove and step back into the world. Here in this grove, she was beautiful and passionate, all the things she was not in the real world.

Jules came to take the satchel, insisting on carrying

it now that she didn't have to hide her surprise. There was no putting off leaving now. Becca took a final look around, committing the space to memory even though she'd been here countless times before with her brother and sisters. But only today with Jules. Only today with a man who thought she was beautiful, who kissed her with passion and intensity, who made her want more than his kisses. That made all the difference.

'I'll never come here again without thinking of you, of today,' she confessed with a final, backwards glance at the falls turned violet-blue in the fading light. She should tell him, he should know. 'It wasn't just a kiss, Jules. It was my first kiss and I'm glad it was with you.'

'I'm glad it was me, too,' he whispered with the slightest catch to his voice as he took her hand and led them out into the dusk.

Chapter Eleven

He'd been her first kiss. Had he ever been anyone's first anything? For a man who'd been experiencing a variety of forms of intimacy regularly since he was fifteen, Becca's announcement should not have surprised him. Kisses, in his experience, were plentiful. Casual, playful things, cheaply come by and easily discarded. But not this one. This kiss had meant something to them both. Kissing her had been like tasting heaven, like treading on sacred, forbidden ground where a man like him dared not go. He was not worthy enough and yet he *had* dared and his reward had been far greater than the satisfying of curiosity.

It had also come with a price. One kiss wasn't enough. Now that he'd started on that path, he wanted to continue down it. But he had to exercise restraint. He was the experienced one here, the one who knew the travails of passion run amok. Mix in the aspect of business with this pleasure, and it had all the potential of a disaster.

Even so, it was hard to think of kissing Becca as that disaster as they made their way back to the workshop. There was enough daylight left to allow them the luxury of a leisurely walk—another simple pleasure in a day that had been full of them. He was glad they needn't rush, glad they could enjoy the warm connection of their hands joined together, the early sounds of the nightbirds and the colours of the sunset overhead. Perhaps the reason it seemed so difficult to think of kissing her as a disaster was that it wasn't—or at least it didn't have to be, that maybe there was a middle path? That somehow things might be different for them?

The thought pleased him and he tried it out as the workshop came into view in the distance. 'I've been thinking, Becca, that maybe we're wrong about us, about the idea that friends can't be business partners.'

Becca slanted him one of her thoughtful looks. 'It's not that they can't be business partners. There's no law that forbids it. They *can* be business partners, it's just that they *shouldn't*.'

'What if they begin as business partners and then *become* friends? That seems very plausible,' Jules argued. 'Business partners spend time together in the course of their ventures. A friendship would be a natural evolution of their relationship, of all that time shared, wouldn't it? There would be shared meals, discussions of the business.' He was warming to his subject now. This was quite a good argument he was making.

'In fact, how could such a thing *not* evolve? I can't *imagine* a business partnership lasting long without a friendship to sustain it.' Then he delivered the coup de grâce. 'I think business partnerships might even *require* friendship in order to succeed.' Today, he believed that. It was just one more sign of how being at Haberstock Hall was changing him, how he thought, how he felt, how he saw the world.

'You're forgetting the other piece.' Becca blew right over his excellent argumentation. 'Even if business partners could be friends, men and women cannot be. There's a reason those friendships, rare as they are, end when one marries.'

'Society's rules only,' Jules scoffed. He had plenty of women who were friends: Madame Clementine, the chorus girls at the Theatre Royale.

You've slept with all of them. Perhaps she has a point.

But he'd not been in business with them, he refuted his inner voice. 'Perhaps we are the exception,' he argued staunchly with Becca. 'Those other friendships you speak of were maintained outside a pre-existing business arrangement. But not ours.' He ran his thumb over the back of her knuckles in a gentle stroke. 'If we were careful, we could find a middle path. Business partners in the morning, but friends in the afternoon.' Friends who kissed one another at waterfalls and asked questions that jarred loose forgotten places in his soul.

'Rules give our world structure,' Becca cautioned. 'Science and society run on them.' Spoken like a true inventor. He expected nothing less from her. She needed order and predictability; they were what made toys like her soldiers possible. The rules of optics made such inventions as her ophthalmoscope a reality. She stopped and turned to face him. 'I'm not a rule breaker, Jules.' It was a warning, a warning about her: the fear that he would find her boring. She did not give herself enough credit.

'No, you're not a rule breaker,' Jules whispered, catching her lips in a soft kiss, 'but I am.'

It wasn't untrue. He *was* a rule breaker. He'd broken rules before: school rules to gain his father's attentions and the kind of rules that society often expects wealthy young men sowing their wild oats to break, rules whose breaking added dash to one's reputation, not scandal. But this rule breaking that he engaged in now was different. These were family rules that he was breaking by kissing Becca, by pursuing a friendship with her, by staying at Haberstock Hall as long as he could. The Howells were never friends with their clients. As such, his betrayal was two-fold. He was not only befriending a client, he was keeping that client's identity hidden from the family. Liking people went soundly against the Howell creed of money first, people second—or possibly third.

Of all the rules he'd ever sought to break before, none of them had been the rules of the family Howell. He might not have broken those rules before, but he certainly hadn't kept them very well either. It had left him in a driftless limbo of belonging but not quite belonging to the family and its business. He'd not considered that before, but as his stay at Haberstock went on, he began to think that his self-imposed limbo had come about because he didn't respect the Howell rules that condoned his father prospering off the ideas of others without paying them for their work and creativity. His father had built a fortune at the expense of others: a Frenchman and his own sons to name a few.

And yet you hang on to that family even knowing their habits and vices, his inner voice whispered the condemning dilemma. *What does it say of you that you don't approve of your father's methods and yet you take the money and you do the work they ask of you and you pretend that you are not part of your father's corruption? You cannot have it both ways. It makes you a hypocrite.*

What would the Peveretts think? More specifically what would Becca think? Becca, who didn't seek fame for herself but help for others with her inventions; Becca, who only wanted to make the world a better place. His own insecurities struck hard and fast. She wouldn't want such a person for a friend or for more.

A few weeks ago, it would not have mattered overmuch to him, yet another sign that he was changing, that a piece of him that had long slumbered, long given up on the world, was waking up, stirring to life, and Haberstock Hall was allowing him to explore the possibilities that came with the awakening. Here, people admired his painting, encouraged his singing, treated him as if he had worth. Here, he was included in everything from supper conversation to the mundane task of raking leaves in the orchard. Only it wasn't mundane when it was done with the Peveretts. It was instead a chance to be together. They turned the mundane into an occasion, like today.

Jules leaned on his rake and surveyed the orchard. A short distance from him, Dr Peverett manned the bonfire, feeding it copious piles of leaves and autumn detritus, and beyond him, Becca and her mother gathered windfall apples into bushel baskets. On the tailgate of a wagon, a hamper sat open with bread and ham for when they got hungry. Easy hospitality.

'Jules, my boy, hurry up with that wheelbarrow, I'm running low on fuel,' Dr Peverett called in jolly tones, and Jules picked up the handles and carted the latest pile of leaves over to the fire for dumping.

Dr Peverett wiped his brow with a handkerchief, sweating despite the crispness of the afternoon. 'We're making good progress,' he complimented as Jules pitched the leaves into the fire by the shovelful. 'You're a hard worker, I like that.'

Jules laughed and wiped his own brow. 'I like it, too. City life doesn't give a man much chance to do labour like this.' He studied the older man for a moment, watching the other man's gaze go out into the trees where Becca and Catherine worked. Becca was dressed in an old brown gown and a knitted wool shawl, her hands in knitted fingerless gloves against the cold that his mother and Mary wouldn't be caught dead in. Her hair was in a tight braid that hung down from beneath a kerchief. She looked like a peasant girl, her cheeks red from the weather, her breath coming in misty plumes as she laughed with her mother. She looked happy, content.

And why shouldn't she be? This was her place, the one spot on earth where she knew in her bones that she belonged, that she was meant for it and for what she did here. She didn't look simply happy, she looked beautiful in a way Adelaide Pembridge never would. The old envy he'd felt in the cottage during that first visit stabbed at him again. Rebecca Peverett had *everything*.

'You are truly a lucky man, sir.' Jules smiled at the doctor.

Dr Peverett cocked his head and gave him a friendly, considering stare. 'Do you think so?'

If his father had been asking the question, Jules would have felt stalked, wary of a trap. One didn't feel that way with Dr Peverett. 'Don't *you* feel lucky, sir?' Jules countered, a bit perplexed at where the conversation was heading.

'I don't feel anything about luck.' Dr Peverett reached for a pitchfork and began stabbing leaves for the fire. 'Luck is not a scientific concept. In fact, there's no such thing as luck. Luck is nothing more than another word for "accidental". All things happen for an explainable reason.' Peverett waved his hand to indicate the land about them. 'All of this happened because back in the 1600s, Richard Peverett made a reasoned decision to eschew court life and be a country doctor because his conscience demanded it.'

Richard Peverett, the ancestor that had started it all. Jules had seen his picture in the gallery, a man with a long nose and the trademark cognac eyes. He fed a few twigs to the fire. 'He gave up court?' Jules asked. That sounded intriguing, mostly because it sounded like a very 'un-Howell-like' thing to do. He couldn't imagine his father and mother giving up a chance to be at court. His father lived to outdo a duke.

Peverett leaned on the pitchfork, warming his hands. 'Richard Peverett had earned the favour of a well-placed noble after rendering him life-saving medical care. In order to discharge the debt, the noble offered him a position at court among the royal family's physicians or this house in the country, run down as it was at the time. Life at court came with the chance for more opportunity, more advancement for the canny man. But court life is a life of constant politicking, deal-making, secret-keeping. It was not an honest life and one that would corrupt any man no matter how good his heart in the beginning.'

'So, he chose the house?' Jules guessed, glancing in the direction of said structure, barely visible in the distance except for the welcoming curl of smoke rising from the chimney.

'Yes, he did. He chose the house and a lifetime of honest service to the community around him. He married a woman from the local gentry, had several children and lived a good life. By the time he died, the house had been restored, the village starting to thrive and enough money in the coffers for his children to live comfortably. His daughters had dowries and his sons had their callings. He didn't miss court. He didn't live a lesser life for choosing to live outside the glamour.' Dr Peverett's gaze held his for a long moment. 'Do you know why? Because he knew his true north.'

Dr Peverett thrust his pitchfork into the leaves. 'I,

too, could have made that choice. When I was younger, I had the opportunity to be a grand surgeon, to publish papers and be famous and wealthy or I could come home and be a country doctor like Richard Peverett and my father. I came home and the wealth, the happiness, has followed. I met Catherine, married her, raised a family I'm proud of and had a career in healing that I am proud of and will pass on to my son, William, some day. I still publish papers, one every few years and present it in London to the Royal College. We have all the money we need—and the fame that had once intrigued me because of the connections it could provide? Well, those, too, have followed. My daughter is married to an earl, another to the son of a duke, another to a member of landed gentry, a former M.P. turned philanthropist and investor. All has happened the way it should, because I followed my heart.'

Jules's father would positively drool over himself to have the connections Dr Peverett mentioned so casually. And yet, that wasn't the point of the story, was it? 'What's your passion, Howell? And don't tell me it's acquiring medical device patents for the company because that's no man's passion. That's paperwork.' He was being polite, Jules thought. It was clerk's work when it came down to it, not the work of a founder's son.

'Painting. I love to paint, to capture a moment, a feeling on canvas.' He felt silly saying it. Would Dr Peverett find it silly, too, as his father had? Dr Peverett saved lives, delivered children into the world—what could be nobler than that?

Dr Peverett merely nodded. 'Very good. Why aren't you painting, then? Surely your family has the means to send you abroad to the art schools or even the schools here.'

Jules shook his head, smiling away his embarrassment. 'Painting isn't big enough for my father.'

Peverett cocked a greying eyebrow. 'Isn't big enough? Or not manly enough? Or not financially productive enough? Apparently, your father doesn't know the current Earl of Bourne, the one who established the Seasalter Academy of the Arts a quarter of a century ago. He's not only married to one of the outstanding female artists of our time, but he's a painter himself and in possession of one of Britain's finest collections of paintings by the English masters. Of course, it wasn't easy for him. Growing up, his father didn't support his painting either. It was something he came back to.'

Peverett reached out a hand and gave him a friendly clap on the shoulder. 'The point is, every man needs their own true north in order to live a purpose-driven life, a life that has real meaning, whether that be his love for his family, his care for his fellow mankind or the need to create something beautiful. When a man listens to his heart, his purpose will follow.'

'That sounds rather whimsical for a man who doesn't believe in luck,' Jules said, trying to resist the allure of the man's words. They were heady and intoxicating and nothing at all like anything his family believed in. His father would think Peverett's ideas heresy. But wasn't this exactly what he'd been trying to tell himself these past few weeks? Only Dr Peverett had put it so much more succinctly.

Peverett was not put off by his challenge. 'Not at all, my boy. For a doctor, the heart is everything, a man's core, the source of his power, his very life. The first thing I listen to when I examine a patient is the force of their heartbeat. Life ceases when the heart ceases, physically, emotionally.'

My boy—the endearments came so easily to Peverett. This was what a father should be, what fathers and sons ought to be to one another together. Helping one another, teaching, sharing life's insights. Jules's own father had never shared such things with him in his whole life as Dr Peverett had shared with him today. It was no wonder Becca was acutely aware of her own calling and her own determination to pursue it. It had been bred into her. She'd been taught to understand herself, to be true to herself and the rest would follow.

Want surged in Jules. He craved that same understanding of himself, hungered for it, hungered for the courage to follow his heart, to be sure enough of himself to *know* that heart, to know he wasn't following a short-lived fantasy. Across the orchard, Becca waved at him, gesturing that he should bring the wheelbarrow to help carry the baskets.

Dr Peverett laughed. 'You'd best go to her. We've had quite the crop of apples. It will be a bumper year for Haberstock cider when we press in a couple of weeks. It's a big event, everyone comes to the hall. We press in the barn, of course, and there's dancing. The Cider Ball, we call it, although it's not really a ball at all.' But Jules wagered, as he pushed the wheelbarrow, it would be tons more fun than any ball hosted beneath the expensive light of a Baccarat chandelier.

True north. The thought stayed with him as he hauled baskets for Becca and her mother, as he ate dinner, laughing at a story Dr Peverett told, as he sat at the piano with Becca, singing as she played that night. Did Dr Peverett guess he'd not yet found his true north? Was that why the man had shared so deeply with him today? Or perhaps he had found it and just needed to claim it. What if it was here? What if it was her? What if true north was Rebecca Peverett? What if he failed to win her? Would he spend his life wandering aimlessly at the beck and call of his family in a life he didn't quite fit? But how could he win her? As he was, he wasn't worthy of her. Not yet. But he could endeavour to be. That started with knowing himself.

Chapter Twelve

Jules Howell, singer, painter, kisser of innocents and rule-breaker, leaf-raker, apple-gatherer. Becca added the last to the growing list of who was Jules Howell. These days, she seemed to know him better than she knew herself. She would never have guessed that her head could be turned by a few kisses, but then she'd never imagined kisses like these, kisses that sent her wits to the four winds and her reason with them. She never should have allowed him to steal that second kiss outside the workshop, never should have allowed him to talk her into the mad idea that it could be different for them, that they would be careful, that somehow they could be business partners and friends, man and woman and friends, where so many others had failed.

Perhaps it was the inventor in her that tipped the scales of reason in Jules's favour, that part of her that loved taking the known rules and twisting them into a new semblance of application. She might not break the rules, the inventor in her argued, but she certainly bent them into new things. That was what an invention was, after all. It was the taking of old technologies and turning them to new uses. Why should the rules of a relationship be any different than the rules of physics?

That argument had carried the day and the weeks beyond. It was all the proof she needed that she was changing because of him. Not *for* him, to be clear. She wouldn't change for any man. But she was changing *because* of him the way rocks change the flow of water, displacing it from its usual beds and sending its currents in new directions. Even her surroundings were affected by him.

Her cottage workshop bore the stamp of him and their changing relationship as well, despite their best efforts at being careful to not let their new roles cross. The workshop was no longer her space entirely, but theirs. Jules had his space now, a table brought down from the Hall's attics to sit before the fire. Jules wrote to his brother from that table, read reports from Manchester at that table. She had made a habit of watching over the rims of her glasses as she drew her plans, fascinated by the way his eyes moved as he scanned letters, the way his hand held a pen when he wrote, the way his brow furrowed when he was thinking, the way his mouth pursed when he drank tea from the chipped mug that had officially become 'his'.

He'd put his stamp on the place in other ways: the way he moved through the space, casually looking through cupboards as he hunted for tins of shortbread to munch alongside his tea, the way his spicy winter scent hung in the air, mixing with the smells of the fire and the workshop. His waterfall painting hung in pride of place over the mantel, a constant reminder of their day together.

They'd gone back to the falls several times since that first visit. It had become their place. The wide rock on which they'd sat and painted had become Painter's Rock. The falls had become Indigo Falls for the way they picked up the late October light at sunset. This was the place where they could be alone, where they could set aside business, where no one would interrupt them or judge them.

It became the place where Jules told her about being expelled from schools in an attempt to gain his father's attention. He'd laughed when he'd recounted his pranks, but she'd seen the hurt beneath the laughter, the lost boy behind the man. It was the place where she'd told him about being envious of her siblings, about feeling she'd never measure up, until now. These contracts proved she could contribute to the world, too.

When the weather had proved too formidable for the hike to the waterfall, they drove the pony trap to the village and wandered the stores. By the first of November, Jules knew all the shopkeepers by their first names and the names of their wives and children. He demonstrated an enormous acuity for remembering names and faces. The shopkeepers invited him to take a drink by their stoves, asking his advice while Becca shopped.

On the second visit, he suggested to Mr Thompson at the mercantile the benefits of a wholesale price on the grey flannel for customers who bought the fabric in bulk in order to reduce the man's overstock. On the third visit, he suggested to Mr Barnes at the bakery the packaging of the bakery's excellent shortbread in decorative tins that bore a winter scene on their lids in order to make the shortbreads into a gift. Then, Jules promptly ordered such tins down from Manchester and made a present of them to the delighted baker.

'You're very good at that,' Becca commented as they left the bakery, having dropped off the tins the moment they'd arrived. Her shopping basket was now piled with wrapped packages of shortbread from Mr Barnes and a bag of liquorice drops from the confectioner's to feed Jules's insatiable sweet tooth.

'At what?' Jules tipped his hat to a passing matron, making the woman blush. Becca knew how it felt to be the recipient of Jules's attentions. She still felt herself grow warm when he looked at her, still felt his touch all the way to her toes, still felt herself come undone at his kisses. Familiarity had not made her immune to the thrill of him, as one might suppose. Instead, that familiarity had made her crave his gaze, his touch, his kiss, that much more.

'You help people see their potential. Mr Barnes is already thinking of how he can add a length of ribbon to those tins in order to dress them up for Christmas. With all the money you spend on shortbread he can afford to buy the next batch of tins on his own.' Becca held up the bag of liquorice drops and offered it to him. 'I think you've been underestimated, Jules

Howell. You're more than just charm. You make people feel good about themselves and that's quite a gift.'

Jules took a handful of liquorice drops and popped one in his mouth. 'Stop, you're going to make me blush.' He laughed, brushing off the compliment, but she thought the remark had touched him, perhaps even that the praise had made him uncomfortable. They rounded a corner and he tugged her hand, pulling her into an alleyway between shops. 'You know what else I'm good at? Kissing you.' He demonstrated the talent with a quick buss to her lips, dancing her back to the rough brick wall of a building.

'Jules, careful, someone might see!' Becca protested with a laugh at his impetuosity, but it was all for form's sake. She didn't mind, although she knew she ought. Kissing him was fast becoming *the* highlight of her day every day. She breathed in the spicy, wintry scent of him, his mouth moving over hers, playful at first, nipping and teasing at her lips before the kiss slowed and deepened. He tasted of licorice and the faint tang of Mr Thompson's visiting brandy. He moved against her, evidence of his arousal obvious as their bodies clung to one another, mouths devouring one another.

She wished they were back at the workshop, where they might be alone, where they might indulge in more than kisses.

At the risk of breaking the rules, a small part of her conscience scolded.

There were to be no kisses in the cottage, the cottage was for business. Afternoons were for friendship, or what passed for friendship between them. She'd never had a friend like this, though, one who could kiss her senseless, who could drag her into an alley and rouse her to recklessness. He put his mouth to her throat just below her jaw and a little moan escaped her, part pleasure, part frustration. She wanted his mouth in other places: at her breasts, at her navel, or even lower where the warm heat he engendered pooled and throbbed. Perhaps his mouth might ease her.

Her sisters had made such allusions when they spoke of intimate things. None the less, they were wanton ideas for an unmarried woman to have, but wanton or not, they populated her thoughts more and more often these days as the calendar marched closer to his departure. What would happen to their kisses once he left? She gripped the lapels of his greatcoat and kissed him hard on the mouth. 'I don't want you to go.' Her voice was ragged.

'Shh…' He pressed a finger to her lips. 'Don't think about it, we have time, another full week yet.' He pushed a loose strand of her hair back from her face. 'We'll manage something.'

The encouragement of his smile warmed her and she let herself snuggle closer in his embrace as he kissed the top of her nose. 'We. I like the sound of that.'

'I do, too.' He kissed her again, softly, gently, taking her face between his hands. She could live on his kisses, so sweet were they, so intoxicating…

'What is going on here?' The sharp tones of her sister interrupted the interlude. Becca startled, her eyes flying open to see Thomasia standing at the mouth of the alleyway. Becca felt her cheeks turn fifteen shades of crimson, never mind that Thomasia was two years her junior. How did she explain this wasn't what it seemed?

Jules stepped forward. 'Mrs Rawdon, how delightful to see you. We were just in the village to pick up some shortbread,' he said as if nothing untoward had been going on. Becca envied him his easy elan under pressure.

'Were you?' Thomasia was less impressed. Her hands settled on her rounding belly while her gaze flicked between them. 'I was hoping my sister might offer me some advice on fabric. Perhaps I could steal her away for a brief time.' It wasn't really a question.

'Of course,' Jules offered graciously. 'Becca, I'll meet you at the pony trap in an hour. Shall I take the basket?' Becca surrendered the basket and watched him go. She counted to three in her head, but Thomasia barely waited until Jules was out of earshot.

'What did you think you were doing? Kissing him in broad daylight?' Thomasia hissed, grabbing her arm and pulling her back out on to the pavement.

'It was hardly "broad daylight",' Becca argued. 'We were well out of sight in the alley.' She winced, seeing her mistake even as Thomasia pounced.

'In an alley does not make it better,' Thomasia scolded, 'only more sordid.'

'No one saw us,' Becca protested.

'*I* saw you and you were definitely *not* tasting the shortbread.' Thomasia fixed her with a sisterly stare. 'I thought there was something going on between you that night Shaw and I came to dinner. He was calling you Becca and feeding you chocolates. So, tell me, what *is* going on?'

They walked past the draper's without going in, confirming Becca's suspicions Thomasia didn't need her help with any fabric. They went instead into the tea shop that also served tea along with selling it. The store was empty, it was a bit too early to be busy for tea, which no doubt ideally suited Thomasia's purposes, alas.

Thomasia steered them towards a table by the window and ordered. 'This baby makes me hungry all the time,' she complained with a smile, rubbing her belly. There was a brief reprieve as they waited for the tea to be brought out. No need to start an interrogation on an empty stomach only to be interrupted, Becca thought uncharitably.

'Well?' Thomasia asked the moment they were left alone, tea set before them.

'We are friends,' Becca said. How did she explain to her sister what she could barely explain to herself?

'You're more than friends.' Thomasia's voice dropped and softened, her eyes filled with concern. 'Have you been to bed with him? Because if you have, you must protect yourself, Becca. You cannot depend on a man to take care with such things.'

Becca blushed, her own voice lowering. 'No, of course not.' It was on the tip of her tongue to say, 'How could you think such a thing?', but she knew how. Thomasia had been one of the premiere debutantes during their brief Season in London a few years back, a Season that had been cut short because she'd been reckless with a young lord who'd promised to marry her, but had reneged once he discovered she was pregnant. Sweet Effie-Claire was the product of that mésalliance. Thomasia might look like the picture of the perfect young matron now, but she'd not always been that way. She knew better than most the perfidy of a gentleman.

'But you want to, you both do,' Thomasia pressed. 'I could see by the way you were standing together, not an inch of space between you, your hands all over each other. Kissing isn't enough, is it?' Thomasia reached for her hands and squeezed them. 'Oh, my dear, what are you going to do?'

'We're going to take it one day at a time. It's all we can do,' Becca offered. 'It's an impossible situation, really. He lives in Manchester, I live here. He's someone I am in business with. To take things further would complicate that.'

'So, he'll leave at the end of his visit and that will be that?' Thomasia queried. 'I suppose that's for the best.' She held Becca's gaze for a long moment. 'I can see you care for him, but you're right. To let this go further would be damaging. I just hope you remember that. In the heat of the moment, men will say anything to get what they want, especially when they know you want it, too.'

Becca nodded. 'I know. We both know. We are being careful, I promise you.'

Jules paced near the pony cart, eating liquorice drops while he waited for Becca. He'd promised her they would be careful, that carefulness would protect them from the foolish mistakes that plagued people who conflated their relationships. But he'd not been careful today. He was lucky it was Thomasia who had spotted them. If it had been Dr Peverett or anyone else, he'd have had to come up to scratch. His brother would have roared over that—his citified brother married to a country girl.

But Jules thought he was the one who would have had the last laugh. He was changing. This place was changing him, or perhaps she was changing him. At first, it had been easier to argue the former. But these days, he was more honest with himself. Becca had made an impact. Her sharp wit and her intelligence were admirable, but her kindnesses were what made her genuine. She listened when he talked as if his stories were the most remarkable tales she'd ever heard, as if his life, as if *he* was interesting. And it was real. She didn't *pretend* he was interesting. She actually *remembered* what he said.

He'd nearly come undone the first day at the falls when she'd produced the paints. Her passion was genuine, too. She kissed with her whole heart, her whole body. When was the last time someone had ever given him that much of themselves? Had anyone ever? His body craved her touch the way his heart craved her kindnesses. She liked him.

Could he ever be worthy of her? This was the question that had taken precedence in his mind of late. He was more aware than he'd let on that the days were drawing short. He would be expected back in Manchester with her inventions in tow. What if he went back to Manchester with her in tow, too? That question went hand in hand with the first one—could he ever be worthy of her? His life in Manchester was not currently worthy of her, he knew that much. He didn't have a place of his own, he lived on the family largesse, earning a haphazard salary for irregular work. Even if he did own the town house, it was not fit for a woman to occupy.

Before he could bring her to town, he had to get his affairs in order and that wasn't even dealing with the issue of having hidden her identity from the family. To bring her to town was to play with a certain amount of fire, to hide his brother's latest inventor in plain sight right under his brother's nose. Jules wasn't sure Win would forgive him for that once the truth was known.

But first things first. He would write to Win tomorrow and ask for the deed to the town house. It would take a large part of the money he had in the bank to buy the house outright and furnish it properly, but perhaps it was high time he did. A thirty-year-old man should have his own lodgings on his own penny. Perhaps, too, this was the first step in claiming the independence he thought he wanted. He'd never be independent if he couldn't stand on his own two feet. He needed to be able to provide for himself.

That meant second things second. He would also tell Winthrop he wanted to draw a regular salary for regular work. It would mean going to the office daily, but that would be a small sacrifice to make if meant providing a life for Becca that she could be proud of and

if it meant working on her behalf to make her dreams
come true. He would advocate for her inventions, perhaps work with other inventors in a more concrete way
than taking them to dinner and signing contracts. That
was Becca's confidence in him coming out, yet another
way she'd changed him. She liked to say that he helped
others see their potential, but she'd been the one to help
him see his own potential.

Across the green, he saw Thomasia and Becca
emerge from the tea shop and hug before Thomasia
went one direction and Becca made her way towards
him. He smiled as she approached. 'Everything all right
with your sister?' He handed her up on to the bench
of the pony cart.

'Yes, she won't tell if that's what you're worried
about.' Becca settled her skirts as he sat beside her and
picked up the reins.

He slanted her a look. 'I'm more worried about you.
I didn't want her to upset you.'

'No, of course not. She didn't upset me. She was
curious and concerned, that's all.' There was more on
her mind—she seemed uncharacteristically distracted,
but Jules did not press for more. He left her alone with
her thoughts, settling instead for the tuck of her arm
through his and the weight of her head on his shoulder.
He liked the feel of her against him. Those moments
in which she gave him her trust both warmed and un-
nerved him. He would try hard to be worthy of that
trust, starting with his letter to Winthrop tomorrow.

Chapter Thirteen

They were down to last things, she and Jules. Becca stood before the long mirror in her room, smoothing down the skirts of her dark green and blue plaid dress and regretting the necessity of it. It was a warm dress, a Sunday-best wool gown for the winter, suited for local occasions like tonight's cider press. It was an event held annually at the Hall. Usually, she loved the cider press evening. But tonight, she'd rather have Jules to herself, something she felt there was little chance of. She had no illusions that she'd be able to claim any privacy with him. This evening, she would have to share him with the village. Once word was out that he'd be returning to Manchester, the event had taken on a dual purpose; to press the local apple crop for cider *and* a farewell party for Haberstock's latest 'citizen'.

It would be a rowdy night, starting early and ending late, a night filled with music, dancing and good food. Village life at its best. Hence the need for a more practical gown like the plaid wool. Her rose silk would be entirely out of place to say nothing of being ruined. And yet, she wanted to look her best.

Since when have you cared so much for your looks? Vanity is superficial. She knew the answer to that: since Jules had started looking at her. *He looked at you before that.*

But she wanted tonight to count—perhaps her momentary vanity could be understood on those grounds. He was leaving in the morning, returning to Manchester indefinitely despite their conversation in the alley earlier that week. Nothing in regards to them, to their future outside the business partnership, had been mentioned since and she'd been too cowardly to bring it up. There'd been several opportunities today to address it. They'd spent the day in the workshop. She'd finished the last of drawings and instructions for the inventions she was sending to Manchester. Jules had spent the day packing up his desk.

It had been difficult to leave the cottage that afternoon, knowing that when she entered it next, it would be without him. Tomorrow, he would be in Manchester, back among his normal life in the city, and she would be here, in a workshop that would never be entirely hers again. His watercolour remained on the wall—he'd refused to take it with him, insisting he wanted her to have it. To remember him by? Did it mean he wouldn't be coming back after all? Was she reading too much into it? Had he always intended for their partnership to continue, but not their unique friendship? Or perhaps he was not exclusive in those friendships? Perhaps he had this sort of arrangement with more than one woman and such women were spread throughout the Continent, waiting for Jules to make an irregular appearance once a year?

You were not raised to be such a woman. You will not wait on any man's favour. Pull yourself together. If this is what falling in love does to your brains, you're better off without it.

But Jules wasn't just any man. She liked to think of him as her man, but in truth, she didn't know that he was. They'd never spoken of exclusivity, of making claims on one another, and now it was too late. Too late for anything but one last night. Becca took a final twirl before the mirror and fastened tiny pearl earrings to her ears. She could either spend this night moping or she could take action. If this was her last night with Jules, what did she want from it? Would she be brave enough to claim it?

The cider press was held in the big barn on the Hall's property, with the press at one end, manned by her father and the local men, the food at the other end and dancing in the middle. The barn smelled of hay and apples, not an unpleasant smell on a cold autumn night, and was filled with the sounds of people enjoying themselves. Becca couldn't help but smile the moment she stepped indoors, her spirits lifting at the sounds of music.

She spotted Jules with her father and the other men at the cider press. He was dressed in tight-fitting buckskins and his shirtsleeves were already rolled up. He was laughing with them, her father slapping him on the back, and her heart gave a queer, wondrous flip at the sight of him amid the neighbours and people she'd known her entire life. He looked as if he belonged here, as if he were one of them.

He's a city man. Be honest with yourself, Becca. Deep down inside, he'll want his comforts. He wasn't made for a place like this. He would tire of Haberstock eventually.

She pushed the reminder away. Her conscience meant well, but she didn't want to hear it tonight, didn't want to speculate on other things attached to those thoughts. If he tired of Haberstock, how long would it be before he tired of her? When would walks to Indigo Falls and spun sugar sunsets lose their ability to entrance him? When would stolen kisses beneath autumn leaves no longer inspire his passion? She didn't want to find out. Best, then, to end on a high note, to make tonight the culmination of their friendship. She would make it clear to him that he needn't feel obligated to continue it outside a business partnership. What happened in Haberstock remained in Haberstock.

Jules looked up as she approached, his face breaking into a grin. 'Haberstock has a talent for cider.' He passed her a tin cup. 'I've been telling the gentlemen how they should be selling this abroad in the cities, Manchester, London, York, instead of keeping it to yourselves.' His face got a thoughtful look as he reflected on that. 'On second thought, if you did keep it to yourselves, it would be a good draw for tourists, bring them up from London. Seventeen miles by train is nothing these days. Day trippers could come

up for the autumn harvest and indulge their fantasies
for country living. You could probably even have them
pay for the privilege of running the press *for* you.'

'Once your brain starts moving it never stops, does
it?' Becca laughed. 'Maybe we won't need people to
run a press. Perhaps I can automate it.'

'Where's the fun in that?' Jules set aside his cup and
grabbed her hand. 'Come dance with me, I've been
waiting all night to dance with you.'

'Just all night?' she teased.

*I've been waiting all my life for a night like this, a
night where I felt like I fit in, where someone wanted
to dance with me, where someone looked forward to
my company, looked at me as if I'd hung the moon
and stars.*

She might never have such a night again, Becca
thought as he led her out on to the dance floor. He
found a place for them in a set just forming and grinned
at her from across the circle.

The best thing about country dances was that you
could dance with the same partner all night and no one
cared, or even noticed. So many of the dances were
round dances or reels where partners rotated so often
it was hard to remember who'd started the dance with
whom. And yet, every time Jules passed her, he threw
a private smile just for her, a reminder that when all
was said and done, he was her partner and no one else's.

She danced until she was breathless and her hair fell
down, danced until she was so thirsty she swallowed
an entire cup of cider in a single gulp and had another
one. Jules pulled her back out on the floor for a fast

polka, his arm about her waist as he swung them into the steps. The polka was delightfully heady, or maybe that was the cider talking, it was hard to tell as they whirled about the floor. Jules was an exquisite dancer and kept them both sure-footed as they flew ever faster.

She'd never danced so hard in her life and the faster they went, the faster she wanted to go. It was as if they truly were flying. There was only Jules's green eyes, the firm press of his hand as he guided their steps, the rest of the world passing beyond her in a blur of indistinguishable colours and she never wanted it to end, wanted to remember always the feel of his hand at her back, the heat of his gaze on her face. But it did end. As the music came to a halt, they stood a little longer on the dance floor, catching their breaths, catching each other.

Jules pressed his forehead to hers, his breath coming hard from the exertion. 'You're like a candle tonight, Becca, all lit up from the inside. You're so beautiful.' He raised his head and looked about, taking her hand. 'Let's go outside.'

She ought not to. Darkness, too much cider and too much dancing were a dangerous mixture for trouble. But tonight was not a night for shoulds and oughts. Tonight was a moment out of time, a night for dreams realised if only for a short while. The cool air fanned her cheeks, and she pressed a hand to her stomach, her breathing returning to normal.

'Here, I don't think we'll be disturbed.' Jules's grin flashed in the dark as he pulled her around a corner, away from the revelry. She felt a wall hard at her back and then his mouth was on hers, her arms about his neck, their bodies pressed together, generating a delicious heat in the cold. She held him to her, her hips moving against him. Kisses would not be enough tonight.

'Be careful, Becca.' Jules's voice was a hoarse rasp between kisses, his own breathing harsh. 'Do not tempt me beyond reason.' He nipped at her earlobe, his teeth raising the hairs on her neck in desire and want.

'Be lost, Jules,' she whispered. 'Be lost as I am lost.' She slipped her hand between them, searching for the source of his hardness and finding it. She closed her hand around the jutting front of his breeches, running her hand along his length. Oh, what a wonder it was to touch a man, to hold a man and know that he roused for her.

Dear lord, she was tempting him beyond the boundaries of his restraint. What sweetness it would be to bury himself in her, to feel her around him just as he felt her hand around his shaft now. Did she understand where this was headed? What it would mean and not mean? What were her expectations? Had she thought beyond the pleasure she was seeking? What did she think he could offer her? And yet wasn't this the very reason he'd written to his brother, so that he could offer her something?

Jules's hand covered hers. 'Becca, do not doubt that I want you, but not like this, not against a wall in the dark, not in the heat of a moment where we might come to regret it.'

She pulled her hand free, bringing them both up to frame his face, her hands demanding he focus on her gaze, to insist that he see the need mirrored there. 'I could never regret you, Jules. I know what tonight is and what it isn't. I ask for nothing more beyond it, no promises, no expectations. You will leave in the morning and the rest is unknown.' Her finger pressed softly against his lips when he tried to mount a protest.

She should not settle for so little. His Becca deserved more and yet, did they not both deserve the pleasure that was possible between them? What would be the greater regret? Taking that pleasure or being too afraid to claim it?

'Would you regret me? Is that why you hesitate or perhaps I have misunderstood, I thought you wanted—?'

'I do want,' he cut in swiftly, harshly, not wanting her to finish. 'I want *you.*' Lord, how he wanted her. He ached for her, he woke wanting her, he spent his days wanting her, waiting for the mornings to tick by so that he might have her in the afternoons, to hold her hand, to kiss her mouth, to listen to her talk about wheels and cogs and mechanisms that made little sense to him. 'But I will not have your first time be against a wall.'

She kissed him softly on the mouth, her own mouth curling into a sensual smile. 'I know a place where we can be alone, where no one will bother us. What do you say to that, Jules?'

He smiled against her lips. 'I would say you're seducing me, Miss Peverett, and I quite like it.' Seduced by a virgin. The old Jules, the one who drank incessantly from his flask and racketed through his days looking for novel adventure to entertain himself with would have seen the novelty in such an occurrence. But the new Jules, the one who didn't want to leave Haberstock in the morning, saw only the seriousness and sincerity behind it. For the first time in his life, he was going to make love tonight.

Chapter Fourteen

The outline of the workshop came into view, dark against the night sky. Of course she'd bring him here. This was the place where she felt most comfortable, most in control. She really did mean to seduce him, then. He smiled in the darkness at the thought of Becca's hands on him, her mouth on him, his body free to respond to her every touch. But there would be pleasure for her, too. 'Are you sure?' he asked as she produced her key. 'We have rules about this place.' He was only half teasing. What they did in here tonight would linger long afterwards. She would have to face those memories every time she entered no mattered how this ended.

She turned to him, tucking her key away. The moonlight caught her face, the light shining on the creamy perfection of her skin, stealing his breath. How had he ever thought Rebecca Peverett a plain woman? She was stunning, innocence and temptation all rolled into one. She took him by the hand and led him inside. 'I'm sure, Jules.'

She lit the lamp and they took the stairs together hand in hand. This was unfamiliar territory for him. In all the weeks he'd been here, he'd not ventured up the steps. The loft at the top was small but neatly kept. Like the rest of the cottage, it bore Becca's stamp; orderly, clean, everything in its place. There was room only for a nightstand and a bed, but the bed was wide, covered in a red and blue plaid comforter that looked stuffed with down. It would be warm to snuggle under. The room had few accoutrements, but the ones it did have had not been skimped on. 'Do you sleep up here?' Jules asked, prompted by curiosity.

'Sometimes, when the house is crowded or if I just want a change. I haven't slept up here for a long time.' Jules knew her well enough now to understand why that would be: because the house hadn't been crowded, because her brother and sisters had all moved away. There were fewer reasons to seek sanctuary these days. Sanctuary was readily available at the big house.

Becca set the lamp on the nightstand, the light catching her from behind, nervous for the first time. Her hands clenched one another at her waist, her earlier bravado now fled. 'What is it, Becca?' Jules took her hands, running his thumbs over their backs.

'I don't know what to do. What comes next?' Her honesty made him smile. He kissed her cheek, then her chin, the tip of her nose, her throat, anticipation rising with his desire.

'There are no rules, Becca. We make it up as we go along,' he whispered at her ear. 'Shall I show you?'

'Yes, please.' Her whispered reply had him hard

and aching as she twined her arms about his neck and pressed her body to his. 'Show me everything.'

He stepped back from her then and for a moment she thought she'd done something wrong. Had she been too bold? Or not bold enough? 'Sit on the bed, Becca.' She tried to launch a protest, but he silenced it with a kiss and danced her about to the bed, his voice rough as if it were difficult for him to make the words. 'No arguing, Becca. You must do what you're told or I can't show you "everything".'

He stepped back from her again, with the lamplight at his back. 'Watch me.' He untied his cravat and drew the length from about his neck, unbuttoned his waistcoat and tossed it aside, his hands working loose the buttons of his shirt, making his intentions clear. He meant to disrobe right in front of her. Becca's mouth went dry as the shirt joined the waistcoat.

She stared at his bare torso, mesmerised by the lean, sculpted lines of him. It wasn't that she hadn't seen a man's chest before. She'd studied da Vinci's drawings and she had a brother. But this was entirely different. This was the body of her *lover* and it was exquisitely made. She wet her lips with her tongue, surprised to find her own voice nothing more than a whisper. 'I want to touch you.' She half rose from the bed, her fingers aching to trace the lines of his torso, the ridges of his abdomen, the planes of his iliac girdle where they disappeared beneath the waistband of his trousers.

Jules shook his head and she resumed her seat. 'Not yet. Good things come to those who wait, my impatient one.' His green eyes glinted with a subtle light, an unspoken promise of pleasure passing between them, a reminder that he was waiting, too. She was not in this alone, not desiring alone. He bent swiftly and pulled off his boots, his hands returning to the waistband of his buckskins, his eyes holding hers as he undid his fastenings and pushed the buckskins over lean hips. He kicked them away with practised ease and stood before her entirely nude, the lamp limning his silhouette in a soft light that turned his skin a warm, pale gold, his hair the colour of coffee. He was all rich, earthy tones bathed in the flame light, primal man in the Garden, every inch of him on display from the elegant lines of his torso to the hard, jutting length of his phallus where it strained upwards from its dark nest, gloriously masculine and powerful.

'Do I please you, Becca?' His voice was like rough velvet, raising delicious goose pimples on her skin. He was making a gift of himself to her and her blood sang with the knowledge of it, of this beautiful man.

'You know you do,' she whispered, letting her eyes show her appreciation, roving the length of him, resting on that most manly part of him. She rose and went to him. He was on offer for her now and she circled him, letting her hand skim his skin, letting her fingertips run over the surface of him, delighting in the pinpricks of delight she raised on his skin, the darkening of his eyes as his gaze followed her circuit about his body. Her hand dropped low, cupping the firm rounds of his buttocks. 'You are my very own Vitruvian Man, the perfection of the universe meeting in human symmetry.' She pressed a kiss to his shoulder blade. 'You're beautiful, Jules.' And hers. He was hers. There was a possessive thrill in the knowledge.

She completed her intimate circuit and stood before him, his hands at her hips drawing her against him, his mouth at her ear. 'Now, I shall undress you, my dear.' His teeth sank into her earlobe and a delicious shudder skittered through her at his words, at his touch. She was fast learning that anticipation was its own aphrodisiac.

'I'll start with your hair.' His long fingers pulled out the pins one by one until she felt the length of it fall down her back, felt his fingers comb through it. He kissed her, a slow teasing tangle of tongues and tastes, his hands loosening her dress until it slid from her shoulders and dropped to the floor. Petticoats followed, undergarments gave way to his proficient fingers until it left her only in her chemise and her mind wondering how she'd got there. She'd been so wrapped up in his touch, his tongue, his words at her ear, she'd not realised, had not felt embarrassed until now. Out of modest reflex, she tried to cover herself with her hands. Her chemise was thin, it was no protection from Jules's green gaze.

Jules captured her hands gently and pulled them away from her body. 'I want to see you. There is no need to hide, I will find you beautiful, I promise.'

'It's just that…' She struggled for words. It was just what? What did she fear?

'That it's the first time you've been naked with a man? You're safe with me, Becca.' Dear lord, he made it sound so natural, so normal.

He reached for the hem of her chemise. 'Will you permit me?' he whispered against her skin. She nodded, fast becoming beyond speech. She'd permit him anything here in this loft, in the private world they were creating just the two of them, and what a world it was—a world full of intimacy, of unimaginable closeness. She'd not realised it was possible to feel this way with another.

He stripped the chemise over her head and tossed it away to join his waistcoat. He stepped back and held her arms out to her side, his throat working as he took her in. 'You are exquisite,' he breathed, and she felt an irrational pride in having pleased him this way. 'Shall we to bed, my sweet? I want to lick every inch of you, taste every inch of you.'

The bed took their weight, the mattress dipping as Jules came over her. Her legs parted, making room for him. It seemed the most natural thing in the world to lie here naked with him, to fit his body to hers, looking up into his face with those sharp cheekbones and green eyes, his hair falling forward. He looked as wild and as primitive as she felt. His mouth began a slow tour of her body, nipping at her neck, sucking at her breasts until they were taut with wanting, licking at her navel and then lower still. Ought she be appalled? His tongue gave a wicked lick along the seam of her fold and she shuddered in abject pleasure. She'd abandoned modesty with her chemise. There was only pleasure and desire now, they were the sum of her new world as he licked at her, his tongue finding a secret nub from which every nerve in her body seemed connected.

She arched, her hips rising against him in supplication, only to find herself caught in a spiral of more wanting. More did not satisfy, more merely spurred the craving for his touch, for the pleasure he wrought and, in a most pleasing but contrary way, it spurred the desire for release. She did not need to understand the dichotomy to want to linger in the pleasure and yet wanting that pleasure to be achieved to claim that release when it found her. It took her at last. Jules's head collapsed on her stomach, his own breathing coming hard and fast, his shoulders heaving in a reminder that her pleasure to receive had been his pleasure to give. He'd not been doing anything *to* her, but that they'd been mutually satisfying one another, and yet she sensed her pleasure was more complete than his. The hard weight of his phallus still pressed against her leg.

She drew him up to her so that they were face to face, his body covering hers once more. 'Come into me, now, Jules. Take your release as well,' she invited, her own gaze searching his face.

'I will go slowly,' he promised. 'You must let me know if I should wait.' Not stop. They were too far gone for that.

She nodded. 'You could not hurt me, Jules. Not ever.' She shifted then, as if to prove her point. She lifted her hips once more to meet his body, smiling when she felt the round tip of him nudging at her entrance, felt the dampness of her own greeting mingle with his. Her body was ready for him just as his was ready for her. He raised up on his arms, letting the lean, sculpted sinews of his arms bear his weight as their hips pressed into one another. Then he was inside her, the length of him pushing forward towards some internal destination, her body stretching around him. What a delicious sensation that was, to feel him inside her, filling her most intimate channel with that most potent part of him. There was the ecstasy of pleasure and the pinch of pain mixing together in the wake of his passage until at last he rested, fully sheathed.

She wrapped her legs about his hips, holding him close, smiling up at him, aware of him in an entirely new way. Then he whispered at her ear, his voice no more than a throaty rasp. 'Follow my lead.' He moved within her then, beginning the roll and glide of an intimate waltz. Her hips answered in pursuit, each movement, each press of him, leading her closer, leading *them* closer, to pleasure's cliff. This was a new pleasure, more intense than the one she'd felt earlier, and her body was hungry for it. She begged with the mewls of her voice, the thrust of her hips up hard into his, the vice of her legs holding him tight within her for fear he'd escape before she could claim what she wanted. But she needn't have feared. Jules knew what she needed before she knew it herself. She had only to claim it.

'Let it take you,' he coaxed, his own body tightening, pleasure nearing for him even as her pleasure crested. She arched against him, hips up, throat exposed as he thrust once more, delivering them both to pleasure's shore. The denouement that followed was exquisite, a place where she had only to float in a sea of bliss, Jules's body wrapped about her as hers was wrapped around his. There was no sense of where one ended and the other began, there was only them. There were no rules, no partnerships, no morning trains to Manchester, only them and the pleasure they'd created. Becca would have stayed in that world for ever. This world made sense.

I love you, Jules Howell.

It had been a wondrous thought to doze off to. It was a more complicated thought to wake up to. What did loving Jules mean? Did she really love him or was that a typical reaction to such an experience? Perhaps what she was feeling wasn't love, but something else born of a response to passion?

'You're awake.' Jules rolled to his side, propping his head up in his hand and smiling at her. Would that smile for ever prompt butterflies in her stomach? He trailed a hand over her hip. 'How are you feeling?'

'Boneless, amazed. I had no idea.' She smiled back at him, unable to find the words. 'Is it always like this? Earth shattering, this sense of completion, this feeling of wholeness?' Something filled his eyes for a moment and she wondered if she'd said something wrong? She bit her lip, realising her error. Perhaps it had only felt that way to her. 'I suppose it's only that I'm new to it...' she amended, wishing she could take back her words.

'What does that mean?' Jules's fingers kneaded her hip.

'Nothing.' She cocked her head. 'Have you had many lovers, Jules?'

Jules drew her close, trailing kisses down the length

of her arm. 'I've had sex with a lot of women, I'm no saint when it comes to that. But lovers? No, my dear. Just you. Trust me, there *is* a difference.' He kissed her again and rolled her beneath him. 'Allow me to demonstrate my point.'

It was a successful demonstration, but it could not change the inevitable. They could not stay in the cottage all night. Someone would be sure to notice their absence. Jules helped her dress and reality returned with each piece of clothing. Jules was leaving in the morning. There was no guarantee he was coming back. What if Howell Manufacturing didn't want her other designs? There would be no reason for him to come back to Haberstock.

There'd be you, aren't you reason enough?

But what if she alone wasn't enough?

Becca twisted her hair into the semblance of a neat bun and poked in a few pins. She'd promised herself no doubts because there was only tonight. What happened afterwards didn't matter. But that was before... before this wondrous experience, before she'd had a taste of what it really meant to be with someone. How could she let him go now not knowing what the future held for them? And yet she'd promised him she would do just that. It was the one rule they'd set for tonight. She could not break it.

Jules came up behind her, wrapping her in his arms. 'You're upset. We should talk...'

'No, we shouldn't. That was not what we decided. You needn't make any pledges, any promises. That's not what this was about.' Becca turned out of his embrace. She stepped back. 'How do I look? Presentable?' She would go straight to the house. With luck, no one would see her. But if they did, she didn't want to give them reason for suspicion.

Something soft flickered in Jules's gaze. 'Presentable,' he assured her with a rueful smile. 'No one will guess you spent the better part of three hours making love in a loft.'

That felt wrong. Surely, after experiencing something so momentous, something so intimate, one should be changed. A sliver of sadness took up residence right next to the joy in her heart, but perhaps it was for the best. No one could know what she'd done. Not even her family. She'd never had a secret from them before. This was the most beautiful thing she'd ever done and she couldn't tell a soul.

'Will I see you in the morning?' Jules asked when they reached the bottom of the stairs.

No, she would cry and tears would give it all away. No one cried when their business partner left. It would be an entirely inappropriate response. Still, it took all of her willpower to utter the necessary words. 'I think it's best we say our goodbyes here.'

Chapter Fifteen

Jules had hoped she didn't mean it, that Becca would change her mind and be downstairs the next morning to see him off. He'd even held out hope she would be waiting in the coach and they'd have one glorious hour together on the way to the station. But Becca had been true to her word and Jules had left Haberstock Hall shortly after dawn relatively unsung. Only Dr Peverett was up to see him off or perhaps the man hadn't been to bed yet. The others remained abed after a late night at the cider press party. Even the November weather seemed to be asleep, the day reluctant to rise above the frosty grey mist that swirled up from the ground.

For a moment, it crossed Jules's mind to use the foggy mist as a delay, postponing his journey another day. People got lost in fog. It might be dangerous. If he thought a delay might solve anything he would have tried it, but it resolved nothing. He *had* to go to Manchester. For both their sakes. That was what he told himself as Haberstock Hall faded from view, lost to the mist. He was still telling himself that an hour later when the carriage pulled into the Broxbourne station and unloaded his trunk.

Becca needed him to be her advocate, to represent her ideas, to see that she got a fair deal for her work. She needed him to protect her identity while making her products available to those who needed them. In that way, he could help her bridge the gap between her dreams and reality. Becca *needed* him. She needed him to get on this train, to go home. He passed his ticket to a conductor and sought his seat.

No one had ever needed him before. His father had never needed him, his brother didn't need him. That a fiercely independent woman like Rebecca Peverett should be the one to need him was heady sauce indeed. Heady *and* heavy, he acknowledged as the train chugged out of the station. To be needed came with responsibility, something he'd managed to assiduously avoid for years, at first to aggravate his father. Aggravation was a type of attention, after all. But then, he'd got so good at avoiding it, it merely became a habit.

He was going to change that. That was what getting on the train this morning was about: proving to Becca that he was worthy of her, or perhaps proving to *himself* that he was worthy of her. The job, the deed to the town house, was all about her, all *for* her.

Not entirely. It's for you, too, part of him acknowledged. *You were tired of drifting through life when you left for Hertfordshire.*

But she was the catalyst, the rudder that was providing him direction.

Perhaps he should have told her? Perhaps he should have discussed the letter he'd written to his brother and why he'd written it. What would she have said if he'd told her?

You think she would have retreated. You think you would have scared her off, lost her. That's why you didn't tell her.

So, yes, coward that he was, he hadn't wanted to risk it. To tell her would be proof that he'd broken the rules, crossed the line of their relationship without her consent.

Of course, they'd broken other rules last night that definitely crossed not only their own lines. They'd made love in the workshop, the one place that was supposed to be business only—but they'd broken society's rules as well. He'd bedded a gently bred young woman without the benefit of marriage.

Jules smiled to himself and settled back in his seat. He closed his eyes, preferring the vision in his head to the scenery outside the window. Last night had been extraordinary. He would carry those images of Becca in his mind always: Becca laughing, her eyes shining as they danced, reckless and jubilant. Becca standing before him, beautifully naked, the defiant tilt of her chin conveying both her boldness and her innocence as her audacity did battle with her modesty.

Jules felt the not so unpleasant stirrings of arousal begin, an arousal evoked not only by the images in his mind, but also by the echo of her touch on his skin, the drift of her fingertips where they'd trailed over him, the drop of her hand where she'd cupped his buttocks.

She'd been bold then, eager to touch him, to learn the contours of him. It boded well for future encounters and where else she might touch him next time…

Next time.

He was sure there would be a next time. In his mind, returning to Manchester was all about guaranteeing there would be a next time. This was about putting plans in place for a future, albeit an amorphous one. What kind of future would that be? They hadn't discussed it. He wasn't very good at discussing futures, given that he'd not spent much time contemplating one and Becca had not seemed eager to. Such reluctance prompted the question—did she see that future the same way?

I don't want you to leave. But what did that mean? Was it the foundation for a new reality they created between the two of them? Was it the sentiment of a moment? A wish whose improbability she'd already accepted? Was one night enough for her to satisfy her curiosity and her desire without muddling the depths of their partnership? One night could be explained or erased as circumstances required. One night would be merely one more secret to add to the secret they already kept between them. Unless they couldn't keep it a secret. Unless there were consequences. Jules's eyes flew open.

A child. The ultimate responsibility as a result of the ultimate irresponsibility. Recriminations flooded. He'd been careless with his body and with hers last night. He did regret that. It had never been his intention to put Becca in harm's way. But surprisingly this morning, he could not regret the potential consequence that could follow such recklessness.

A child would certainly settle the unknown between them. He *would* marry her if there was a child: a dark-haired child with inquisitive eyes, quick hands and an agile mind like his or her mother. Such a child would be welcomed and loved by them both. He'd seen Becca with Effie-Claire, seen the care Becca put into the toys she crafted for children she didn't even know. Becca would be a splendid mother.

But what of yourself? You imagine being a husband and a father, but what do you know of such things? What do you know of love? You pay women to love you, you ply them with expensive champagne and trinkets in return for their attentions. That is not love. Would they love you if you were a poor man? You know the answer to that.

Today, he would not give such self-doubt an anchor. *I would know enough,* he told himself fiercely. Love had filled Haberstock Hall and, for a short time these past weeks, he'd lived in its milieu.

Jules made quick work of the station routine, hailing a cab and collecting his trunk in short order. The leather cylinder containing Becca's sketches had never left his side. It was far too precious to trust to anyone's care but his own. Inside the cab, he began to order his plans. He consulted his pocket watch. There'd be time to send Winthrop a note inviting him to drinks at the Union Club later this afternoon.

His blood was humming with purpose by the time

he arrived home. Home. He liked the sound of that as he jumped down from the cab. He looked up at the town house with its red-bricked facade and long windows. Soon, this place would be his very own. A new sense of pride surged through him as he mounted the front steps, the door held open for him by his long-suffering butler, Steves.

'Just the person I wanted to see.' Steves had no idea what was in store for him. 'I'm about to grant you your most fervent wish, Steves,' he greeted the poor man with a grin. 'We're going to turn this place into a home. I think it's time we started decorating to *our* tastes.' He laughed at the look of shock on Steves's face. 'But first, have a bath drawn, send my valet up. I need to dress and shave. I need a note sent round to my brother to meet me at the Union Club. We have business to discuss. I need to meet with Mrs Harris, too. There's housekeeping to be taken care of.'

'Housekeeping, sir?' Steves trotted after him up the stairs to his chambers. The man was struggling to keep up on all fronts. Housekeeping hadn't been discussed for years at this address. Not that the house wasn't in good shape. Mrs Harris did a fine job without his direction. Mary had hired him good servants when he'd first moved in. But there was more to do.

'Yes, you heard me, Steves.' He was enjoying this. Who would have thought after years of trying to shock his butler with his rowdy antics about town all it really took was a little attention to the house to entirely discombobulate the man? Jules stripped off his cravat and set aside his pin, catching sight of Steves in the mirror. 'Is that a smile I see, Steves?'

'It might be, sir. Welcome home, sir.'

Welcome home indeed. Jules smiled. Who would have thought that he'd found a purpose at last and that purpose was a person?

The Union Club with its stark Greek Revival facade dominated Mosley Street. What it lacked in decoration, it made up for in size. The club had moved here twenty years prior when Jules's father and other similarly minded businessmen decided they'd outgrown the original premises on Norfolk Street. Richard Lane had converted an old warehouse into the most prestigious club in town. Not that anyone would guess from the outside. Unlike other clubs, the Union Club was sans entrance portico. Jules had always thought the absence of the portico made entering a rather casual experience for the member. One could simply walk up to the door straight from the street. There was no place in particular to be let out from a cab or carriage.

The doorman held the door for him, and Jules gave him a nod, handing his greatcoat and top hat to a waiting valet. He scanned the ground-floor coffee room and spied Winthrop by a window overlooking the street. This was it. Showtime. He'd dressed carefully in a pressed dark suit and a subdued dove-grey waistcoat and black neckcloth. He hoped the effort would not go unnoticed with Winthrop. He pulled at his cuffs and straightened his jacket one last time and strode towards the future.

'Jules, you're looking well. The country air agrees with you.' Winthrop rose and shook his hand.

'It does, Win.' He smiled broadly at his brother. 'Thank you for meeting me on short notice. I wanted a chance to discuss my position at the company with you as well as R. L. Peverett's opportunities.'

A waiter came to their chairs as they sat. 'Brandies, sirs?'

Winthrop ordered coffee. 'What will you have, Jules?'

'Coffee for me as well,' Jules replied, earning a sharp look from Winthrop as the waiter hurried off.

'Coffee? It's after two o'clock. That's fairly late for coffee for you. Are you sure the country hasn't addled your wits? I did expect you back much sooner.'

Jules shrugged and crossed a leg over one knee. 'There was a lot to do. But we can discuss that in a moment. You received my letter, I assume? What do you think?'

Winthrop shook his head. 'I don't know what to think. I'm thrilled. I'm sceptical. I'm surprised. You have been a reluctant employee these past five years. What's changed?'

He had changed. But how did he explain that to Winthrop? Winthrop understood money. Winthrop did not understand emotions or people. He put it in terms Winthrop could comprehend. 'I think we've been using my talents on the wrong end of the business. What I really want to do is work the back end and sell our products. I want to take the ophthalmoscope, for instance, and show it to doctors, show them how it can change the way they treat patients. I think that's where

I can be the most use to the company, not in securing contracts from individuals, but in mass marketing our products—in short, adapting people to ideas, *our* ideas—and ideas to people, to paraphrase Isocrates.'

Winthrop nearly spewed his coffee. He choked and wiped his mouth with a napkin. 'My brother quoting Isocrates? Now I know you're an impostor. Where is the real Jules Howell and what have you done with him?'

Jules laughed, tolerating the dig. 'A man *can* change, Win. It just took me a while to work out what I am good at.' And he had to love himself. A man couldn't be respected by others if he didn't respect himself first. He had to be his own change.

Win nodded. 'I like the idea. You can start with more specialised products like the scope and then we can have you branch out, if all goes well.'

'It will go well.' Jules smiled confidently. No doubt Win was wondering how long the change would last. Jules couldn't blame him. This wasn't the first time Jules had been excited about something, only to cool his interest in a couple of weeks. The waiter came with fresh Italian coffees and lengths of almond biscotti.

'So, who is she?' Winthrop asked when they were alone again.

Jules dipped his biscotti in the coffee and took a bite before answering, wary of where the conversation was headed. 'What makes you think there's a woman?'

Winthrop pointed his biscotti like a sword. 'Because I know you, Brother. You have a woman in every town. I don't think for a moment the wilds of Hertfordshire were without their comforts. You were gone for three weeks and now you come home wanting the deed to your house—a place you've shown no interest in for the last five years—wanting to take an active role in the company, also something you've shown no interest in, and you haven't reached for your flask since you've been here. If that's not the essence of being reformed, I don't know what is. Men don't tend to reform themselves. So, who is she?'

'Rebecca Peverett.' This was one area where he was not prepared to engage in deception. He would not lie about her or his feelings for her although he could see the answer did not entirely please Winthrop.

'The inventor's daughter?' Winthrop drummed his fingers on the table in his customary show of irritation. 'So, you're not entirely reformed, then,' he scolded. 'That creates a potential conflict of interest, surely you can see that? It puts us in a difficult position, Jules, when it comes time to do business.' Not nearly as much difficulty as her actually being the inventor, though, Jules thought.

'She's an extraordinary person, Win,' Jules said firmly in her defence and in his.

'She must be if she has you wanting a deed to a house and regular salary.' Winthrop smiled. 'What are your plans in regards to Miss Peverett?' Jules could already see the wheels of his brother's mind moving, trying to work out how best to use this latest development, perhaps thinking a conflict of interest could work in one's favour, and he didn't like it.

'My personal relationship is not to be about business,' Jules warned and looked to redirect the conversation. 'Shall we talk about R. L. Peverett's other inventions?' Winthrop's eyes lit up. Nothing pleased a Howell more than discussions of money.

'Did you bring the plans?' Winthrop looked about.

'No, I'll bring them by the office tomorrow.' Jules felt possessive of those as well. 'There are three items that have potential, but I want to be sure Peverett is treated fairly. These are good, original ideas and Peverett is trusting us with them, trusting us to pay well for them since we'll be the ones who will hold the patent and will benefit over the long run from the sales.'

'Of course,' Winthrop agreed, but Jules wouldn't let Becca's designs go so easily.

'It will not be like the Frenchman, Win. Howell Manufacturing studied his designs, rejected them and then a few months later miraculously produced something remarkably similar.'

Win sat back as if struck, his voice low and angry when he spoke. 'Are you insinuating that Howell Manufacturing stole the design?'

'Well, when it looks like duck…' Jules did not back down. He'd given Becca his word. She wasn't just trusting Howell Manufacturing, she was trusting him, which mattered a great deal more.

'The timing was unfortunate,' Winthrop explained, 'but nothing illegal occurred. That's business and that's the world of invention in this modern day and age. There are multiple people at any given time working on the same things, often unbeknownst to each other. Who is the "first" to do anything is quite subjective. It's hard to be sure. Others may be working on similar designs, but how is anyone to know? In the case of the Frenchman's telescope, we got the patent first. If the Frenchman's design had been any good, it might have gone differently for him. As I recall, his articulating piece wasn't reliable. Howell Manufacturing simply did it better.'

'I like Peverett,' Jules said baldly.

Win raised a brow. 'This is business, Jules. *Liking* our clients is inconsequential, or have you forgotten? We cannot let liking our client or our client's daughter—' Winthrop gave him a sharp look '—interfere with good business deals.' That was the difference between the Howells and Peveretts. The Peveretts had treated him like family, not like business. He'd sang with them, played cards with them, gone to church with them, pressed cider with them.

He'd worked side by side with Becca, she'd treated him as an equal, been impressed with him, taken him seriously, trusted him in so many ways, with her body, with her work.

Jules met his brother's gaze with his own. 'No, I've not forgotten, that is why I must insist that Peverett be treated fairly.'

'He will be,' Winthrop assured him solemnly. 'If you can't take your brother's word on that, whose can you take?' He smiled. 'I have good news for you. The ophthalmoscope is ready for production. The first ones should be rolling out of the factory in two weeks. I was thinking, we could make a celebration of it. Perhaps Peverett would like to come to Manchester for it. Mary was already planning on holding an early Christmas ball. We can easily incorporate the launch of the scope into the celebrations and at that time, perhaps we can talk about the new inventions and celebrate a new contract.'

'I'm sure that would be wonderful,' Jules answered because it was the only answer to give. 'I'll contact Peverett in a few days once the production schedule is certain and see if a trip is possible.' It wouldn't be, of course, but perhaps Becca would be able to attend as R. L. Peverett's representative family member. It would mean adding a few more lies to the carefully spun web he and Becca had already created. There would be no signing of a contract. He'd have to find a reason to postpone the signing until he could go down to Haberstock.

Winthrop finished off his coffee and rose. Shadows had fallen outside the window and evening approached. They'd talked the afternoon away. 'Come to supper, Mary will want to see you.'

'Yes, I'll be by in a little while. I need some time to think.'

Winthrop chuckled and slapped him on the back. 'Careful, Jules, you're dangerously close to becoming a man of integrity.'

Not too close, though, Jules thought after Winthrop left. A man of integrity didn't find himself in the unenviable position of lying to his family in order to protect the woman he cared for. But what could he do? Becca had put her trust in him and he could not fail her. Failing her would be like failing himself all over again.

Chapter Sixteen

Becca failed to get the paint exactly right on the little soldier and a drop spattered on the tabletop. Drat it. She grabbed a rag and scrubbed at the blob. She'd never have all the toy soldiers done in time for the Royal Military Asylum in Chelsea. Christmas was forty-odd days away and she wasn't going to be ready at this rate. This rate being, attempting to paint soldiers in the workshop only to be distracted by any little reminder of Jules. She spent as much time staring at the waterfall painting over the fireplace as she did painting the soldiers and she hadn't touched any of her other projects.

Becca set down the paintbrush and went to the hearth, retrieving the kettle. Perhaps a cup of tea would help, although the odds were against it. A cup of tea hadn't helped all week since Jules had left. It only served to remind her of all the tea he'd drunk as he sat at the now-empty table in front of the hearth. She hadn't had the heart to move it, so she'd thrown a checked square of fabric on the table and took her tea at it. But every cup of tea, every tin of shortbread, only acted to rub salt in the wound. He was indeed etched into the very fibres of the workshop, his presence echoed in the wood and stone. But mostly she felt the echo of him in her heart. It was hard to work, hard to concentrate on anything but Jules and what they'd shared in this cottage, not just the one night, but for the entirety of his visit.

Becca wrapped her hands around the chipped mug. What they'd shared was more than sex. It was the stories they'd told, learning one another as they sat before the fire, or how they'd worked together to prepare her plans and select ideas for him to present in Manchester. There'd been talk between them, but also there'd been silences and there'd been comfort in that silence, each doing their own work and yet still aware of each other. Perhaps that was the truest sense of partnership.

And now his absence suggested another aspect of partnership. She didn't feel complete without him. Nothing had gone right since he'd left. It was hard to be in the workshop, the one space that had always brought her solace. She heard his voice, easy and laughing, in her head as she worked. She carried on conversations with him in her mind. Was he doing the same? Was he missing her or had she already faded to a pleasant memory? One of many? Was he already flirting shamelessly with a pretty blonde in Manchester, dazzling her with his charm? It was one of the many ways in which she managed to torture herself since his departure. To top it off, she'd got her courses this morning, those messy, inconvenient things that left her feeling crampy, grouchy and entirely out of sorts.

Becca sipped at her tea. By rights, it ought to be a cause for celebration. There would be no repercussions from their one night together. But what should have been a relief had been met with tears on her behalf. She'd actually cried when she'd woken up this morning. It was an entirely illogical response. She was not ready to be a mother, certainly not an unwed mother. Nor was she ready to be a wife, which ought to come before motherhood. And there were other things which should come before both of those, like love and courtship. Not a one-night affair. That was hardly the grounds on which to start a meaningful marriage.

Marriage, motherhood. She was being overly fanciful this morning. She'd cast herself for so long in the role of doting aunt, she wasn't used to thinking about herself in those other roles. She'd quite given up on them, but perhaps not as much as she'd thought. They'd slid back into her psyche so subtly she hadn't even noticed they were there until this morning's reminder that they were not for her. There would be no child. No little boy that had Jules's green eyes, who would run in the spring fields of Haberstock with his cousins. He would have been a middle cousin. There'd already be three cousins older than he and there would doubtless be more cousins to follow. He'd be a middle child in that regard, just as she was. But she'd have made sure he didn't get lost in the crowd.

Becca set the mug down with a hard, sloshing thump

on the table. It was back to work for her. She was only thinking like this because it was nearly Christmas, the season of children. It was for the best that there was no child given that there'd been no talk of a future between them. She could not sit here indulging in such idle fantasies over a child that would never be. She needed to focus on real children, the children at the military asylum. She returned to the worktable and picked up her paintbrush, determined to make a good effort today. This missing Jules would get better with time, she assured herself. It could hardly get any worse.

She'd like to say the emptiness she felt, the distraction she felt, was all his fault, but in truth, the fault was all hers. If he was gone with nothing settled between them but business, that was her fault as well. She'd been the one to set the rules: just one night with no expectations beyond that; no goodbyes in the grey dawn, no mixing of their two roles as business partners and short-term romantic interests. She'd done it to protect them, but mostly to protect herself. From rejection.

Would he still have wanted her if he'd felt obliged to follow up that wanting with a fulfilment of traditional social obligations? She'd not wanted to lose him, to lose this chance at passion. At least this way she couldn't be rejected. She wouldn't suffer the indignity of Jules trying to let her down gently. She'd got exactly what she'd asked for: no commitment, no discussion of a future.

And he'd agreed to it.

Perhaps her conditions had been a relief to him. He'd made no secret that he was a rule breaker, that he followed his own dictates, not society's. He'd not hidden the fact that he was accustomed to many lovers. He was not the marrying sort. And neither was she, although for different reasons. This had worked out just as it should have. But that ending had not made her happy. He should be here, helping her paint the soldiers.

There was a knock at the door and for a wild moment she entertained the idea that it *was* him, that Jules had come back. But it was only Thomasia wrapped in a cloak, her rapidly expanding belly poking through the folds. Six weeks to go and there'd be a new addition to the family.

'Sorry, it's just me.' Thomasia smiled and shut the door behind her. 'Missing him?' Thomasia didn't mince words as she pulled a stool up to the table.

'Was it that obvious?' Becca winced. She'd not meant to be so transparent. It would only invite questions and Thomasia never shied away from difficult discussions.

'The two of you disappeared for a long while the night of the cider press.' Thomasia picked up a spare brush and began to work on a soldier. 'Did you come out here?' Thomasia didn't wait for an answer, but perhaps the answer was obvious, too. 'It's no wonder you miss him. This place is full of him. Do you want help putting away the reminders?'

'Would it help?' Becca asked sadly.

Thomasia shook her head with a soft laugh. 'No, it doesn't.' She rubbed her chest. 'He'll still be in here.'

'I can't decide,' Becca admitted, 'if I want to exorcise him from the workshop or if I want to keep him close, wrap myself up in the memories.'

'Memories? That sounds quite final. Don't you think you'll see him again?' Thomasia got up and wandered towards the cupboard.

'The shortbread is on the top right shelf,' Becca offered. Thomasia was always hungry these days. 'It is final. We did not talk of the future, not romantically at least.'

Thomasia returned with the shortbread tin and held it out to her. 'Just one night to satisfy longing and curiosity and hopefully scotch the desire for more?' she said matter-of-factly, saving Becca the embarrassment of confessing what had happened upstairs. Thomasia sighed and sat back down. 'That sounds remarkably similar to the situation Shaw and I found ourselves in.' She took a thoughtful bite of her shortbread. 'We promised ourselves one night, nothing more. Then one night became two weeks. We'd have two weeks and then we'd let each other go—Shaw to London for Parliament and me to wherever.'

Becca looked up from her painting. She'd not heard about this hidden detail behind Thomasia's romance last autumn with the man who was now her husband. Thomasia smiled. 'It wasn't something to discuss out loud. You and Mother and Father had left for London to see Anne and Thea. Shaw and I had the Hall to ourselves. I wanted no promises between us. I couldn't bear the idea of breaking those promises or putting Shaw in a position to break them. I knew I'd ruin him if our association became known.' Thomasia had been a mother to a child born out of wedlock at the time, absolutely anathema to man looking to make a career in Parliament.

'It's not like that between Jules and I, though. Shaw *wanted* to marry.' Becca couldn't think of a man more different to her upstanding brother-in-law than Jules. 'Jules is charming and flirtatious, he's handsome and wild. He has a woman in every town. He's not looking to settle down any time soon and I knew that. I always knew that.'

Thomasia took a thoughtful nibble of the shortbread. 'You think he's too good for you. You think you can't hold on to a handsome man.' She reached for Becca's hand. 'Look at me, Sister. You have long underestimated yourself. What makes a man handsome is that he sees your true worth, who you are on the inside. What I love about Shaw is that he sees *me*, Becca. He's not like those men in London who danced with me because I was pretty and popular.' She frowned. 'Becca, does Jules make you feel beautiful?'

Becca blushed, but found the courage to meet Thomasia's gaze. 'Yes.' She'd felt like a queen in his arms—no, not a queen, a *goddess* and he her reverent supplicant. 'He doesn't look *through* me like the men in London did. He looks *into* me.' He saw her, the person who was satisfied working in the cottage, the person who was happy to forgo instant fame in lieu of serving the greater good with her creations. 'We complete each other, I think. I am the quiet to his loud, the thought to his ideas. I fill in his gaps and he fills mine.' She'd not thought about it that way before. They weren't opposites, though, not entirely. Beneath their differences, they were the same: two people looking for some place to belong, to fit in, or maybe they were looking for *someone* to fit with. But what happened when one person thought they'd found that fit and the other didn't? Would she be doomed to spend the rest of her life missing that piece of herself?

Thomasia squeezed her hand. 'Does he know how you feel?'

'No, we promised not to talk of it.' That seemed the height of foolishness now in retrospect.

Mischief lit her sister's eyes. 'Then you must tell him. If he knows how you feel—'

'No, absolutely not!' Becca was quick to interrupt. 'That might send him running for the proverbial hills.' She couldn't bear that. It would colour her memories of all the good that had passed between them and it might ruin the future of her business prospects with Howell Manufacturing. He wouldn't want to be in association with a woman who was hungering after him.

'Or it might send him running right back into your arms.' Thomasia was undaunted. She leaned forward and Becca did not like the look in her sister's eyes, it always boded trouble like the time Thomasia had plotted for them to steal some tarts from the kitchen before dinner. They'd been caught red-handed. Sort of. What they'd thought would be sweet strawberry tarts had been sour instead. Cook had been prepared for them and swapped the real tarts out with a decoy. They'd not stolen dessert again. 'What if you went to him?' Thomasia began to plot.

'That would be terribly forward. I can't just show up in Manchester. Besides, the factory doesn't know I'm R. L. Peverett. I can't go even under the guise of checking on work.' Thomasia might have the aplomb to show up unannounced, but Becca could never see herself pulling it off.

'All right, what if you had a reason?' Thomasia pulled a letter from her pocket. 'I came down here to deliver this. It arrived with the post while I was visiting Mother. Maybe this is your reason?'

Becca grabbed for the letter. 'Did you read it?'

'Becca, would I do that?' Thomasia feigned shock.

Becca shot her a sharp look as she slit the envelope open. 'Yes, you would.' She scanned the note, revelling in the sight of Jules's handwriting. She swallowed, hardly daring to believe it. 'He wants me to come to Manchester.'

Thomasia beamed. 'He misses you, too.' She nearly crowed. 'I knew it.'

'No,' Becca cautioned, unwilling to let herself get too carried away, 'it's for business. Of course, I can only come as a representative of R. L. Peverett, but they want to celebrate the first production of the ophthalmoscope. There will be a ball and other activities.' She would get to see Jules again. Her heart did a happy skip at the thought before other considerations took over.

'I know that look.' Thomasia sighed. 'This should be good news, but it's not. What is it?'

'The ball, the city. We'll be on his ground. What if I don't measure up? What if he realises I'm just a country girl? I'm no good at such events and he'll be…

dazzling. Perfect and I'll be…not perfect.' It would be London all over again and he'd see her limitations once she was away from Haberstock Hall.

'Nonsense, I won't hear any of that talk.' Thomasia rose and dragged her by the arm. 'We're marching straight up to the house and going through your clothes at once. There's no time to lose. You have clothes still from London. We can pay a visit to the dressmaker in the village for ribbons and lace to trim them up a bit. Remember, it's Manchester, not London.'

It was hard not to be buoyed by the twin prospects of Thomasia's enthusiasm and seeing Jules again, but also it was difficult not to worry—there was the deception to consider. She'd be walking into the lion's den, facing the people she was deceiving. When she'd devised her plan, she'd not considered that. Nor had she considered actually falling for her business partner. A week of preparations flew by until at last her trunk was packed and there was nothing to do except to get on the train. Becca was full of nerves as she boarded the train. Despite Thomasia's encouragement, her head was swimming with what ifs. What if his family discovered she was R. L. Peverett? What if Jules discovered she was nothing more than a country mouse? What if she embarrassed herself and him? The whole world she'd built over the last months would come crumbling down. But there were other what ifs, too. What if she told him how she felt? That she didn't want just one night? What if she said the three words in her heart: *I love you*? What would happen then? Did she *want* a proposal? All she was certain of when she boarded the train was that no matter what happened in Manchester, her life was going to change. Nothing would be the same afterwards.

Chapter Seventeen

What if she'd realised her folly in the intervening weeks? What if she was only coming because of the ophthalmoscope? Jules was plagued by what ifs as he stood on the bustling platform of the Manchester station waiting for the train to disgorge its passengers. Two weeks without Becca had been…well, it had been too long and he'd leave it at that. To name it otherwise was complicated. Was this love? He suspected it might be and that scared him.

What did he know of love? Could he make her happy?

He saw her first. She emerged from the train car and paused at the top of the steps before disembarking, her gaze sweeping the station. Looking for him? Or simply surveying the new territory? He stepped back, wanting a moment to watch her, to have her to himself. She looked quietly stunning in a plum-coloured two-piece travelling costume trimmed in black braid he'd not seen before. Her glossy walnut tresses were tucked up beneath a fetching but decorative hat, her hands sheathed in black leather gloves. He drank her in, letting the details of her wash over him before he waved and wove his way through the crowd to her side.

'Becca, you're here. I'm so glad.' He hazarded a quick kiss to her cheek, a gesture that would go unremarked in the busy station. He tucked her arm through his and ushered her through the crush of people.

'It's much busier than Broxbourne.' Becca had to raise her voice to be heard and he laughed, but there was no chance for conversation until they were settled in the coach. Did she feel it, too, he wondered as he took the seat across from her—this thrum of excitement between them and the undertone of tension, too, the kind of tension that came once the initial thrill of reuniting passed, especially when a relationship was new and people were still learning one another.

Who are we together?

That was the question that hung unspoken between them in the carriage. And they *were* together, whether Becca wanted to admit it or not. They'd been lovers. He'd told his brother about her. He'd taken steps to plan a life worthy of her: the town house, the job. Some might consider that the cart before the horse when so much lay undiscussed between them, but before he could ask for more from her, he had to show her he could offer her more than a smile and charm. Perhaps he had to prove it to himself as well.

'How is everyone at Haberstock Hall?' Jules asked as the coach moved into traffic. 'Thomasia is well?'

Becca smiled, perhaps grateful to ease into things

with small talk. 'She's huge but, yes, she's well. She's eaten all of your shortbread stores at the workshop.' They laughed together at that and Jules felt some of the tension leave them. They talked of little Effie-Claire's latest antics, a letter Becca had from Anne and news from the village.

'Mr Barnes has his colourful shortbread tins in the window of the bakery with big bows on them. They look lovely and there's a crowd outside the window every day to admire them,' she told him. 'And the ladies' church auxiliary has bought the last of grey flannel at wholesale prices. They plan to make shirts and dresses for some of the children in less fortunate families this winter.' Becca leaned forward. 'The ladies' auxiliary couldn't have afforded to do that without your idea of the wholesale pricing. Children in Hertfordshire will have you to thank for warm clothes this winter.' She smiled and he felt as if the sun had come out just for him.

'I'm glad to hear it. What of your toy soldiers? Have you made progress on them?' He was aware that this trip to Manchester would take her away from her own Christmas projects. He hoped it wouldn't put her too far behind.

'Yes, I worked double time this week, but I think I'll make it.' Becca reached into her reticule. 'I brought you one, as a *gift*,' she emphasised, handing him one of the toys. 'Not for business. Just for you.' She paused, and he could see she was gathering herself. He braced. 'I should have given it to you before you left Haberstock.'

He studied the little soldier, pulling at its string and

watching its arms raise. 'Thank you, Becca. I'll treasure it.' It would always be a reminder of the happy
weeks he'd spent at Haberstock and of the woman he
spent those weeks with. 'I hope when I look upon it
in years to come, I will think about how it marked the
beginning of...*us*.'

It was bold statement. He watched her for a reaction.
But why not say it? Why not confront the real question: who were they together? Had she come only for
the thrill of seeing her ophthalmoscope? Or had she
come for another thrill? The thrill of him? The thrill
of who they were together? Did she understand that it
was the latter which had prompted his own invitation?
He put the question to her. 'Tell me the truth, Becca.
Did you come for business or pleasure?'

'Which one have you invited me for?' she parried,
and he sensed the nerves behind her question. Did she
fear that his attentions had waned in their time apart?
That he would not be constant?

He reached for her hand, his fingers working the
buttons of her glove loose. 'For pleasure, my dear.
Do not doubt it.' His mouth found the merest spot of
bare, tender skin at her wrist, his body revelling in
the chance to touch even the smallest part of her after
weeks of wanting to hold her, revelling further still
when he felt her pulse leap beneath his lips, proof to
them both that the magic was still there.

'The business of the ophthalmoscope was a very
convenient mechanism to orchestrate your visit around.'
He looked up, his gaze holding hers. He needed her to

see that his desire was real, not some fleeting fancy. 'I wanted *you* here.'

'And I want to be here, with you.' Becca met his gaze and he saw the truth of that in her eyes, but also reluctance.

He released her hand and waited for the other shoe to fall. 'But?'

'There is more to this visit than just being here with you. How am I to be? Who am I to be? I don't want to disappoint you.' All of her insecurities were wrapped up in those short sentences and yet her worry was for him. Her concern was on his behalf and it touched him deeply that she'd risk so much of her own personal comfort for him.

'I have told my brother that I care for you. He knows that you're here in R. L. Peverett's stead and that you are the woman who has captured my attentions. We needn't hide what we are to each other.' The announcement did not bring the relief he expected it to.

'But there is still the question of the deception.' Becca played with her glove. 'When I suggested it, I never dreamed I'd be seeing the people responsible for producing my ophthalmoscope face to face. Neither did I anticipate you, us. I have put you in an unenviable position with your family. I regret that.'

That was Becca at her finest, always thinking of others. It wasn't the lack of fame she was regretting, or that she could not outright claim her invention. It was the position she'd put another in. 'My deception was selfish and I must apologise for that.'

If it was selfish for her, then it had been selfishly

motivated from his end as well. He would not let her bear the entire burden of that alone. 'You forget, Becca, that I agreed to it. We are complicit in this. You couldn't have done it without me. And it is a temporary deception, just as we've always planned. It needn't last for ever, just long enough.' Long enough to secure future projects, long enough for the ophthalmoscope to be a success in order to soften the blow when all was revealed.

'I think no harm has been done, but a great deal of good has been achieved, for you and for me.' It was the argument that soothed him the most when guilt poked at him. He'd cut up at Winthrop about the Frenchman while he was perpetrating his own deception. *If you can't trust your brother, who can you trust?* Winthrop's words had taken on a certain haunting intensity when considered from his position.

'Good?' Becca queried.

'Yes, your scope will help change the medical world for doctors and patients, and this project had changed things for me for the better. Surely, those two items outweigh any concern over a small, short-term deception.' They were nearly to his parents' town house and there were still things he wanted to tell her.

'My brother and sister-in-law plan to fete you in style, as do my parents. They'll all be at my parents' town house to greet you today, by the way.' He wasn't pleased about that, but his father had insisted and Winthrop had allowed it. 'We've a box at the royal theatre and the Christmas show season is just beginning. My sister-in-law is holding a ball at which you will be the guest of honour.' Would Becca be amenable to such events? 'I know it's a lot to take in. Life moves a bit faster in the city,' he said, half apologising. Becca was a woman who preferred long hikes and painting at waterfalls. What would she think of life in Manchester? Could she see a place for herself amid its hustle and bustle?

'No one needs to go to all that trouble for me,' Becca said, her hands twisting nervously in her lap. He'd been so eager to show her what he could give her here, but now he wondered if it would please her?

'It's how things are done here. I'll be with you every step of the way, you needn't worry,' Jules assured her. 'My family will like you.' Maybe. He was pushing it there. She wasn't Adelaide Pembridge and his parents didn't love anyone but themselves.

'For a while, perhaps.' She smiled to soften the blow of her words. 'Once they learn of the deception, they may not. You're family, they will forgive you. But I am not. I'm an outsider.'

'You overestimate them.' Jules gave a laugh. 'Make a Howell enough money and they'll forgive you anything.' It had even worked for him, the prodigal brother returned to the fold. The coach rolled to a stop and he drew a breath, his parents' town house appearing through the window. 'We're here. Showtime.' He smiled at her to give them both courage even as he ran through the lists in his mind. He'd covered everything, right? There should be no surprises.

It was one surprise after another, each revelation bigger than the last. They'd started at the train station and they just kept coming. Not all of them bad, Becca told herself as she took tea with the Howells, *all of them*, in their opulent drawing room. Her wrist still burned with the memory of Jules's mouth on it. It had been a potent reminder of how his mouth had felt on other body parts and how much she wanted to feel his mouth on her again. Jules wanted her. Jules had feelings for her. Such revelations should have relieved her. Most of her worries had stemmed from what it would be like to see him again. But instead, they left her with one overarching burning question: What did it all mean? Where was all of this headed to? Or, more importantly, where did she want it to lead to?

The second surprise had been the extent of the Howells' wealth, or perhaps not the extent of it—the Peveretts were more than comfortable and her sisters had married into the households of peers. Perhaps it was more the way in which the Howell wealth was displayed that caught her off guard. Where she was used to a more subdued show of wealth, the Howells flaunted it. Expensive art hung on the walls of a newly redecorated drawing room that boasted silk wallpaper and velvet floor-to-ceiling curtains that were so new they'd probably not yet been beaten for dust. The carpet beneath her feet was also new, evidenced by the bright vibrancy of its colours. Every tabletop, shelf and mantelpiece was crowded with an expensive figurine or artifact for which there was an acquisition story—a story Stefan Howell or his wife was more than happy to tell. Not even the tea was immune from the Howells. It was a blend Jules's father had invested in from India.

'A black Kashmir Tchai,' Stefan boasted as his wife handed around the teacups—Wedgwood's latest pattern. 'It goes best with a little sugar to take off the bitterness and, of course, cream. Perfect for cold winter days, something the Russians knew long before Britain discover it.' Stefan regaled her with a brief history of the tea on the Silk Road as she sipped.

Perhaps this was going to be easier than she'd thought. She needn't carry the conversation or worry about small talk. All she had to do was admire an object and Stefan and his wife or Winthrop and Mary would take it from there. They *all* loved to talk, as did Jules. Talking must run in the family, but where Jules had the knack of knowing when to listen and step back, those nuances escaped the others. It wasn't that Jules's father wasn't an intelligent man—intelligence oozed from him. He tried very hard to put that intelligence on display. Too hard. He wanted everyone to know.

After tea, they journeyed to Winthrop's town house where she would stay and Winthrop's wife, Mary, showed her to her room, talking the whole way up the long, elegant white staircase. 'I've put you in the blue room,' she said in a tone that indicated the blue room was special indeed. 'It overlooks the street.' Mary opened the door and Becca followed her inside a spacious bedchamber. 'But it is from this very balcony that we watched Queen Victoria pass down the street during her visit a few a years ago.'

Mary threw open the French doors that let out on to a small Juliette balcony. The sounds of the street filtered up as she dutifully admired the view and Mary could shut them again. 'What a momentous occasion that was.' Mary sighed. 'There hadn't been a monarch in Manchester for one hundred and fifty years.' Becca braced for a monologue, but in doing so Becca was taken off guard by Mary's next comments. 'A monarch in Manchester is much like Jules bringing a woman home to meet his family, a rare occurrence indeed.'

A maid entered to unpack Becca's things and Mary took a seat in a chair near the enormous white marble fireplace that warmed the room. 'So, tell me, Miss Peverett, now that it's just us women, how did you manage to tame our Jules? He's a wild one. We never thought he'd settle down with just one woman. We'd quite given up hope and so had most of the young women in town. Hearts will be breaking to know his affections are engaged, especially Miss Pembridge's.' Miss Pembridge? Jules had said nothing of her, but there was no time to contemplate that bit of news with Mary racketing on to more revelations.

'When Winthrop sent him to Hertfordshire, it was do or die. Winthrop was determined to wash his hands of him if he came back empty-handed. Goodness knows how Jules would have survived then. The company pays for all of his expenses. Of course, the company can afford to, but that's not the point.' She fluttered a hand. 'Listen to me run on, when I want to hear all about you. You and Jules.'

'There's not much to tell,' Becca said carefully, her mind reeling over the latest revelation. So, that explained the depths of his desperation that first day when she'd argued with him on the porch. Had that really only been two months ago? It seemed a lifetime, not a handful of weeks. 'We discovered we had much in common the longer we spent time together and developed an affinity from there. We both enjoy music, painting and hiking in the woods.'

'Jules? Hiking in the woods?' Mary laughed, pressing an affected hand to her bosom. 'I can hardly imagine it. He's a city man through and through, can't go a day without his creature comforts.'

Becca felt the urge to argue, the urge to defend Jules from what seemed like an attack, but she was saved from perhaps the folly of arguing with her host by the maid's unpacking of her rose silk. 'Oh, dear, is this the only silk you've brought?' Mary's attention focused on the gown. 'We're to have a ball. Perhaps Jules did not tell you? That would be just like a man. They don't understand how difficult it is to pack for a visit. Well, don't worry. We'll visit the dressmaker tomorrow and she'll have something whipped up for you by the ball.'

Mary went to the wardrobe and sorted through the gowns. 'Perhaps we'll have her make few day dresses as well,' she said, the topic of Jules forgotten in the wake of this latest fashion crisis.

Mary left her shortly after that, so that she could rest before dinner. Becca didn't think she'd actually rest, but she was grateful for the peace. She sat before the fire, letting it warm her as she let her mind play through the revelations. She'd not truly believed Jules when he'd told her his family was focused exclusively on money or that they were going to cut him off if he'd failed with her. She wouldn't have believed it if she hadn't heard it put so bluntly from an actual family member. But that was not the most concerning revelation. It was the things underneath that were most troubling: the mysterious Miss Pembridge whose heart was about to be broken and, primarily, that the Jules she thought she knew was not him at all.

The picture Mary's words painted was of a man who was a wastrel, living off his family's money, the very epitome of a hedonist, not a man who enjoyed simple pleasures in the country. It raised a powerful question. Who was Jules Howell? Citified wastrel, or the man who'd become an important part of the Haberstock community in the short time he'd been there? It also raised the question of who was she? She hardly knew herself. She, who was so very reserved and cautious, had bedded a man she barely knew. And she would do it again. What did that say of *her*?

Chapter Eighteen

It was a question Becca was asking herself more and more often as her stay progressed. Each day was busy, filled with dress fittings, dress deliveries, outings with Mary to pay calls where all she had to do was smile because Mary did the rest, and every conversation ending with, 'And of course Jules adores her, which is quite enough for us.' That would always bring a smile and a speculative gaze from their hostess and after a while, Becca began to think the last bit about 'being enough for them' was something of an insult, as if her antecedents weren't good enough for the nouveau-riche Howells or if her preference for the countryside was something to be frowned upon.

She was missing the countryside these days. Missing the chance to take long walks by herself, to immerse herself in the quiet of the landscape. She was missing the sanctuary of her workshop as well. There was no quiet in Manchester, a city that seemed to never sleep, thanks all the factories, and there was no sanctuary from which to escape Mary and Jules's mother's ambitious social schedules. Despite his promises to be with her every step of the way, Jules was scarce during the days, spending his time at the Howell Manufacturing offices. He did show up at his brother's town house in the evenings and he did escort her to evening entertainments. But during the day, she was entirely on her own to manage his sister-in-law and his mother.

'I think we need more lace at the hem and the sleeves,' Mary instructed the modiste, circling Becca on the raised pedestal. 'The gown is so plain. Perhaps more trim on the bodice as well, maybe sequins or crystal beads that would catch the light.'

'Yes, ma'am.' The modiste nodded for an assistant to fetch more trimmings. Becca sighed. At this rate, she'd look like an overdecorated cake. She didn't have this much trim on *all* of her dresses combined.

'We have a lovely blonde lace that would look divine.' The modiste held up a sample for Mary's consideration. That was the last straw. Mary wasn't the one wearing the dress. She was and she would decide what she appeared in public in.

'It's my dress,' Becca spoke up, drawing all eyes to her. 'I don't want any more lace.' Becca met Mary's gaze in the long pier glass. She would have to stand firm on this. 'I like the gown as it is. I prefer less, um, decorated clothes. Simple lines, simple features. That's what I like.' She turned to the modiste. 'The gown is fine the way it is. Please help me out of it so we don't take up any more of your time.'

Mary looked positively peeved and a glance passed

between Mary and Jules's mother. Mary sighed and presented the image of a long-suffering woman who'd tried her best. 'This is the city, dear. Certainly, you want to look your best for the ball.'

'I'll look fine.' Becca gave a tight smile.

'For Haberstock society, perhaps.' Jules's mother entered the conversation with a patronising tone. 'You want Jules to be proud of you. My son represents the family.' The message was unmistakable: by extension she'd represent the family, too, if she was attached to Jules. No wonder Jules felt stifled here.

'He will be pleased with me. He likes my rose silk,' Becca said, implying that she might not wear the new gown at all. It was the only piece of leverage she had and it wasn't much. Deep down, she was starting to wonder if Jules would be pleased? Perhaps he would find her simple style lacking in the city. She stepped out of the gown and began to dress in her own clothes.

Mary gave her a pitying stare. 'Let me speak frankly. Jules is a man used to beautiful women in beautiful clothes. How long do you think your plain ball gown will hold his attention in a room full of the finest silks and satins? You *do* want to hold his attention, don't you?' A reminder that there was no official understanding between them, nothing to anchor him to her.

Becca looked up from her dressing and said with a confidence she only partly felt, 'I would like to think that Jules's attentions are held by something stronger than the cut of my clothes.'

'Miss Peverett, I am trying to help you,' Mary insisted, 'Jules is…'

The bell over the shop tinkled and a male voice floated behind the curtain.

'Jules is what, dear sister-in-law? Is everyone decent? May I come through?' Becca had never been so glad to hear Jules's laughing tones than she was in that moment.

'Yes, we're decent,' Mary called, holding aside the curtain. 'You are just in time to be of use for once. Perhaps you can persuade Miss Peverett to be guided by those who are more familiar with city fashions. We're trying to decide on lace for her ballgown.'

Jules flashed a look her direction, a brow raised. 'Is that so, Becca? A dilemma over lace?' Becca smiled, her gaze meeting his. He was not fooled. It warmed her to be understood, to know that he knew she would not be in a dither about lace and her worries dissipated.

'No, I've decided against the lace,' Becca said firmly, coming to stand beside Jules. 'I'm quite happy with the dress the way it is.'

Jules turned a charming smile on his sister-in-law. 'Splendid! All is settled and Becca is free to take tea with me.' He threaded her arm through his. 'Shall we be off? Don't worry, Mary, Mother, I'll make sure she's back in time to change for the theatre.'

The modiste approached Jules with a box wrapped with a wide pink satin ribbon. 'Will you want to take the finished gown with you? The lady intended it for the theatre tonight.'

'More good luck.' Jules beamed and Becca had the sense that he was having far too much fun needling his sister-in-law and mother. Whatever plans they'd had for her afternoon had just been upended. 'We'll take it.' He had her out of the store in moments, setting a brisk pace with the dress box under his arm until they were a street away. 'I think we're safe now.' Jules slowed down and let her catch her breath. 'We had a narrow escape.'

Becca laughed. 'You were masterful. You couldn't have shown up at a better time.'

'You were holding your own just fine.' Jules's eyes danced with green lights. 'Are you enduring? I apologise for being gone during the day. But there's just the ball and the presentation of the ophthalmoscope to get through.' He steered her out of the way of an oncoming pedestrian to avoid being bumped, but it was suddenly all too much: too much noise, too many people, too many unknowns. Out of nowhere tears began to sting. She wanted to go home to Haberstock and she wanted to take Jules with her, back to where she understood him and understood herself. She was out of her depth here and she wanted her family.

'Becca? What is it?' Jules stopped before the door to the tea shop. 'Are you well?'

'No, I'm not. Jules, I need to be alone. I need…'

'I know exactly what you need.' Jules hailed a cab and gave an address to the cabbie and helped her inside.

'Where are we going?'

'Somewhere quiet. I am taking you home, to my house.'

He did indeed know what she needed. He sat beside her in the cab, his arm about her, letting her lean her head on his shoulder. He seemed to know, too, that silence was more welcome than words at the moment, and more precious, too, given that she'd been surrounded by Mary and Winthrop and Jules's mother endlessly.

The drive was not far and he helped her down in front of a red-bricked town house with long windows. 'It's not overly large like Winthrop's and my parents,' he said, but Becca hushed him.

'Thank goodness.'

Inside, Jules ordered tea to be served in a cosy sitting room located at the back of the house away from the noise of the street. The room was practically furnished much in the way Haberstock Hall was furnished, with comfortable, overstuffed pieces that a person could sink into and feel at home in. One need not stand on ceremony in this room and Becca didn't. She took off her half-boots and tucked her feet up underneath her. She gazed at the picture above the mantel, a painting of a countryside scene; fields and a thatched cottage. The initials J. H. were in the bottom right-hand corner. One of his own works, then. She liked it even more. 'Your family doesn't believe you paint,' she commented. 'Or sing.'

'No, I imagine they wouldn't.' Jules took the chair across from her and crossed a leg over one knee. 'Those things don't make money therefore they are not worth mentioning.' He nodded towards the picture. 'I painted that six years ago while I was on a walking tour of the Cotswolds.'

Tea arrived and Jules did not press her until she had a hot cup in her hand. Then he fixed her with his green eyes. 'Well? Tell me all about it, or shall I guess? Winthrop and Mary talk too much and listen too little. They've worn you out.'

She smiled, starting to feel better. She was not alone. Jules understood, at least in part. 'Yes, but that's not all of it,' Becca said honestly. 'I am not myself here. Spending days at the dressmaker's, paying calls, making conversation with women who spend the afternoon appraising each other's gowns, these are not things I do or enjoy. I will not *learn* to enjoy them.' She sighed. 'And I am afraid you will be disappointed in me, Jules. I can't be a city girl, a society girl. I don't know who I am here, but this is not me.'

Jules sat still for long moment, thoughtful, watching her the way he'd watched her in the workshop. 'Do you think that makes me like you less? That I need you to be those things?'

Becca met his gaze evenly. 'Yes, I think you might.' This was the other piece of her upset and harder to articulate. 'Mary says I'm not your sort. That you prefer pretty women in pretty clothes, that I can't possibly hope to hold your attentions, not like Adelaide Pembridge can.' Her eyes followed him as Jules rose and began to pace.

'Mary talks too much. Since when does she think she's an authority on what I prefer? As for Adelaide Pembridge, I've met her precisely once.' He fixed her with a strong look. 'I've no eyes for Adelaide Pembridge, only for you. I promise.' She wanted to believe that.

'Mary knows you better than I do. I've known you

for six weeks and since coming here, I'm not sure I know you at all. Mary told me you were going to be cut off if you failed in Hertfordshire. Mary said you're the family black sheep, a wastrel living on the family money. But that's not who I saw. I saw a man who liked the countryside, who liked painting on the rocks, who was happy to sit in my workshop. That's the man I made love with and now I don't know what to believe. Who is the real you, Jules? I thought you'd told me enough… Maybe it's not that Mary talks too much, but that you haven't talked enough. I should have learned all that from you, not her. Is it no wonder I feel out of my depth here? I don't know you and I barely know myself.'

She was feeling betrayed and for all he'd tried to do to prove himself to her, he'd ended up failing her. Jules raked a hand through his hair and stood silent before the fire, his thoughts filling with self-recrimination. How had he not seen it? She'd been so brave in coming here, but she was alone among strangers with only him to count on and he'd abandoned her to the wolves. All for the sake of proving he could go to work at the offices, that he could hold a job, provide for her in some distant future. But in doing so, he'd not taken care of the present. He hadn't even told her why he was doing it.

What do you know of love?

Apparently, very little because he'd ended up hurting her instead.

Confession was supposedly good for the soul. Perhaps it would be good in mending broken fences, too. Perhaps it would allow him to redeem a little of her trust in him. It couldn't hurt. She already knew the worst of him. But he had to own it and he'd never been so ashamed of himself as he was facing her. 'How could I tell you what sort of man I was? You would have had nothing to do with me.' Jules sighed and knelt before her, reaching for her hands and hoping she would let him take them. 'Is it too late for me to talk?' He was rewarded with a shake of her head. He had her hands and he held on tight.

'I am all those things that Mary said. At least I was until I went to Haberstock, or more precisely, until I met you. My life had no direction. My days lacked purpose. I drank. I gambled. I spent evenings with expensive women on my knee at the gaming tables and later in a bed in a brothel, but they were only there because I had money to spend on them. I had no interest in the family company. I did whatever Winthrop occasionally compelled me to do. I didn't earn my own money, pay my own way. All that is true.' And it was embarrassing as hell to admit to her.

'When I came to Haberstock, I was planning on going to Italy afterwards, to paint, I told myself. But in reality, I was just running away. Somewhere new, but still the same old habits. My only hope was that the money might last longer somewhere cheaper. But then, you wouldn't let me fail. You offered me a way to go home successfully. I'd never met anyone like you. You saw the world and wanted to make it better.

You had a purpose and I coveted that. You amazed me from the start.

'It was hard to leave even at that first visit with just a couple days under my belt. But when I got home, my brother was pleased with me for the first time in ages and I leapt at the chance to come back to Haberstock. But it wasn't Haberstock I was coming back to, it was you. Always you, Becca.' He watched her face; those expressive eyes softened with emotion.

'Part of me hoped that when I returned to Haberstock, I'd discover you were less than I recalled, that perhaps familiarity would put you into perspective. But it wasn't like that. The more time I spent with you, the more amazing you became. Not just your inventions, but the way you see the world, the way you move through it with kindness and compassion. I want that for me, I want to be like you, Becca, and if I can't be like you, I at least want to bask in your shadow in the hopes that it might rub off on me. You have changed me. I've been trying to prove myself to you, and to me.

'I bought this house outright from my brother when I returned. I didn't want my brother paying my rent any more. I go to the office every day and draw a salary because I want to earn my keep. I'm doing sales for the company because I think I might be better at that, more useful like I was to Mr Barnes at the bakery. I hope that will become my passion.' So far it hadn't. Going to the office was tedious, but he'd stick with it because he hadn't stuck with anything ever. It probably took some getting used to.

'I furnished this house for you, with you in mind.'

He drew a long breath, his grip on her hands tight. 'I'm not sure I know what love is, there wasn't much of it growing up. But I care for you, Becca. All this is for you, because of you. I'm sorry I didn't know how tell you, or how to show you. I didn't want to lose you.' Although he might have lost her anyway.

'You did all of that for me?' The idea seemed to amaze her. She offered him a soft smile. 'You're not the only one who is afraid. I don't want to lose you either. I didn't want to make demands of you in Haberstock for fear you'd get on the train and never look back. I thought one night was all I could have. You were so dashing, I could hardly believe you were interested in me. In London, everyone was always interested in Thomasia.'

'Their loss.' Jules leaned forward to find her lips with his mouth. 'Tell me I haven't ruined everything? Because I want you, body, mind and heart, Rebecca Peverett.'

'And I want you, body, mind and heart, Jules Howell,' she murmured. 'But I must have all of you. No secrets, no holding back.'

Of course she'd want it that way, it was the only way she knew how to be and she would demand the same from those whom she loved. 'You shall have all of me, Becca.' He drew her to him, pulling her down to the floor and rolling her beneath him. There was no better time than the present to show her he meant every word of that promise.

Chapter Nineteen

This was what she'd come to Manchester for. For him. For this. Jules came into her hard and fast, both of them frantic to join, to be together physically in a way that would obliterate the earlier misgivings of their minds. At his touch doubt was replaced with clarity. He was what had drawn her to Manchester, the ophthalmoscope was secondary. She was here for him. She rose up to meet him, hips to hips, her arms wrapped tight about him, holding him close to assure him with her body the truth of her spoken words. She would not let him go.

'I need you, Becca.' His own words came hoarse and panting at her ear as they came together, swift desire consuming them. When climax found them, it was as a thunderous, pounding storm of emotion unlike anything she'd experienced before. This was what it meant to feel alive, to be at life's core itself, so raw and overwhelming were the sensations it stirred in her. And in him. Jules collapsed against her, spent, his heart pounding beneath his shirt.

There'd been no disrobing this time, no lingering seduction. This had been primal and fierce. But now, before the fire, their passion sated, there was time to savour one another, to lie in each other's arms. Jules reached out to tug the throw pillows from the sofa down to the floor. In another reach of his long arm, he grabbed a blanket. 'Now, we can be comfortable.' He smiled and made to draw her close.

'Comfortable? Dressed like this? I don't think a woman is ever entirely comfortable with all these clothes on.' Becca sat up. 'Will we be interrupted?'

'No,' Jules assured her, a slow smile claiming his sensual mouth as he guessed the direction of her thoughts. 'Shall I play lady's maid?'

She turned and gave him her back. 'If you wouldn't mind.' They made short work of her many layers, both of them eager to lie back down before the fire together in their nest of blankets and pillows. She slid beneath the blanket, feeling very decadent to be lying before a fire, undressed beside a man. She held a corner of the blanket up for Jules, but he shook his head.

'Not yet, I am feeling distinctly overdressed.' He grinned, stripping out of his clothes until he was entirely nude. She ought to be appalled at such a blatant show of nakedness, but Becca could rouse only extreme appreciation for the masculine vision before her. Even in a state of recovery, his phallus was an impressive sight. More impressive, however, was the feel of his warm skin against hers when he joined her beneath the blanket. 'There, now we're equals,' Jules murmured, drawing her close, and this time she went, nestling against the crook of his body.

'How is it that this is deemed the height of decadence and yet it feels so natural?' Becca drew a circle around the flat of his nipple. 'Sin ought to feel wrong, not right.' She'd lie here every afternoon, given the choice.

'I've long thought sin was a convenient man-made fiction created to steal all the fun out of living.' Jules chuckled. 'I try not to let it stop me, though.'

'Hmm. So, you *are* a hedonist at heart, after all,' Becca teased gently, drawing a new pattern on his chest with her fingertip.

'I try to enjoy living.' Jules laughed.

'Are you enjoying living now?' Becca raised up on one arm, propping her head in her hand. 'Do you like going to the office?' It had seemed at odds with the Jules she'd come to know. Working within a schedule didn't suit him, neither did the confines of an office. He was far too wild for such staid pursuits.

'It's what a responsible man does,' Jules replied. 'I will learn the rhythm of it. It's only been a few weeks.'

'You are evading the question.' Becca levered herself up, sitting astride him. 'Do you enjoy going to work at the company? When I first met you, you didn't enjoy it.'

'But that was before you.' He smiled up at her, his hands resting warm at her hips. 'I enjoy it *for* you, for what it can allow us to have if we choose.'

'So, it's a means to an end and as such is justified?' Becca placed a kiss to his chest, one kiss and then another, her lips creating a soft trail down his sternum, to his navel as her body slid down the muscled length of his.

'Is this to be an interrogation by kisses?' Jules's voice took the rasp of want.

'It might be.' She looked up at him. His green eyes were twin flames of desire and she revelled in the ability to move him like this. What delightful power that was and what a revelation. To think this man, who could have anyone, was enthralled by her.

'Be careful, Becca,' Jules warned. 'You might wake the beast.'

Becca slanted him a coy look. 'Are you saying I shouldn't do this?' She blew a light breath in his navel and his skin pimpled in delight. 'Or this?' She moved lower still, indulging her curiosity. He'd put his mouth on her down there, something she remembered with extraordinary clarity and pleasure. Would he like the same? She placed a kiss on the tip of his phallus, her hand stroking his length, feeling it harden in the wake of her ministrations. 'Or how about this?' She reached the heavy sac hidden behind his phallus and squeezed gently.

'Yes, no, I mean yes,' he groaned, the muscles of his throat standing out as he swallowed hard. 'By the saints, Becca, you'll have me unmanned in no time.'

'I'd like that, to see you undone, to see you come apart,' Becca teased in a throaty whisper she hardly recognised as her own. She was a temptress come to life with him, a whole new person she was discovering. She had her way with him then, licking and liking, tasting and teasing with the skim of her tongue, the nip of her teeth, until he was iron hard against her lips, his sac drawn up tight in aching response to her hand, his body taut in search of release.

She gave that release to him, holding him in her hand as spasms of pleasure racked him. This was intimacy at its height, she thought, the warm seed of him soaking her hand. To see this man in the throes of his quickening, to share that quickening with him. In those moments they were a world unto themselves. There was no thought of inventions, of ophthalmoscopes, deceptions, of overly talkative brothers or bossy sisters-in-law. No talk of a future that remained undefined. None of it mattered.

Their eyes held, emotions passing unspoken between them. Jules reached for a length of her hair and sifted it through his fingers before gently draping it over the swell of her breast, his fingers lightly brushing her skin. 'You are magnificent like this, Becca. I could look at you like this all day, but what I really want is to have you back in my arms.'

She snuggled down beside him and they slept, the sleep of the truly sated, the contented. When they awoke, the fire had gone out and the room had taken on a slight chill. She opened her eyes and sighed. Afternoon had gone. Gone! She sat up, the warmth of the blanket slipping from her. 'Jules! Wake up, what time is it?'

Jules was groggy. He groped for the watch in his discarded waistcoat pocket and flipped the time piece open. 'It's seven.' They'd slept the early evening away.

Their eyes met and the thought occurred to them simultaneously.

'The theatre!' Mary and Winthrop and his parents were likely already there and waiting on them.

'The curtain doesn't rise until eight, we have time. Thank goodness we have your dress.' Jules threw on trousers and shirt. 'I'll ring for some hot water.'

'In here?' Becca wrapped the blanket around her, suddenly self-conscious.

'Did you want to walk through the house in a blanket to reach a bedroom?' Jules argued with a laugh. 'While I wouldn't mind seeing that, I think this will be more expeditious.' And more modest in the long run. At the door to the sitting room, she heard Jules giving instructions to a servant for hot water and for his own things to be brought down.

They made quick work of their modest toilettes, Jules playing the lady's maid for her once more and she acting as his valet, tying his neckcloth and spearing it into place with a stickpin. 'How do I look?' Becca stepped back for his inspection, shaking her skirts for any wrinkles. 'It's not too much, is it?' She'd chosen a deep rose silk for this gown trimmed in beige lace that dripped in elegant folds from the puffed sleeves, but nowhere else.

Jules smiled in appreciation. 'I think rose silk is your signature colour. This silk is slightly darker than the gown you wore at Haberstock, but I like it. It suits your colouring.'

She fingered the lace. 'Is it too much?' Her other gown had very little in way of trim on it and even trimming the sleeves of this gown had seemed ostentatious to her.

'It's perfect, as are you.' Jules pulled at the lapels of his dark evening jacket. 'And myself? Do I meet with your satisfaction? Neckcloth straight? Stickpin straight? Not a speck of lint in sight?' There was a scratch at the door announcing the arrival of the carriage.

'Will we make it?' Becca asked as he handed her into the coach.

'Yes, the theatre isn't far and with luck the curtain will be slightly delayed.' Jules shut the door behind him and gave the signal to the driver to make all haste possible.

This was possible. Life with Becca was possible. It was the one thought that occupied Jules's mind throughout the evening, which ought not surprise him. That thought had been at the forefront of his mind since returning from Haberstock. It had been the driving impetus behind the decision to take a job with the company, to buy the town house. Building a life with her was *possible*. But it came with a price.

Jules glanced at Becca sitting beside him in the front row of the theatre box. She had come exceedingly close to that price this afternoon with her questions. Was he happy at the office? No, he was not. Working on a schedule was confining. Even though he was focusing on sales, the actual work wasn't as exciting as he'd hoped it would be. There were letters to write and an swer. Most of his day was taken up with correspondence, not with creativity.

Yet, when he thought of what the job allowed him to do, to provide for Becca and later for a family of his own, perhaps it was a small sacrifice to make. For her, for the true north Dr Peverett had spoken of, for love—the one thing that had been elusive in his life to date—for more afternoons like this one when they'd made love before the fireplace in the sitting room. He felt complete with her—perhaps that was his purpose in life, to be with her and all else could go hang.

In the dark, he slipped his hand around hers where it lay on her lap and felt her glove-clad fingers grip his in return. *We are together*, he thought. In all ways. But to what end and for how long and in what ways? He had yet to discuss it with her, to put the question of a future to her. What did that future look like? Perhaps he was going about it all wrong. Perhaps he didn't need to build the future and present it to her as a fait accompli, as much as he needed to build that future *with* her. It occurred to him as the curtain went down on the first act that his Becca was an inventor—she wouldn't want to step into a world someone else was handing to her, she'd want to build a world of her own, of their own.

The lights came up and people began moving about to pay visits to the boxes of friends. Winthrop rose. 'Shall we see about some champagne? Ladies, we'll be back with refreshment.' Jules tossed Becca a smile that said, *I'm sorry*. He hadn't wanted to leave her alone, especially since they'd not parted on the best terms with Mary that afternoon, but there was no help for it.

In the salon set aside for the box seats, Winthrop clapped him on the back. 'You were late tonight and you had Miss Peverett to yourself all afternoon. Mary told me you whisked her away from the dress shop.' He lowered his voice. 'One might speculate as to what you've been up to since then.'

'One might,' Jules offered blandly without embellishment. 'People speculate all the time.'

'Jules, she's a good girl, from a good family from what you've shared. Mary's concerned. Miss Peverett is not one of your expensive ladies. There are expectations to be considered,' Winthrop said, but Jules interrupted.

'I am not sixteen years old, Win. I know what she is owed,' Jules ground out. She was owed a man who could provide for her, who could keep her in the style to which she was accustomed. He could do that, all he had to do was give up a little freedom.

Winthrop seemed to relax. Perhaps he'd not wanted to lecture his brother on manly conduct any more than Jules had wanted to hear it. 'Very good, then. No time like the present. She's already here in town. Ask her tomorrow after the ophthalmoscope ceremony. We can announce it at the ball. Mary is amenable to having the occasion become an engagement ball and it will be the talk of the town. Grandmother's ring is in the vault. We can have it brought out.' Grandmother's ring was a heavy, clunky piece of jewellery, known for its sheer worth and not its style. Jules couldn't imagine such a piece on Becca's slim, nimble fingers.

'Tomorrow?' Jules stared at his brother. 'I need

more time.' Time to get a decent ring, time to make arrangements. Becca needed more time. She would feel rushed, especially coming on the heels of the ophthalmoscope ceremony. Becca would *hate* the idea of having their engagement announced at a ball. Too much attention. 'When I propose, I'd thought to do it at her home after I've talked with her father,' Jules countered. He wanted to give himself the best odds possible for success.

He'd imagined a very different proposal than the one his brother had in mind. He'd thought of walking down to the waterfall with her, taking her hand and asking her in the place where he'd kissed her the very first time. They'd go back to the Hall and celebrate privately with her parents and perhaps Thomasia and Shaw over dinner, sipping Dr Peverett's son-in-law's excellent red wine. It would be a quiet, intimate event that suited Becca and suited him, truth be told, although such a realisation would have stunned him two months ago.

The brothers retrieved champagne glasses from the refreshment table and made their way back, but Winthrop wasn't done with the subject yet. 'Just think about it,' Winthrop said as they reached the red curtained entrance to the box.

'Perhaps *you* should think about it,' Jules replied. 'There *is* a flaw to your idea. Have you considered she might say no?'

'She spent the afternoon with you and showed up to the theatre looking well ravished. She won't say no.' Winthrop was smug.

'But what about the conflict of interest?' Jules didn't care for that smug tone in his brother's voice. Win hadn't been in favour of an intimate connection with Becca at the start and now he was pushing for a proposal.

Win gave him a wink. 'I think marriage resolves that, don't you?' No, he didn't think it resolved anything. Instead, it made for more complications, especially when he couldn't ignore that marriage to Becca would involve business as well as pleasure. Neither could he ignore that he felt his brother was up to something. The volte-face on his relationship with Becca seemed out of character for Winthrop. He was never one for rash or quick decisions. He thought things out, always played the long game. But a handful of days ago Win had been cautioning him against dallying with the inventor's daughter and now he was pushing marriage. It made him wonder what was at the heart of Win's redirection? Jules hoped it wasn't his father, pulling strings through his brother.

Inside the box, they handed around the champagne and Win raised his glass in a toast. 'Here's to a lovely evening, lovely company, and our big day tomorrow and all that it holds.' He sent a wink in Jules's direction as if everything had been decided. That worried Jules very much.

Chapter Twenty

Jules was worried. He was smiling, but he seemed distracted, as he had been all day. That distraction continued as they gathered for the big revealing of the ophthalmoscope at the Howells' ball—the second reveal, truth be told. There'd been one earlier at the factory, a reception at the offices attended by the workers. This second reveal was for the guests at the ball. It seemed like half of Manchester was here.

But Becca's attentions were fixed not on the scope or on the crowd, but instead on the man beside her, her senses attuned to the emotional turmoil that he hid behind his smile and his easy manner since the afternoon. His touch was light at her back as they listened to Winthrop make a speech about the latest product Howell Manufacturing was excited to put out. It was the same speech he'd given once already today, the difference being that tonight, waiters circulated among the group with trays of cold champagne and canapés—a new style of finger food popular in France, Mary had been quick to tell everyone.

It was the sort of occasion Thomasia would have loved, Becca thought. The festivities had involved two changes of gowns: a change for the supper that had followed the reception at the office and then a change after supper in to the newly sent ball gown. The town house had been buzzing all day with florists and caterers setting up tables and chairs and Christmas floral arrangements which had only served to underscore how much she was not looking forward to the evening's events. She hadn't had a moment alone with Jules since the theatre the prior evening. She would have given anything to return to yesterday afternoon's fireside tryst.

She felt Jules's hand surreptitiously grope for hers and she smiled, twining her fingers with his, hidden in the folds of her gown. Even in public, this was small private way to be connected in a crowd. Jules slanted her a look and their eyes met with the same message: *surely Winthrop would be done soon.*

'A portable ophthalmoscope will become an important component of any doctor's bag, allowing physicians to take better care of their patients at home,' Winthrop boasted proudly. 'All thanks to the efforts of R. L. Peverett. We are pleased to have his daughter, Miss Rebecca Peverett, on hand for the occasion. Miss Peverett, would you join us on the dais?'

It had not hurt to go unacknowledged as the inventor until that moment. Perhaps it was the patronising look in Winthrop's gaze that did it. It had been all too easy to perpetuate her ruse, far easier than she'd thought it would be. No one even contemplated that the inventor might be a woman. A flicker of anger flared to life as she stepped up to the dais beside Winthrop and the cloth covered form that would be the ophthalmoscope, *her* ophthalmoscope. She looked out over the assembly and found Jules with her gaze. He had made this moment possible. There was victory in what they'd done together. She needed to remember that.

Winthrop removed the cover, revealing the scope with its sleek handle and its head, made of a lightweight metal, the vital concave mirror that allowed it to be portable, protruding from the side with an adjustable arm. Her breath caught. It was beautiful, truly beautiful. She reached for it and held it aloft, revelling in the light weight of it, the compact shape. This would fit easily into a doctor's bag.

There was applause and Jules beamed at her, the only one there who knew how much this meant to her, and then the moment was over. Winthrop ushered her off the dais and the orchestra took up their positions. Dancing would commence shortly. She and Jules would be leading out the first dance in honour of her attendance.

'You're disappointed,' Jules said softly as they took up their position on the floor and the music started. 'You're regretting the subterfuge.' He moved them into the opening measures of the waltz, flawless and sure.

'Yes. Why is it so hard for people to believe a woman could have come up with this idea? With any of my ideas?' That was something else that was bothering her. Those other ideas had not been mentioned since her arrival. Even if she could not own the ideas, surely, the potential for future business could be discussed at least in passing.

Jules navigated them through the turn at the top of the ballroom. 'It will come out right in the end, we'll see to it.' He smiled at her and she relented. She was dancing with Jules, the handsomest man in the room, and she wasn't going to squander the opportunity by wasting it on complaints.

'Are you happy, Jules?' she asked. 'You seem off form today.' In fact, he'd seemed off form since he'd come back from fetching champagne at the theatre.

'Why wouldn't I be? I'm dancing with the incredible Rebecca Peverett.' His smile was dazzling, too dazzling. But Becca let it go. There was much to sort out between them, perhaps tonight wasn't the night. Perhaps she needed to let herself live in the moment.

When the dancing ended, Jules tugged her towards the table where the scope had been left on display for the curious. 'Show it to me up close. Give me the grand tour, as it were.' He picked up the scope.

'Jules, you can't just take it,' she gasped.

'Of course I can.' He grinned. 'Let's go find a place where we can be alone.'

That place was the library, located down at the end of the hall a long way from the ballroom. The music was barely audible when they shut the door behind them. It was a large room, as all of Winthrop's rooms were, but it was warm, a low fire burning in the grate. They took up seats on the turquoise velvet sofa before the fire and he handed the scope to her. 'Tell me all about it. I want to know everything.'

'The scope needs three things to function,' Becca explained. 'An illumination source, a reflective surface and the ability to correct for an out-of-focus image. If it can do that, it can show a physician the back of the retina of the eye.' She laughed. 'I can see I shall have to educate you about the eye as well, but perhaps another time?'

'Why would we want to see that?'

'It helps detect things like detached retinas and senile amblyopia, er…um…eye disease,' she simplified. 'You really didn't read any of the reports, did you? Well, anyway, it was the lack of illumination that in general prevented significant work on the scope, as you know, because I've told you that before.' Back in the workshop, back in Haberstock. Oh, how she wished she was there now, that they were in front of her fire at the cottage.

'Once Helmholtz, who improved the scope a few years ago, found that source of illumination, other factors could be focused on. I got to thinking about how the reflection surface was critical to making it a portable tool.' She played with the protruding arm holding the lens and grimaced. She didn't like that. 'Jules, move this piece. Does it seem stiff to you? As if you have to force it to move?'

Jules moved the piece, carefully. 'Yes, it does. Perhaps some lubricant would help. It *is* new.'

Becca frowned. 'It needs to be sturdier than that. This piece is going to eventually snap right off. I must speak with Winthrop about it tomorrow. Such unreliability cheapens the product. It should be durable.'

'Like us? Are we durable, Becca?'

The question caught her off guard, but she knew the look in his eyes. 'What are you asking, Jules?'

'Something I should have asked you weeks ago.' He trapped her hand in his. 'In a couple days you will be returning to Haberstock and I want there to be an understanding between us. I would like to come and speak to your father, but only if it's something you want.'

Her breath caught. There was no mistaking what this was. A proposal. Something she'd not thought to ever receive. That it came from this man with whom she'd shared so much, and that he'd thought to ask her first, to give her the choice, touched her heart in unexpected ways.

'Certainly, this is not a surprise, Becca?' Jules prompted. 'When we made the love the first time, I should never have let you get away with defining the rules. A gentleman knows his duty.'

Becca froze. 'I do not want this to be about duty, Jules.' She struggled to retrieve her hand. He didn't let go.

'It's not about duty. It's about love, Becca. I have fallen in love with you and I want to share my life with you. Everything I've done since I've been back in Manchester is to assure us a good future, one in which you can live in the style to which you are accustomed. I must work for a living. I'm not an earl or a duke's son like your sisters' husbands, but I do know how to make money. Howell Manufacturing will not fail you in that regard.'

'Shaw works, my father works. You needn't be ashamed of working. Most of the world does it.' Becca's heart twisted at the sight of the earnestness in his gaze. He truly meant this.

'Rawdon invests. His *money* works. Your father is a doctor, I don't think that counts. Doctors are different. You know what I mean. I need to go to the office every day, work nine to five in order to draw a salary. I may need to travel for business.' In order for them to have the cosy, red-bricked town house. In order for them to have more evenings like tonight, dressed in silks and satins, swilling champagne with other nouveau-riche industrialists who paraded their wealth about like calling cards.

She could not see herself in that life, nor could she see him in it. 'Jules, I want you to listen to me very carefully because everything depends on it. Did you like today? Tonight? Do you like going to work in the office? Be honest with me and be honest with yourself. Why are you doing this, Jules?'

'For you. For us.' Jules looked perplexed and her heart sank a bit.

'Is this truly what you want our lives to look like? Balls and parties, the theatre, endless suppers with Mary and Winthrop.' Perhaps Mary was right and in the end Jules did need his comforts. What if she lost the argument because it was never hers to win? If she had to choose between Haberstock and Jules, living in Manchester, living as Mary Howell did, what would she choose? Could she trade the life she loved for the man she loved? If she could not make that trade, what right did she have to ask him to make that same choice? To trade Manchester for her?

Jules's dancing green eyes went still. 'How else would I support you? This is my family's business. This is what I can do to give you a good life. I'm not sure what else I'd be, Becca.' He let go of her hand and rose, walking away from her. He was starting to think and there was hope in that.

'You'd still be Jules, still be the man I've come to care for.' She couldn't bring herself to say love, not when everything hinged on these next moments, these next words. 'You'd still love to paint, love to sing. You'd still want to take walks in the woods. Contrary to what the Howells believe, money does not make the man. Character does, though. A man is the sum of his actions, as is a woman.'

Her character was being sorely tested right now with this latest temptation. How much was she willing and able to give up of herself in order to marry Jules? Should she have to give *any* of herself up? Marriage ought to make a person whole, not fracture them. Anne, Thea, Thomasia—none of her sisters had given themselves up in order to wed. Yet it seemed very plain to her that marrying Jules and living in Manchester would require it.

'What are you saying, Becca? Is this your way of refusing me?' His throat sounded choked. His fist clenched and unclenched at his side. 'You're not making this easy on me.'

'I will not apologise for that. Marriage should not be an easy decision.' She wanted a little space, too. She took refuge behind the desk set before the long, wide windows overlooking the little garden. It was a working desk; someone had been using it earlier. Perhaps Winthrop. It seemed unlikely Mary would work in the library. She fiddled with the paperweight. 'I want you to think about everything marriage is requiring of you, of everything you're giving up.'

He preferred to think of what he was gaining. 'I'm *getting* a lifetime with you. Isn't that enough? Is a lifetime with me not enough for you?' Had he somehow misread her?

'You know it is, but not at the price of our freedom. We would come to hate each other.' Becca took up the seat behind the desk. 'Do you like your job, Jules? Do you want to go to that office every day for the next twenty-five years?'

'I would do it if it meant coming home to you.'

'But you shouldn't have to. Jules, don't you want to have it all? I don't want to take that from you. I don't want you to have to work in a job you don't like because you think you owe it to me.' She looked down at the papers on the desk and shuffled through them, a frown creasing her brow. 'Jules, come look at these.'

Jules strode to her side, the argument temporarily tabled. She held up the papers. 'These are copies of my drawings for the hypodermic needle, the two-sided stethoscope.'

A cold hand gripped his belly as he stared at the pages. 'Are you sure they aren't your originals? Winthrop could have brought them home from the office to look over.' But why he would have brought them home troubled Jules. He did not like how this looked.

'No, I signed mine. My initials would have been in the corner. Has he said anything about them to you? Are there any plans to produce them?'

Jules shook his head, 'No, it hasn't come up.' When he had tried to bring it up, Winthrop had neatly side-stepped the topic in lieu of other issues. He didn't like this at all. Was Winthrop looking to appropriate the designs as he'd done with the Frenchman despite his promises to the contrary?

'I'll ask him about them tomorrow when I speak with him about the arm on the scope.'

'No, Becca.' Jules was quick to intervene. 'Let me talk with him about both. I'll speak with him in the morning, first thing. I promise.' If his brother was looking to swindle the woman he loved out of her designs, Winthrop would have to answer to him.

'I can handle it,' Becca insisted.

'No, you can't,' he reminded her. 'You are not R. L. Peverett here, you have no authority. But I do and I will see it done.' He drew her to him, stealing a soft kiss. 'As for the other question, you don't have to answer it tonight. Will you think about it? We can make each other happy, Becca, that is no small thing in this world.' He knew, he'd lived in a world devoid of such happiness for too long. Now that he'd had a taste of it, he would not relinquish it, or the woman who provided it, without a fight.

Chapter Twenty-One

There was a fight brewing. Jules felt it before he even sat down in the study, facing both his brother and his father, who looked completely put out at the early summons. Jules had asked to speak with Winthrop immediately after breakfast. He should have made it clear that he wanted to speak with Winthrop alone, but perhaps it was best this way if his father was involved. Better to do it here at home, too, instead of at the office. Unpleasantness was best managed privately. The last thing he wanted to do was raise a scandal around the family and have it pinned on him, or—worse—on Becca, who could easily become a scapegoat for the present situation.

You are family, they will forgive you, but I am not.

She had warned him. He'd tried to change that last night with his proposal. He could *make* her family.

'Well, has she refused you? Is this what this is about?' Winthrop was in a sullen mood this morning despite the success of the ball last night and the big revelation of the portable ophthalmoscope.

'She has not exactly refused.' But she hadn't accepted either, on grounds that seemed to have little to do with how she felt about their relationship. He did take heart from that. He'd always admired Becca's ability to think of others first, but he wasn't particularly admiring it now that it was an impediment to getting what he wanted—her, for ever.

'Then what is this about?' Winthrop was brisk. 'I have meetings today with lawyers over patents. Business never sleeps, Jules.'

'There's a concern over the quality of the ophthalmoscope,' Jules said, splitting his gaze between his brother and his father. It was as good a place to start as any and perhaps the easiest. Surely Winthrop would want to produce a superior product. 'The arm that manipulates the mirror for reflection seems fragile. Becca was disappointed in the design. She fears it will break too easily.'

Winthrop's briskness seemed to ease. He waved a hand, dismissing the notion. 'What does she know? She's a woman, she has no notion of how things are made.' He gave a chuckle. 'Besides, breakage is good for business. We can't have a long selling tool if people only buy it once, especially when that tool has a limited audience. Only doctors will want it. So, their scope works for a while and then, after five years or so, they replace it.'

Jules took a moment to digest that. 'You mean you *want* it to break?' He shot his father a sharp look. This had all the hallmarks of his father's ethic.

His father met his gaze with a stare of his own, his

tone patronising. 'Yes. Not right away, of course. I want it to work and to last, but eventually to break. I want doctors to love it so much they'll replace it with the same. That kind of construction takes a certain genius, a careful balancing of durability with terminal life expectancy.' His father smiled, pleased with himself. 'You'll learn how it is as you do more with the business. It's an important concept to keep in mind in your position with sales as well.'

'That sounds dishonest to me,' Jules replied. It would definitely sound dishonest to Becca. He wondered what she would make of such practices? What did Winthrop think? He cast a quick look in Win's direction. 'Did you know about this, Win?' His brother seemed to have shrunk into his chair.

'It's a clever idea,' his father continued before Winthrop could answer, not the least bothered by the concept. 'In fact, we're probably doing them a favour. I've done some reading on the ophthalmoscope.' Implying that Jules had not. Becca had implied as much last night and the guilt stabbed at him again. He'd not done his research. He'd relied on his charm instead of on the facts and now he was at a disadvantage.

Well, no more. Part of this new leaf of his would need to include reading scientific articles and staying up on the latest developments. He cringed inwardly. That would mean more time spent not actually selling. Just as his days now were spent burdened with correspondence. He'd not anticipated that. *Do you like your job, Jules?* Becca's voice was clear in his mind. No, he did not. She might be his true north, but this job, this pathway to her, was not.

'This is a device that is likely to be improved on over time,' his father was saying. 'It's a device which relies on technological advancements for its improvement. As soon as the technology is available, this device will change, it will be refined, a constant work in progress.' Hadn't Becca said as much last night? Something about illumination being limited for a long time and once that problem had been solved, other advancements had been possible.

'By the time the current scope breaks, we'll have a new and improved version to sell doctors and they'll be happy to purchase a newer model.' For a higher price, of course. Jules could see that much at least. He could also see that doctors would be less likely to want the newer model if the old one was working fine. But a broken ophthalmoscope would create a convenient window of opportunity to upgrade. There was a certain genius behind such a strategy—an evil genius.

'You can assure Miss Peverett there's nothing to worry her pretty head over.' His father offered a patronising nod. 'This is why women don't do business. They simply can't fathom all the angles we must consider.' The comment made Jules's blood boil on Becca's behalf. No wonder she preferred the solitude of her workshop. Had this been what her previous experiences had been like seeking patents? She'd mentioned it once and he'd not fully considered what it must have been like for her to sit and listen to a man not only refuse her on grounds of her gender but also to degrade her intelligence on those grounds as well.

Perhaps it would be best to just move on. 'It's not only the ophthalmoscope I wanted to discuss.' Jules held Winthrop's gaze. 'We were in the library last night.' He watched for any tell-tale sign that their presence in the library would concern Winthrop.

'Oh, so that's where you disappeared to. I noticed you were gone. I thought you might be proposing. I had hoped you'd return with an announcement. It would have been the perfect way to top off a great evening for the Howells.'

Jules overlooked the idea that an engagement was a source of entertainment instead of a lifetime commitment and pressed on. 'Becca found copies of her drawings on the desk. Copies, Winthrop, when we have not even discussed the future of the three inventions I brought back with me. Winthrop, you promised me we would be fair.'

Winthrop's face went still and for a moment Jules thought he'd struck a worthy blow. Winthrop's words came slow. '*What* did you say? Copies of her drawings?'

'Yes, copies.' Exactly so. Jules knew a moment's relief. Winthrop hadn't known they were there. Whatever was happening he was not behind it and now Winthrop could put a stop to it.

Winthrop pushed a hand through his hair, disbelief on his face making him come to life. 'Copies of *her* drawings? She drew the sketches?'

Jules squared his shoulders. After weeks of being

careful to hide R. L. Peverett's identity, he'd inadvertently revealed it. Did he brazen it out, come up with an excuse? Perhaps Winthrop would believe she drew to support her father's efforts. Would his father? Or did he say enough with games and lies and tell the truth? He thought of Becca's disappointment last night. If he meant to stand up for her, and in a way, stand up for himself and his own independence, he needed to tell the truth. 'Yes, hers.' He met Win's gaze firmly. 'Rebecca *is* R. L. Peverett. Her gender does not change the quality of her designs.'

'It most certainly does!' his father roared through gritted teeth before he reined in his anger. 'Who will buy a woman's device? Certainly not a learned, educated man like a doctor. In fact, he would be least likely to buy it *and* he's our only audience.'

Winthrop drummed his hands on the desk, his eyes darting nervously between him and their father, looking for the peaceable middle ground. 'Well, there's nothing for it. It's too late now. We've already begun production and marketing. No one can know. We could lose a substantial amount on this if word got out and I can't afford that just now. With the war in the Crimea concluded, our munition contracts aren't as lucrative as they have been.' He smirked at Jules. 'You don't have a war up your sleeve, do you? We could definitely use another one.'

'No, sorry, clean out of wars,' Jules replied drily, his mind latching on to the idea that all was not as well as he thought with the company. His brother's look of desperation was about more than easing the tension between him and his father.

'You've put us in a difficult situation, Jules. Not the first time, of course.' His father gave a long-suffering sigh, but Jules refused to feel guilty over this. 'The best thing we can do now is have you married as soon as possible.'

'I don't see what that has to do with anything.' Jules studied his father looking for a clue. Apparently, he'd been right, though, and the pressure for him to wed had come from his father via Winthrop.

'It has everything to do with the current situation. None of this will matter if she's married to you. Her property becomes yours. Coverture means her legal identity is determined solely through her husband's identity. She'll have no rights to stand on to claim her inventions. But you will.' His father halted with a harsh laugh, a thought occurring to him.

'Why, you slimy bastard, you've been planning that all along, haven't you? Of course you have. You knew from the start *she* was the inventor. So you hid it from me, from all of us, and got the company to patent her tool, because she couldn't get a patent on her own. Then, the company produced it and sold it, while you seduced her. You'll marry her and reap the benefits of that income and whatever other income she can produce for you. No wonder you're so eager to discuss her other inventions. There's no money in it for you if the company turns the inventions down.' His father grinned. 'You might just be a Howell after all.'

Horror crept over Jules. He did not want to be a

Howell, not if that was how Howells did things. He shook his head against the scenario his father painted. One had to be entirely corrupt to think along such lines. *This is what our life will be like...* Becca's words came back to him as did his own—*I could do it if it meant coming home to you.*

What else could he do? What else was he capable of? He glanced at Winthrop, a thought occurring to him. Was this what had happened to Winthrop? Had he started down the path slowly and gone so far there was no point of return?

He'd not seen it last night when Becca had challenged him or perhaps he'd not wanted to see it then. Becca *was* right. Happiness shouldn't be bought through compromise. Dr Peverett had counselled as much. He thought briefly of Richard Peverett choosing the country over court and the reasons for it. If he was willing to give his days over to a job he despised, what else might he eventually give up as well? Perhaps something far more fundamental to who he was than his time. He might give up his integrity, something he'd just begun to reclaim. Becca would never love a man with no integrity, no self-respect.

'So you *do* mean to take the designs and patent them on your own,' Jules accused. The incident with the Frenchman had not been an accident. How many more times had such a thing occurred? He felt sick to his stomach. How often had his efforts in wining and dining potential clients been complicit with such schemes? Who had he cheated out of money and hard work? Even if he hadn't known, he'd been part of it.

'Yes, absolutely,' Winthrop said, entering the conversation. 'The hypodermic needle is full of potential, although the two-sided stethoscope seems limited. What we're doing is *not* illegal, I assure you.'

Jules shook his head. 'Is this how we've made our money?'

His father laughed. 'It's a bit late to develop such a fine-tuned conscience, Jules. It didn't bother you when you were spending our money. It's not so bad. We're not doing anything illegal and neither are you. You've a bit of Howell genius in you—seducing the female inventor to steal her designs and then marrying her in order to live on her profits. It might have worked, too, if we'd bought her designs. You're a sly one, Jules. That's why you wanted the job, isn't it? I see it all coming together now. You wanted to keep steering us towards R. L. Peverett's work. Very canny of you. You were covering yourself there even if you were deceiving family. Tsk, tsk on that level. But we can all keep a secret.' His father smiled approvingly. The one thing he'd wanted his whole life. He finally had it and it was worth less than nothing to him. Not at this price. Not at the price of Becca's admiration and respect.

His father laid out quick terms in typical fashion. 'I'll cut you in on the commission from anything we sell from her designs and we'll keep her identity a secret. She'll be none the wiser and you can live off the profits and your salary here at the company. She'll make you a rich man, Jules. Well done, my son. I never suspected you had such treachery in you.'

'I don't. I'm not like you. I'll never be like you.'

Jules snapped, his gaze going to his brother. 'Are you going to allow this to continue, Winthrop? Are you going to sit there and be counted as part of these practices?' He wanted his brother to side with him. Perhaps together, they might stand up to their father and right the crooked ship that had become Howell Manufacturing.

Winthrop looked away with a shake of his head. 'It's not illegal, Jules, and there are things you don't understand.'

Jules rose, disgusted with the pair of them and with himself. His world was reeling at the implications. He'd failed in so many ways and now he needed to think through what to do next, how to protect Becca even if it meant sacrificing his true north. He could not make her part of this family. They would destroy her by inches, but ultimately what would break her would be her misplaced faith in him. Best to do it now while anger and disappointment offered him a false fortitude to see through what must be done.

He found her at the piano in Mary's music room crowded with furniture and knick-knacks. Jules did not announce his presence at once. Instead, he took a long moment to watch her, to listen to her, letting his heart recall the musical evenings they'd spent together at Haberstock Hall. She was wearing blue today, a lighter shade than her usual fare. It looked good with her dark hair, but it was slightly fussier than her normal gowns. A new dress, then, something Mary and his mother had foisted upon her. How had he ever thought her plain and wallflowerish?

That seemed a lifetime ago, the thoughts of a different man. In a way they were. She had changed him.

I won't go back, I won't go back to being that man, a man who gave up too easily, he promised silently.

He was going to lose her, lose true north, but there were other things she'd given him that he could keep like his pride, his sense of rightness. He wouldn't hide from that again. She finished the piece and he cleared his throat, his fingers clenching around the warm wrap he'd brought for her in his hands.

'Jules!' She turned, smiling at the sight of him. Then her brow furrowed. 'I thought you'd be at the office by now.'

He shook his head and held out his hand, mentally counting down last things: the last time she'd smile at him, touch him, take his hand. 'Come walk in the garden with me.' They were in two different worlds. In her world, everything was still fine, they were still together, everything was still possible. In her world, she didn't know he'd already lost her. But in his world, she was already gone.

She studied him with those eyes that saw too much, letting him drape the wrap about her, her smile fading. 'What is it, Jules? Has something happened? You sound serious.'

He waited until they were outside and he was certain there were no listening ears. He would give her the protection of absolute privacy at least. He led her to a small stone bench at the back of the garden where they'd be invisible to those in the house as well as inaudible. He was aware of how tight his grip was on her hand. He was holding on to her, his anchor for a short while longer until he had to cast her adrift.

'I have been thinking about what you said last night, about the life we would lead here. I think I may have been impetuous in my proposal.' He felt her body still and he had no illusions about how hard she'd take this news. Becca Peverett loved with her body and soul and she'd loved him. This was going to wreck her. For a while. Her family would put her back together and she would see it was for the best.

'Impetuous? In what way?' Becca asked softly, but he was not fooled as he once might have been by her quietness. She was on full alert, missing none of the implications of his words. He could see in those beautiful cognac eyes that she knew where this was headed.

He would make it as gentle as he could. He did not want to hurt her, but to marry her would hurt her more. 'I cannot give you a life that would make you happy and you deserve happiness. I took unfair advantage last night, catching you in a vulnerable moment. It is only right that I release you from any promises we might have made or implied last night.' He'd failed to protect her, to protect her inventions from the avarice of his family. Marriage into the Howell family would corrupt her. All he could do now was set her free.

Chapter Twenty-Two

He was letting her down gently, she saw that immediately, and the pain, too. Oh, she definitely saw the pain. It was there, stark and obvious in those lovely green eyes of his. He was setting her free, but against his will. The only question was how to go? Should she make it hard on him and fight or should she go quietly with acceptance and understanding in order to ease his pain?

'I know it hurts now, but it would hurt more if we were to..' He groped for the word. *Marry*, she thought. The word he wanted was marry. 'To continue,' he found a less emotionally charged word. 'I see now that I was wrong. I can't make you happy here.'

He was being kind. He couldn't make her happy here because she didn't belong here. She didn't fit into the glamorous world of Baccarat chandeliers and over-trimmed ballgowns. She preferred the solitude of her workshop to the bustle of shopping expeditions and a calendar crowded with teas and at-homes. Wasn't this what she'd counselled herself against from the beginning? That a handsome, charming man would soon see that she was no match for him? She was too plain, too quiet, too uninterested in city life and material things. A life of the mind had no place in the Howells' world.

While that last did not disappoint her, losing Jules did. It disappointed her a great deal. To never see him again, to never laugh with him, to never dance with him, paint with him, make music with him. She felt her eyes sting and she blinked back the tears. She was not going to cry, not yet. She didn't want to make it hard on him. He was only acknowledging the truth. He should not be castigated for being honest.

She managed a tremulous smile. 'I understand, Jules. Truly, I do.' She hoped he wouldn't require her to say more. She didn't think she could manage it. It seemed Miss Pembridge would win him after all and perhaps for the better. She was eminently more suited for life in Manchester.

'I'm sorry, Becca. I didn't mean for things to turn out this way,' he said, at a loss for words. 'I will see to the inventions so that you have all you're entitled to.'

'But we knew it was how they'd probably turn out. We should have expected this.' She said it as much for him as for herself. Bluestockings and dashing rogues were an unlikely combination. It had been nice while it lasted. She rose so that he could rise, too. 'I trust you will see right done by my inventions.' It gave her a sense of control to direct the conversation towards business and away from her heart. This was all there would be between them from here on out.

'Yes, I will be in touch. I promise.' His jaw worked

as if he were fighting back emotion. 'Becca…' Her name was a plea on his lips and she could not give in to it.

She shook her head, finding a new reserve of strength. 'Miss Peverett would be better, I think. And no more promises, please. If you would allow me a moment alone.'

'Oh, yes, of course. Pardon me.' He made a small bow, his charm suddenly clumsy. 'I must be away to the office. We'll talk more when I come home.' But there was nothing to talk about. It would only prolong the agony.

She watched him go back up the path towards the house. When she was certain he was out of sight, she sagged on to the bench, her breath coming in gasps, her legs like rubber. Dear God. She had lost Jules. The hurt of that knowledge was unbelievable, absolutely overriding what should have been the bigger hurt— that her invention had been betrayed with substandard design and her other inventions were in the process of being stolen. She'd hardly been able to focus on that in the wake of the devastation of losing Jules. What to do now? She was in the city, alone, far from home and all she wanted to do was cry. She could *not* cry. She had to think. The brain she so prided herself on having needed to work.

She *had* to get out of the garden. She didn't want to be caught out here crying. She didn't want to see the look on Mary's face or his mother's when she told them Jules had broken with her. They would offer patronising 'I told you so' looks, they would say if only she'd tried harder, bought a different dress. She'd been so foolish to think this could actually work, that someone like him would want someone like her in his world. She rose on unsteady legs, letting anger at herself combined with a breaking heart propel her up the quiet back stairs to her room undetected.

In her room, her mind knew what to do. She must escape, she must leave. As soon as possible. Before Jules came back from the office. She dragged out her trunk and blindly began to pack. She had to get back to Haberstock Hall, to her family. Thomasia would know what to do, Thomasia would understand. If she could just get home, she could start to put herself back together. To think she'd nearly said yes last night! How much she'd wanted to say yes, to believe in the dream of him, of them. Recrimination flooded hard and fast. Everything had been a lie, a beautiful, deceitful lie they'd willingly spun between themselves, all of it a fantasy: the afternoon beside the fire, the night in the loft. Two of the most intimate experiences she'd ever had and they'd all been part of some unreal world that couldn't last, that was lost.

The grief that followed such a realisation nearly overwhelmed her. She stumbled against the bed and clutched the bed post, dropping the clothes she carried on the floor. She steadied herself. She was making a hash of this. How was she even going to get the trunk downstairs without anyone seeing her? She wasn't. There would be questions, someone would call Jules, there would be a scene.

Thinking about details settled her anger to roiling

simmer long enough to make a decision. She changed into the plum travelling costume she'd worn on arrival, took a warm cloak and her reticule, which held plenty of money to see her home. She left the rest. She told the maid she was going out for a walk, opened the front door and didn't look back. She would cry later, she told herself. But first, she had to buy a ticket and get on the train. When she was home, then, and only then, she would allow her broken heart to grieve over the enormity of what she'd lost.

Chapter Twenty-Three

Jules did not allow himself to accept the enormity of what had happened until he saw her room—the clothes on the floor, the open trunk, the garments thrown in and spilling out haphazardly, the mess uncharacteristic of Becca's usual order and organisation. 'What did she say, again?' he interrogated the poor maid for the fifth time.

'That she was going out for a walk.' The same eight words the maid had shared all the times before.

'When?' Jules ran through it all again and again, surveying the chaos of Becca's room.

'Half past ten, sir.'

He dismissed the maid who fled the room with alacrity. Jules sank into the chair set before the fire, his head in his hands as he pieced the morning together in his mind. Half past ten, after he'd gone to work, leaving her so forlorn in the garden. He'd broken her heart and he'd left, because she'd asked him to when all he'd wanted to do was gather her in his arms and find a way to make it better, to take back the hurt he was inflicting on her. But there was no way to make it better other than to send her away from his toxic family. He was saving her. She would never know, but it was the most selfless thing he'd ever done.

He'd come home for luncheon only to find her gone, the maid telling him she'd gone out for a walk. But by tea, she was still gone and he was genuinely worried. He'd queried the maid again. Had Becca said where she was going? He'd asked Mary if Becca had any appointments—perhaps she'd gone to the dressmaker? Neither enquiry had borne fruit. That was when he'd gone up to her room and seen the mess and he'd known she'd not just gone out for walk. She'd *gone*. She was not usually a mercurial creature, but her departure bore all the stamps of flight, rapid and swift and unpremeditated—a sign of how deeply she was hurting.

She was not alone there. He was hurting, too. The day had been overwhelming from the morning discussion with his brother and father to breaking with Becca, and now ending with her absolute desertion. Although it should not have come as a shock. He'd hurt her deeply and he could see the narrative playing out for her that capitalised on her vulnerabilities. For all her belief in her abilities as an inventor, Becca had little confidence in herself as a desirable woman. It had been beautiful to watch that change over the past weeks and to know that he'd given her that confidence. His break with her today would have decimated that.

He rose and paced about the room, stopping to pick her rose silk off the floor. She'd been his blooming rose. He remembered the first night he'd seen her in it back at Haberstock, the night the contract was official. She'd been lovely. He raised the gown to his nose and breathed her in, all cinnamon and vanilla, and the grief that came with regret racked him. She'd left too hastily to even take her favourite gown. There was no more damning condemnation than that, no more proof needed as to the depth of hurt that had sent her flying so precipitously.

He'd failed her in love

Should that surprise you? You've never been good at it.

But he was good with her. He was a better version of himself when he was with her. He'd had purpose with her, his days had direction. His own natural talents had been valued. She'd loved him for who he was. He'd not had to pretend with her. She'd loved the painter, the singer, the man who talked to storekeepers.

Grief and frustration ripped through him at the use of past tense. *She'd loved.* Was it truly all in the past? She might have left, but he knew where she'd gone. She'd gone to Haberstock, to her home, her family, to her strength. They would put her back together. But what of him? Who would put him back together after today? Not his family. His family was the reason he was emotionally bloodied, the reason he'd lost his true north.

You give up too easily, Mr Howell. Her words were as clear as if she was in the room with him. But she was miles away. Only her wisdom remained. He could go after her, chase her down. He could be there tomorrow. While her anger was still hot? While she was still hurting, perhaps not even able to process that hurt or listen to reason? When he had very little reason to offer her? What could he tell her tomorrow that he hadn't told her today? He could not go to her empty-handed.

He thought about Thomas, the dog in the stable, the one she'd rescued through patience and perseverance. Perhaps he ought to take a page from that book. He'd failed her in love, drawn her into the toxic environment of his family and then broken her heart. All to save her, came the refrain. But who would save him if he stayed here and continued to contribute to the family Howell's corrupt practices? Who would save other inventors who would inevitably fall prey? Who would save Winthrop? That last whispered through his mind. His brother had been desperate and frightened today. Win might be beyond saving. At what price could he save himself and his brother and those who might come after? If he gave up his family, would it even be enough? Would Becca want him after today? These were decisions that required a man to take a leap of faith into the unknown.

He thought of Richard Peverett choosing between court and countryside, of Dr Peverett who'd given up fame and fortune for family and found both. The thought gave him comfort. He was not alone in this. He knew what Dr Peverett would say. A man needed purpose, passion. Becca was both to him. He would not fail her in business. He'd promised to protect her inventions. He would see it done. He could not go to her otherwise. It was the only thing he had left to give her, to show her he might be worth a second chance.

Jules forced himself to sit, forced his brain to work. He would pack up her trunk and have it sent to her. Then, he would dedicate himself to getting her back. It would not be an easy task. First, he would need to sever ties with his family, he saw that now. Perhaps he always had. He was not like them, he could not engage in the practices they engaged in—legal or not, they did not resonate with him. He did not want money associated with such practices.

Severing would be simple. He could do as Becca had done and simply leave. But that wouldn't be enough. It wouldn't protect Becca's drawings from becoming uncompensated property of the company. Neither would it protect other inventors. An idea began to form, one that might see her work compensated and one that might generate a bit of money for them to start their lives on. They *were* going to need money, something he'd not given much thought to in general until lately. Even so, he was not going to take family money, tainted money.

He would sell the town house and those proceeds would last a while. But eventually that would be gone, unless it could grow into more money. Rawdon might be useful in helping him invest, that was always a possibility. But it did not ensure he'd win her back. None of these plans did. Still, he had to try.

Jules shifted in the chair, something in his pocket digging into his side. He put his hand in his pocket and pulled out the little soldier Becca had made for him. Even as he faced the prospect of losing Becca, the solider made him smile. It brought to mind watching her work in her cottage, of how she laboured over each figure, painting special uniforms on each so that a child might have a soldier wearing the same uniform as his father. For a child who'd lost his father to war, the soldier would be a toy and a token of remembrance, the embodiment of a story. Because Becca always saw beyond the immediate, always saw the bigger significance of even the simplest things.

He turned it over in his hand. Toy soldiers from the Crimea. He could imagine whole battalions of them, dressed as the tragic Light Brigade, mounted on horses, others dressed as the dreaded Russians. After all, what was the use of an army if there was no enemy to fight? Perhaps a miniature cannon that fired or made a popping sound? Such things existed, but not for the masses—they were too expensive. But now, with quick production possible... Another idea took root. A toy company featuring Becca's creations. Maybe Rawdon would invest, perhaps it would be something just for them. But none of that would matter if he didn't win her back. First things first. He moved about the room, packing her trunk. Then, he'd take a good long look at the family financials. He'd want to be sure of all the details before he confronted Winthrop.

'The company is losing money.' Jules strode into the offices of Howell Manufacturing and tossed the account books on Winthrop's desk. 'The reason is Father's overspending and possibly yours. The remodel of the town-house drawing room—those curtains alone cost a small fortune. There's the parties and the extravagant entertaining.' It had taken two full weeks

of poring over ledgers to work it all out. The Howells were living beyond their means and financing it
with credit and with inventions they didn't pay for. No
wonder Winthrop was concerned about the war ending too soon.

'Keeping up appearances is expensive work. Since
when are you a financial wizard, little Brother?' Winthrop's gaze narrowed. 'You didn't mind the finances
when they were paying your bills.'

'I regret that,' Jules said sincerely. 'But that is not
the point. I want the company to pay Becca for her designs and I want her to receive a royalty on all sales
from them. If you choose not to produce them, so be it,
but she will at least be paid for her ideas.' He named an
appropriate sum. 'You know it is the right thing to do.'

Win gave a small nod and reached for the cheque
book in his desk drawer.

'Why didn't you say anything the day after the ball?'
Jules ventured the question carefully. 'Why didn't you
stand up for me? With me?' He would have his answers before he left. This might be the last time he
saw his brother.

Winthrop looked up from his cheque writing. 'It's
complicated. I have a wife, I have a home, I have bills
to pay. I don't have the luxury of the high ground,
Jules.'

There was more to it than that, there always had
been. 'He doesn't respect you for it, for following his
rules.' Jules played with the paperweight. 'He's using
you, Win, and I'm sorry to see it. I never thought you
would pick him over me. How did it come to this, Win?

We were so close, I used to look up to you.' But that brother had been gone for years and the man in his place bore little resemblance to the brother Jules had once known. Here sat a man starting to go grey and careening towards middle years, a man who was beginning to show the marks of living without a conscience.

'Jules, I'm sorry—' Win said, but he was interrupted before he could say more.

'What is going on here?' Stefan Howell strode into the office, eyes narrowed.

'I'm just paying for the Peverett inventions,' Winthrop said in a surprising show of backbone.

'We don't have to pay for them and we can still use them. I'll just have my team modify them.' Stefan Howell nodded at Jules. 'I was told you were here. Come to speak poison into your brother's ear, have you? Your little bird has flown the coop and now you're trying to save yourself.' He was, in fact, trying to save himself, but not in the way his father thought.

'Besides, we're in tight straits for money as you've surmised. Why would I pay out funds?' Stefan challenged.

Jules was ready for the response. 'You will pay because I will tell the newspapers and those in the business what happens here at Howell Manufacturing. I do not think that will help sales or the keeping up of appearances. Inventors won't want to do business with you.'

Stefan studied him with a slow nod of his head. 'I see, you're asking for hush money. We pay you for Becca's inventions and you keep your mouth shut.' Very clever. Still swindling that poor chit and she's not even here. We've woefully underestimated you, Jules.'

'No,' Jules clarified, not liking himself associated with such an insinuation. 'You're buying the designs from *her* and you're buying silence from *me*.' He would turn that money over to Becca as proof of his pure intentions. There was no sense in getting the designs back, the damage had already been done. Who knew how many copies were floating around? He couldn't stop that, but he could ensure she'd be compensated.

'And then what? Does this become an annual thing? You come in every quarter and demand tribute for your silence?' Stefan frowned.

Jules steadied himself, his temper rising. 'No, that would be extortion, I believe. The designs may only be bought once. She should only be paid once.' Becca would not want it any other way.

'You should know I've sold the town house. I am leaving on the next train to Broxbourne and I do not intend to be back. As long as Becca is paid her royalties for the ophthalmoscope, and potential royalties from these other inventions, and other inventors are paid fairly for their designs, I will have no need to return.'

Stefan raised white brows at that. 'You mean to cut ties with your family? For a country chit?'

'Not for a country chit. For love. Having found it, I am loath to let it go.' Assuming she'd have him back, but he did not dwell on that for fear that thinking such a thing possible might make it so.

Stefan grunted at the notion. 'Winthrop, do not give him that money.' To Jules he said, 'Is that all you've got for leverage? Going to the papers?' His father studied him. 'I'll deny it and I'll tell them your little woman made it all up because she got turned down. Who do you think they'll believe? Me or a woman who claims to be an inventor and you?' He gave a cruel laugh.

'They'll believe me,' Winthrop spoke. 'I've been the head of the company. They'll believe me.' He glanced at Jules and Jules felt something warm unfurl in his gut. Winthrop nodded. 'I'll confirm everything he tells them, how we've not paid for designs, how we've supposedly turned designs down and then put together our own.' A long look passed between Winthrop and his father.

'You would not dare, Winthrop.' Stefan Howell skewered his older son with a stare. 'You would lose everything.'

'In many ways, I already have.' Winthrop rose, slanting a look in Jules's direction 'Take the cheque, Jules, and let's go.'

'What?' Stefan spluttered as Winthrop came around the desk to stand with Jules.

Jules faced his father squarely. 'It is us who should have been done with *you* a long time ago. We've spent our lives trying to earn the impossible from you: Winthrop trying to follow the rules and me trying to break them. We both got the same results. But no more.'

'This is *your* doing, Jules.' Stefan's voice rose in anger. 'You've ruined your life and now you want to ruin your brother's. Winthrop, be sensible. If you walk out of here, I won't take you back, neither one of you.'

He snarled at Jules, 'Take your hush money and go. You never were one of us.'

Thank goodness for that. Jules tucked the cheque into his pocket and with his brother by his side, he went straight to the train station, each step taking him closer to a new beginning, to Becca. At the platform, Winthrop embraced him. 'Write soon. Invite me to the wedding.'

'I don't know if she'll have me,' Jules said.

'When she learns what you did today, she'll have you. Miss Peverett knows a good man when she sees one and I do, too. Thank you, Brother. I'll see you soon.'

He'd imagined seeing her again a hundred different ways. Perhaps he'd put the money into her hands like he had the first time. Perhaps he'd simply pull her into his arms and kiss away her misgivings. Misgivings was too tame a word. Misgivings would not have sent her fleeing. What had sent her fleeing was a breach of trust, a betrayal of the faith she'd put in him. Those were far larger things and they needed to be handled with care and respect if he hoped to win her back.

Never in all his imaginings did he expect to arrive at Haberstock Hall and find her gone. Yet that was precisely the situation which greeted him.

'What do you mean she's not here?' Was she at the workshop? Perhaps she was at Rosegate, visiting Thomasia and Shaw. Maybe she was shopping in the village. He was instantly deflated. He'd come all this way, worked over a week on making the arrangements to come to her, to step into a new life with her, and she wasn't here. It was unfathomable. All this time he'd been picturing her in her workshop, heartbroken, and she wasn't here.

Dr Peverett put his hand on Jules's shoulder, a kindly, fatherly gesture. 'She's in London, my boy. She's working with Anne and Ferris at the children's Military Asylum.' He paused and drew a breath before braving the difficult topic. 'I don't know all the details of what happened in Manchester, but I do know she's as crestfallen over it as you look. You've come a long way. Come in, have a drink. Stay for supper. Rawdon and Thomasia are here and in the morning you can take a train to London if you're so inclined.'

Jules followed Dr Peverett into the music room, let him put a tumbler in his hand and seat him near the fire. The kindness nearly broke him. It was easy to see where Becca got such generosity from. He was the enemy in this camp. He'd broken Becca's heart and yet her family welcomed him with all the customary Peverett hospitality. Well, most of them did. Dr and Mrs Peverett were friendly and considerate, Rawdon was interested to talk business about the toys, but Thomasia was politely frosty. She spent the evening playing with Effie-Claire or resting her hands on her belly and staring daggers at him when her mother wasn't looking. Well, good. He deserved it. He would be sure to tell Becca how loyal Thomasia had been when he caught up to her. Still, it was good to be among…family. At least he hoped they'd be family very soon.

Chapter Twenty-Four

Her family had been good to her. As a result, Becca was starting to feel a little bit more herself. Not much. Just a little. She made the walk from Anne and Ferris's house on Cheyne Walk, past the physic garden to the military asylum where she'd spend the afternoon playing with the children and making more presents of her little soldiers. She looked forward to her afternoons at the asylum. It was a chance to be out of the house *and* on her own. It was the 'on her own' piece that Becca treasured about the walk. She was out of the house quite a bit with Anne. Her sister took her on rounds with the mobile health cart she and Ferris had designed to serve poorer communities. But Anne watched her with hawk-like intensity and worried over her, asking questions she had no good answers to. How did she feel? Did she feel like things were starting to get back to normal? What was normal? What would ever be normal again?

She might never feel 'herself' again, not in any

complete sense. Jules had a part of her that she would never get back—the part that had dared believe in love against the wise counsel of her mind and past experiences. Love was not for her, she'd known better. Men like him didn't fall in love with a brainy girl like her. She could not be entirely angry at him. He'd only taken what she'd been so willing to give.

Becca approached the gates to the asylum's grounds and found a smile. Christmas was approaching. These children had precious little to look forward to, they were counting on her to make their days bright. Her time in London would be brief. The family would all depart for Haberstock this year, mostly in the hopes of being on hand for Thomasia's baby. But London had been good for her. She'd not been able to face the daily reminders of Jules at Haberstock. Perhaps surrounded by family and a new baby she would be able to face her workshop again. Perhaps time would also have softened the memories.

'What did you bring!' A child spotted her and ran up, tugging at her hand. The day was crisp but fine and the children were enjoying a rare treat of playing outdoors in winter.

'I've brought oranges and toy soldiers.' She took the child's hand and let him draw her into a game of tag with the others.

The afternoon sped by in breathless games of tag and delighted screams of children when she caught them. It was possible to forget her own hurt a while as she played with them, focused on their needs. Tired and happy, they collapsed on the ground on old blankets that had been spread out and gathered about Becca as she handed out oranges. A small boy plopped in her lap and she helped him peel the fruit while she told them the story of the Christmas orange. 'Oranges symbolise bags of gold, you know,' she said, and the children listened, enrapt. 'Once upon a time in the Mediterranean—do you know where that is?' They took a moment for a geography lesson and she continued, 'There was a poor man. He had three daughters who could not wed because he had no money for their dowries...'

'Miss Peverett,' one of the children spoke up. 'Why is that man watching us?'

Becca twisted around, her gaze going to the gates, her heart stopping at the sight: the long wool coat, the hair that trailed over his collar and blew in the winter breeze. The tall figure, the broad shoulders. Surely her eyes were playing tricks on her. She wished for her eyeglasses. What would Jules be doing here in London?

A pit formed in her stomach from a flutter of excitement and then the remembrance of hurt. She didn't *want* him here. Was he here for her? Why couldn't he just let her be? Hadn't he taken enough? And now he'd tracked her down where she was alone and vulnerable, no family around her to drive him off.

One of the caregivers at the facility bustled out to bring the children inside. It was time for them to wash for supper. Becca gathered her basket. She had to face him. But she need fear nothing. She was armed with the truth now.

He began to move towards her. 'Let me take that

for you.' He reached for the basket as he had so often during their shopping trips to the village or visits to Painter's Rock.

'No, it's fine. It's empty. Besides, I think you've taken enough.' She held his gaze, letting him see the depth of her resolve. She would not be so easily won this time as she had in the past.

'You are not pleased to see me,' Jules said.

'No, I am not. You broke my heart. I've spent the interim trying to put that heart back together.' So few words, yet they conveyed so much. 'Why have you come now? Business can be conducted by letter.'

She began to walk briskly, but he fell into step beside her. The wind off the river had picked up and it grew cold as dusk fell. Jules's hand was at her arm. 'Look at me, Becca. Do I look like a man who has had an easy time of it these past weeks?'

She turned to face him, steeling herself against the sight of his dancing green eyes and the charming smile he put to such effective use. But those were not the features she saw. There were dark circles beneath his eyes, their sparkle dimmed. His laughing mouth was a grim line. The pallor of his skin further evidence of sleepless nights. 'You're hard on a man, Becca Peverett. You take a man's body, his mind, his very soul, and you claim him for good and then you run away. Do you not trust your ability to effect lasting change?'

He did indeed look like a man who'd suffered and something in her began to reluctantly, cautiously, soften. They approached the physic garden. 'I need to get some things here for Anne. If you wish to ex-

plain yourself, you have until I complete the errand.'
She stepped into the park, searching for Anne's herbs.
She could listen to him. She didn't have to agree with
him. It didn't have to mean anything, change anything.

His boots crunched on the gravel pathway beside
her. 'I broke with you to protect you. My father was
going to reject the designs and not pay for them. He
was going to have his own team draw up similar designs and claim them for his own. It is also true that
he designed the ophthalmoscope to break for the purpose of selling replacements. Those are not things I
can countenance whether it is you or another who is
victimised by such practices. Once I understood what
my father was about, I knew I could not marry you and
drag you into that. It would only have been a matter of
time before he turned us against each other and ruined
what happiness we'd managed to find.'

He toed the dirt with his boot. 'My father accused
me of seducing you to steal from you. He would
have put such a claim to you at some point as leverage against me to make mischief between us. You deserve better.'

'So you let me go.'

'Yes, so I let you go. To save you. But I need you to
save me. It came down to you or my family. I choose
you. I have broken with my family, Becca. I will not be
a party any longer to the way they built their fortune.
Actually, my brother has broken with them as well. It
was a big step for him, for both of us.'

Hope began to rise in her. He'd broken with his family for her? Stood up to corruption for her? Did she dare

let herself believe? His hand was at her sleeve again. 'Becca, stop walking. I have something for you.' She made him demand it. She was deliberately not looking at him. It hurt too much.

'Close your eyes and hold out your hands. Please. This one thing, please, Becca. Let me prove to you that I kept my promise to protect your inventions.'

She did so reluctantly as she'd done all else since he'd turned up at the asylum, but the tug of memory was too powerful. She remembered another time, a happier time when she'd met him at the train and he'd put...pound notes in her hand. Her fingers closed around the papers in her palm. Her eyes opened slowly. 'What is this?' she asked sceptically. 'There are no other contracts.' It was a lot of money. Much more than she'd received for the ophthalmoscope.

'This is what you're owed for the other three. If they're ever produced, you'll have royalties as well. I promised you. I'd failed you at love, I could not fail you at business, too.'

His confession moved her, melting the hard shell she'd put around her heart. Was that a crack she felt? 'You never failed me at love, Jules.' She folded the pound notes up and put them safely away in her coat pocket, feeling self-conscious.

'I've sold my home in Manchester,' Jules said quietly as they began to walk again. 'The proceeds will provide us a start. I do not come to you empty-handed.'

Yes, that was definitely a crack she heard. He'd sold his home, walked away from his family, ensured that she was paid for her work and tried to prevent others from being hurt in the same way, all in an attempt to prove that he was worthy of her.

He grabbed her basket and set it aside. He seized both of her hands, his grip hard. 'You're not the only one who is hurting. Do you know how it felt to come home and find you gone?

She stared at him, emotions rocketing through her. She'd not thought of it that way. 'I was protecting myself,' she stammered. The crack was a full-blown fissure now.

'You're very good at that. But I am good at it, too, Becca. I can and will protect you, always.' His eyes shut for a moment and his jaw tightened. 'I was devastated when I arrived at Haberstock and found you gone. I felt devastated because I'd wanted to find you so badly, to be with you, to sort everything out, but also because you were hurting—hurting so much that the one place you love more than any other place in the world had become a source of grief to you and that was my fault. You left Haberstock because you thought everything we'd shared there was a lie, that I had seduced you with no feeling. And that broke me all over again, Becca.' His eyes fixed on hers. 'I would not hurt you for the world and yet I had, twice.'

'And I hurt you,' she breathed, 'I didn't mean to.' She shook her head. 'I don't know what life together looks like.'

'We'll work it out. Together. I've been talking to Rawdon about investing...' he paused, adding '...in you. More precisely, in your toys.' He dropped her hand, reaching in his pocket. He pulled out the toy soldier. 'I want to start a toy factory. Rawdon will invest and he thinks maybe the Treshams will, too, with their connections to the Prometheus Club and Winthrop knows business. I can sell things, Becca, and there's enough help in the family to figure out how to run a business. You can invent toys and anything else you want to your heart's content. I've also talked to Rawdon about how best to protect you. I will not claim a single coin from your work. There are papers we can draw up. I insist.'

'I am overwhelmed.' Becca groped for words. 'You've given up everything.' The enormity of what he'd done began to swamp her, seeping in and around and through the anger and hurt she'd sustained herself with.

'I've given up nothing, Becca. I have hopes, however, of gaining everything. A life in Haberstock with you and with myself. A life where I am who I want to be, doing what I want to do, with the person I want most to do it with. You've awakened me, Rebecca Peverett, and I want to live every day with my eyes wide open, but I must have you to do it. May I have hope of that?' There was that charming smile she adored so much.

'Yes,' she whispered, twining her arms about his neck and drawing him close, letting the spicy winter scent of him fill her as her mouth found his in a promise of for ever. He was not the only who'd been awakened. 'You've redeemed me, too, you know.'

He laughed, his nose brushing hers playfully. 'How long do you think it might be before we can fulfil those hopes? And where? At Haberstock before Christmas, perhaps?'

'Definitely. I can think of no place better than where it all started.' Becca smiled. 'I'd say I was going home, but I think I'm already there.'

Epilogue

W inter weddings were the most beautiful, Mother Nature turned out in spectacular bridal glory, Becca thought as she climbed into the Peverett coach to join her sisters on the journey to the Haberstock village church. There was snow on the ground and crystal icicles hanging from the roof of the Hall. Inside the coach, there was more laughter than space, all of their skirts taking up the room that wasn't already occupied by Thomasia's stomach.

'It's a perfect morning for a wedding! The world is dressed in white for you, Becca.' Anne fussed with the bouquet of tiny pink hothouse roses, a splash of colour against the white landscape outside the coach window. 'Oh, my dear, you look lovely. Grandmother's dress never looked so good.' There'd been no time for a new dress, but Becca had always admired Grandmother Peverett's ivory wedding gown with its long sleeves, high neck and tight waist—perfect for a December wedding.

'Are you excited? Nervous?'

Becca smiled at her sisters and shook her head. 'I'm happy.' Today, she was marrying the man she loved, a man who'd defied his family for her, who had helped her see herself more completely than she might ever have on her own.

'You should be happy, you deserve it. He's a wonderful man.' Thea, who'd travelled home from Germany for Christmas, reached across the space and squeezed her hand. 'Look at us, all four of us happily married, or at least soon to be happily married.'

'I wish William was here,' Becca offered in the silence that followed. 'He's missed it all.' And he'd likely miss the birth of Thomasia's second child and yet another Christmas.

'Some day, we'll all be together again.' Thomasia smiled softly, her hand on her belly, and the four sisters held hands all the way to the church. At the church, though, they left her to join their husbands already in the Peverett pew and for the first time since she'd awakened that morning, Becca was alone.

I want to remember this, she thought, looking about at the snow, the village where she'd grown up and where she was going to make her adult life with Jules.

Her pulse sped up at the thought of that life, that love, they'd share. There was so much to look forward to, but first she had to get through the ceremony, had to walk down the aisle with all eyes on her, something that she would have been supremely uncomfortable with a few months ago.

'Are you ready?' Her father was at her elbow. 'This

will be my last walk down the aisle. All my girls married.' He kissed her cheek.

Becca smiled and fiddled with her gown. 'I never thought I would be a bride.' She felt her throat tighten at the words.

Her father grinned and patted her hand. 'I did. You never did give yourself enough credit, my sweet, beautiful, tenacious girl. Nothing stops you.' Thanks to Jules, she saw that now. She didn't have to compete with her siblings, that was all in her mind. She'd always been enough for her family, for her village.

They stepped inside the church and started down the aisle, her father smiling at the villagers as they passed the pews decorated with white bows with long satin trains, but Becca only had eyes for the man at the end of the aisle. Jules stood there, dressed in a dark suit, his hair combed back, his green eyes fixed on her.

Her father placed her hand in Jules's and Jules whispered, 'You look beautiful.' She felt beautiful. Love did that to a person. It changed them from the inside out. She would not remember much of the service, only that she'd looked into Jules's eyes the whole time and saw her future there, and that he'd looked into hers and saw his as well. She'd remember the kiss, though. Jules took her face in his hands and took her mouth in a soft, simple kiss that shook her to her toes in the very best of ways. 'Our first kiss as husband and wife,' he murmured.

'You've always been my first everything,' she murmured back. Her first kiss, her first love, and he'd be her last, her only.

It was the last time they were alone until much later in the day—a day filled with well-wishers. After the ceremony, the whole village—at least it seemed that way—came back to the hall for a wedding breakfast that went well into the early evening. There were end-less kegs of cider, a wedding cake from Mr Barnes's bakery topped with a shortbread bride and groom frosted for the occasion as an homage, Mr Barnes said, to Jules's sweet tooth.

Best of all there was laughter and family. Winthrop and Mary were there for Jules, having taken up residence over a shop Winthrop had purchased in the village from which he hoped to sell cider. Jules had quite sold him on the idea of transporting the excellent local cider to London especially when Winthrop heard about Shaw's plans to establish a branch railroad, cutting down the time it took to travel the seventeen miles to London.

'They seem happy,' Becca whispered to Jules as Winthrop and Mary came to the bridal table to wish them well.

Jules nodded. 'I think they are. Haberstock agrees with them.' He grinned and stole a kiss. 'It agrees with me, too. I'm happy beyond words, Becca.'

'I am, too. How soon do you think we can slip away?' They wouldn't have to slip very far. They'd decided to live in the workshop while their new house was being built on the Hall's property. It would be quite cosy quarters until summer when the house would be done. Not much building could happen in the winter, but they were newlyweds and didn't mind. All that mattered was that they had the bed in the loft and each other.

'Soon.' Jules laughed. 'Perhaps we might start making our farewells.'

There was a small commotion at the door, heralding the arrival of the lad left in the village to watch the telegraph office. Becca watched her father take something from the lad and gestured for the boy to help himself to the food. She glanced about the great hall—her sisters and their husbands were on the move, gravitating towards her father. 'We have to go to him.' Becca was already up, making her way towards her parents, Jules at her back.

'It's not bad news, is it?' Becca asked, reaching her parents and her sisters.

Her mother smiled. 'Why does it always have to be unwelcome news, Becca? I thought we'd talked about that.' The little knot in Becca's stomach eased. She squeezed Jules's hand.

'It's good news.' Her father beamed at the family gathered about him. 'It's from William. He's coming home for Christmas.'

'We'll all be together,' Becca exclaimed, smiling at Jules. 'I think that's the best wedding gift we could ever have.'

'At least until tonight,' Jules whispered at her ear, just for her. That was her cue to hug her sisters and say goodnight. His new brothers-in-law thumped him on the back and the sight of Jules welcomed so thoroughly into the family warmed her. They were home, both of them.

* * * * *

*If you enjoyed this story, be sure to read the other
books in Bronwyn Scott's
The Peveretts of Haberstock Hall miniseries*

Lord Tresham's Tempting Rival
Saving Her Mysterious Soldier
Miss Peverett's Secret Scandal

*And why not check out her other great miniseries,
The Rebellious Sisterhood?*

Portrait of a Forbidden Love
Revealing the True Miss Stansfield
A Wager to Tempt the Runaway